ABOUT THE AUTHOR

Lexie Winston has been an astronaut, rock star, princess and time traveller. In her dreams. But none of the dreams have lived up to what becoming an author has been like. She gets to live in a world of pure imagination, and her heroines get to do the things she's always wished she could.

When not writing books, Lexie is a mother of two gorgeous teenagers and the wife to a patient and understanding man. They live in Western Australia and are lorded over by a black toy poodle. She loves camping, reading and if her Kindle was stolen, her world would explode.

And you can find all links at

www.lexiewinston.com

UNWILLING QUEEN

KINGDOM OF ARAMIS BOOK ONE

KINGDOMS SERIES
BOOK ONE

LEXIE WINSTON

ALSO BY LEXIE WINSTON

The Collectors Division

(Paranormal Reverse Harem Series)

Guardian

Guardian's Blood

Guardian Ascending

Collector's Division Omnibus

Seductive Sins Collection

(Reverse Harem Series)

Glorious Gluttony

Gangs, Guns, and Glory

Glory Glory Hellelujah

Crowning Glory

What's the Story, Morning Glory?

(Seductive Sins Omnibus)

Neighpalm Industries Collective

(Contemporary Enemies to Lovers

Reverse Harem)

Abandoned Girl

Broken Girl

Tormented Girl

Wanted Girl

Cherished Girl

Loved Girl

Superficial Girl - Jacinta's Story Part 1

Superficial Girl - Jacinta's Story Part 2

Neighpalm Industries Collective 1-3

Neighpalm Industries Collective 4-6

Galaxy Circus

(Sci-Fi Reverse Harem Series)

Apprentice

Stagehand

Whisperer

Mama - Galaxy Circus Novella

Performer

Ringmaster

Interlude

Spectacle

Ovation

A Night Most Wicked - Galaxy Circus Novella

M.I.T.H.O.S

(Contemporary RH)

Spies Like Me

Spies Like Us

Broken Promises

(Dark Poly Romance Series)

Secrets Kept

Lies Untold

Trust Broken

Storm View Stories

(Contemporary Standalone RH)

Ice Me Out

<u>Kingdoms Series</u>

(Fantasy reverse harem)

Kingdom of Aramis Duet

Unwilling Queen

Ardent Queen

First published by Neighpalm Publishing in 2024

Unwilling Queen

Mobi format: 978-1-7636228-6-9
Print: 978-1-7638409-0-4

Cover design by Covers by Aura

Editing by Elemental Editing

Colbie

I shove my hands deeper into my pockets as I make my way down the cold, quiet streets toward my bakery. The thud of my sneakers echoes on the pavement. The days are getting shorter, and the temperature has really started to drop in the evenings, even if the days are still sunny. Soon enough, I'll need my hat and gloves as well as my warm winter jacket, but not yet.

The pale streetlights seem to flicker, the slight fog in the air giving my path a creepy vibe, but I don't hurry. I'm mostly safe in the neutral zone. Curfew dictates that everyone is indoors or returned to their own side by a specified time. Only those of us with special permission are permitted to be out after curfew. That doesn't mean people don't disobey the zones directive, but the punishment of imprisonment if caught seems to do its job in deterring both shifters and humans alike. It helps that the night watch are a visible presence as well, though none seem to be patrolling this particular area at the moment. Made up of highly trained shifter and human teams, the night watch is a formidable deterrent to anyone looking to flaunt the pack and human agreement. Of course, this only applies to the neutral zone, so those who want to party on into the night are free to do so in their home zones.

The yawn that leaves my mouth makes my jaw click, and despite the chill in the air, my mind is still foggy with sleep. I didn't get home until late, and with my early starts, I'm functioning on less sleep than normal. All the preparation in the lead-up to the shifter royal pack's retirement has sent many of the businesses in the neutral zone into a flurry, trying to use it as an excuse to boost sales—me included.

I have two recipes for a dedicated royal retirement cupcake special, as well as the cutest little marshmallow animals to float on top of coffee and hot chocolate. For the humans, I have a cupcake with a surprise filling, as well as one with "good luck" written on it, because of course all humans are praying that they become the next shifter king or queen. Well, most of them, because I'm certainly not. I am very happy with my life in the neutral zone, running my bakery, visiting with my mother, and occasionally hanging out with the few friends I have.

Living in the neutral zone and having to obey its curfew doesn't really lend itself to making friends or socializing. The neutral zone doesn't have a lot of permanent residents unless you own a business like my mother and I do, but it serves an important purpose.

It came into existence when the humans and shifters were at war. Both sides realized they couldn't go on like that any longer, so they called a ceasefire, and an amnesty was held to split Aramis into two territories, with a small neutral zone for trade and socialization. This agreement also caught the goddess Aramis's attention. The creator of both races didn't believe that would be enough to stop the antagonization, so she declared that the shifters would have a king or queen, who would rule for forty years before a new king or queen would be selected by her magic. This ensured that both races behaved, which they have.

The end of the current King Lucas's and his three queen consorts' rule is coming to an end, and everyone is eagerly awaiting the next step. Aramis not only selects the new royal, but she also marks a number of possible mate candidates from the shifter population, and then the king or queen will decide from those selected—hence the humans' excitement and my bakery's new desserts. Every human in the human zone of Aramis is on tenterhooks waiting to see if they get chosen.

The whole thing seems a little medieval to me. If and when I decide to marry, I want it to be someone I choose, not because someone has decreed it, but by all intents and purposes, the royals seem deliriously happy. Once they retire, they will become advisors to the new royals for the first few years. They will be known as the former king and queens, and any children from their unions will carry titles but have no ties to the crown.

Apart from that, I don't know a lot about shifters. I don't even really know how many types there are. I've occasionally seen some in shifted form, since they are allowed to wander around the neutral zone like that, but they mostly take their human form. The only way to tell a shifter from a human is by their eyes, which glow with an inner light, unlike that of a human.

I hurry across an intersection, not bothering to look either way. It's starting to drizzle, and I'd rather get to my shop without being soaked by the deceptively fine rain. Traffic isn't allowed in the neutral zone, apart from electric scooters and public transport specifically to prevent shifters from being hit by cars, so I don't have to wait for lights to change.

While adult shifters are usually pretty safe from that fate, they occasionally bring their children over in shifted form, and nobody wants to hit a shifter child. Shifter children are considered precious, since their birth rate is low because they have such long lives, and harming a child, whether human or shifter, is considered a crime punishable by death.

I pull the key out of my pocket as I get closer, wanting to get out of the rain as quickly as possible. I turn down the alley that sits between my store and the one next to it—a quirky bookstore that caters to the romantics in both races. When Brock decided to open the Romance Nest, he and his partner Niles installed a cozy little downstairs reading room. People are encouraged to bring food and drinks and settle in to read their purchases. Luckily for me, instead of opening their own café to compete, we came up with an agreement to offer them a discount with proof of book purchase, and so far, it's been working well for both of us. Brock and Niles are shifters, but I don't know what type of shifter they are. It's rude to ask, and I'm not as close to them as I wish I was. They seem like such a sweet couple, and I think they would be fun to hang out with, but in the six months they have been open, I haven't worked up the guts to ask them.

As I put my key in the door leading to my kitchen, a noise at the end of the alley catches my attention. I turn to look, peering into the darkness. I wonder if it's just a rat shuffling around in the dumpster, but then a small, keening sound reaches my ears. I drop my keys back into my pocket and pull out my phone, turning on the flashlight so I can see as I step farther into the alley. There's nothing down here but a dumpster and a stack of cardboard boxes, but I keep going farther into the darkness, and I can't stop the surprised gasp that leaves my lips as the boxes tumble over, revealing the cause of the noise. A small black and orange tiger cub is curled up behind the pile, shaking like a leaf. I would bet my last dollar that this is no run-of-the-mill tiger cub, but what is a shifter child doing here in the dark early hours of the morning on its own?

"Oh, you poor, sweet thing. Where did you come from?" I crouch down and inch closer to it. It whimpers and shuffles backward under the boxes. I pause, not wanting to scare it, worried that it will make a run for it. I rack my brain for a solution. I'm not just going to turn my back on it and leave, but I also don't want to be scratched if they aren't happy with me picking them up. My eyes catch on one of the cardboard boxes, and I scrunch up my nose. I really don't want to catch them like a wild animal, but I have too much work to do today to have to worry about seeing a doctor if the cub injures me.

I purse my lips as I look between the box and the cub. How is this cub even here? I didn't see anyone on the walk from my apartment to the bakery. Not a single person was out on the streets, and certainly not a frantic shifter parent looking for their child. I'm surprised the streets aren't filled with worried shifters searching for this little one, curfew be damned.

Sighing, I reach for the box, knowing this is probably going to traumatize the child even more, but I slowly lift it and quickly bring it down over the shivering animal. A small, adorable snarl is muffled by the cardboard, and I feel them scrape at the walls of the box with their tiny sharp nails. Yup, glad I decided to protect myself. Looking down at my hands, I grimace, wishing it was cold enough for gloves. I know I'm probably not going to be able to get out of this without an injury or two, but I'm also not leaving the cub here. I slide my hand under, and in one quick movement, I flip the box. More snarling sounds, louder this time now that it's not muffled, and when I peer down, the cub is glaring up at me with bristled fur, but it has stopped fighting.

"Come on then, let's get you warmed up," I tell it and tuck the box under my arm, using my phone to light my way to the rear bakery door. I turn off the flashlight, shove my phone into my pocket, and retrieve my keys, opening the door to my second home. A rush of warm air brings the scent of yeast, flour, and yesterday's sweet treats with it. I don't bake a lot of bread, mostly just pastries and savory treats to have with coffee in the café, but I do make all the rolls we use, as well as bagels. I flick on the lights and slide the heavy box full of tiger cub onto the counter before turning the ovens on. It won't take long for the kitchen to heat up.

"Just stay there for a moment, and I'll find you

something to eat," I tell the cub, who has settled and is now looking up at me with intelligent eyes. I'm not sure how old the child is, but it seems to understand me, so I'm praying it isn't an infant. Shifters are understandably tight-lipped about their children's development.

I slide my jacket off then hang it on the coat hook in my office, replacing it with a clean apron that covers my simple leggings and T-shirt. Work clothes aren't anything fancy for me. I'm just going to get dirty, and once I start prepping for the day, I won't be cold at all.

I pull out some towels I use when I want to shower before going home—my office has a small, attached bathroom—and then I return to the kitchen. The cub has done as I asked, staying in place. They are resting their head in their paws and waiting patiently. I put my hands on my hips and look down at them, smiling gently.

"Well then, I appreciate you listening to me. How about we dry you off and find you something to eat?" I suggest, and their ears twitch like they are listening to me. "But you need to keep your claws and teeth to yourself. I don't want to drop you by mistake if you hurt me, okay?" I ask, and the cub's little head tips to the side like they are acknowledging me.

I breathe out a sigh of relief and reach into the box, sliding my hands gently under the cub's tummy. It's not as rounded as I expected, and I frown. Surely a growing cub should be fed well to help with their growth. Slowly picking it up, I move it onto the towel I spread out on the bench, then I use the towel to vigorously dry them off. It yowls and squirms but keeps its claws and fangs to itself.

Once I'm happy it isn't going to shiver to death, I pull away. "Right then, I'm sure you're probably hungry and thirsty. Let's get you something to eat. My name's Colbie, by the way. I guess you can't really tell me yours, so I'll just call you cub for now." The cub's eyes widen, and it quickly nods its head. I'm not sure if that's in acknowledgment of the name or wanting food, but I'm going to go with the latter.

"Can you shift?" I ask it, and it tucks its body in defensively, its tail sagging and its ears flattening against its head. "I'm going to take that as a no. How about I set you up a little nest and you can wait in there while I fix you some food?"

I take the other dry towels I have over to the side of the oven, which is starting to warm up nicely, and arrange them in a cozy little nest. "Right, so don't touch the metal, because it might be hot, but this should chase away the rest of the cold," I tell the cub gently, then I lift them up and transfer them to the pile of towels. Before I can pull my hand away, it bumps into it with its head, and a chuffing sound comes from its mouth. I give them a little pet on the top of their head, marveling at how soft it is. I expected the orange and black fur to be bristly, but it's not, it's like feather down. A little tongue swipes roughly across my wrist, and I smile. "What would you like to eat?"

Standing up, I go over to the industrial fridge and open it. I grab a bottle of milk and pour it into a little saucer before checking what other offerings I have that might be suitable for a tiger cub. There's a large roast beef I have been planning on cooking for rolls and sandwiches, but I'm happy to sacrifice it to the small creature, hoping it's old enough to be eating this kind of food.

Shrugging, I head back to the prep table and pull out a cutting board and knife before I cut off a chunk of the meat, dicing it into small, cub-sized pieces. I wrap the rest up and return it to the fridge before grabbing the offerings and placing them on the floor in front of the cub. It looks between me and the food with wide eyes. "Go on then. Eat up. I need to clean and start getting ready for the day." I turn around, but I smile when I hear the greedy sounds of the cub scarfing down its food. "Not too fast, you don't want to be sick," I caution, cleaning up the mess on the prep table and wiping the surface with cleaner so it's ready to go.

I need to think about calling the night watch to come and get the cub so they can find whom it belongs to, but first, I need to get my initial batch of muffins in the oven.

TWO

Colbie

The kitchen is filled with the scent of baking muffins, cupcakes, and boiled sugar as I prepare the first batch of marshmallows. I'm deciding which of the adorable little marshmallow animals to make first when Olivia, my assistant, walks through the door at six.

"Good morning," she greets me as she takes off her jacket and hangs it next to mine. She's wearing leggings and a shirt similar to mine, and she puts an apron over the top of them. Her pixie cut black hair is sticking up at all angles from wearing her helmet, and it makes me smile. Pushing her glasses up her nose, she faces me and frowns. "The streets are super empty this morning. I didn't even get a peek of the night watch on my way over here today." Olivia lives in the human section of Aramis and has to travel a lot farther to get here than I do.

"Hmm, something is going on," I grumble. "I tried to call them earlier to report something and the operator blew me off. I couldn't even tell her what I wanted before she hung up."

Her eyebrows jump on her face. "Why did you call the night watch. Is everything okay?" She comes around and leans on the prep table, crossing her arms to grill me for gossip, but then she catches sight of my problem. The cub is curled up fast asleep in its little nest and didn't even notice her come in. The poor little thing really must be exhausted. Olivia's eyes go wide, and she pushes off the prep table in a hurry, pointing at the little bundle of fur.

"That's a fucking tiger!" she shouts, and I wave the thermometer in my hand to keep her quiet.

"Shh, don't wake it. It's had a rough night," I tell her before sticking the probe into the bubbling sugar mix to check the temperature. I need to dissolve the gelatine and then add the hot mixture to the whipped egg whites and sugar in my stand mixer.

"Where on earth did you get a tiger cub?" she whisper-screeches, her eyes locked on the little creature. Her face softens when she realizes it isn't going to attack her. Heck, it still hasn't woken despite her being super loud.

"I found it huddled up under some of Brock

and Niles's boxes near the dumpster in the alley," I answer, studying the gauge on the probe. The sugar is at the right temp, so I turn off the stove and carry the pot to the prep table, dumping in the softened gelatine sheets and whisking furiously to dissolve it. "That's why I called the night watch. I have no idea where it came from, but some poor shifter parent has to be going out of their mind with worry."

A small whistle escapes her mouth. "I'll say. There's nothing more precious to a shifter than their child. Even us humans know that."

"I'm just going to make this batch of marshmallows, and if they still haven't arrived, then I'll call them again, and this time, I won't let the operator blow me off."

"Yeah, good plan. The last thing we need is to open and have a shifter come in for something and find us with a shifter cub in the kitchen. Apparently, their sense of smell is so good, they'd probably smell it over all the other scents in here."

The timer on the oven goes off, and she grabs some pot holders and pulls them out, stacking the hot ones on the top rack. There are already a couple of batches cooling on there, ready for her to frost and decorate.

We work in comfortable silence for another hour. This isn't the first time I've made marshmallow animals, so I know what I'm doing, but they do take a little bit of concentration. I'm planning on doing a bear, tiger, unicorn, and a cute little penguin, but I can only make the marshmallow in small batches, otherwise it hardens, and I can't pipe it.

When it's time to open the store at seven for the early morning coffee crowd, I'm covered head to toe in starch and powdered sugar. Thankfully, Olivia finished icing and filling all the muffins and cupcakes and setting up the front display. I would be lost without her.

There's a knock on the back door as I'm shaking off the last of the powdered sugar and starch from the penguins. I look up, but Olivia is already in the front of the store, turning over the sign and unlocking the door. I brush off as best as I can using a tea towel and go over to see who it is. It's probably just Niles or Brock coming to grab their first mug of coffee for the day.

Smiling and pushing a strand of my black hair off my face, I open it. "Hey, guys, just in time. Olivia should almost have the coffee ready." When I look up, I meet a pair of glowing green eyes, and all the breath in my lungs wooshes out. I take a step back, gasping. "You aren't Brock."

The glowing green eyes belong to a man in the night watch's uniform. He's a tall, golden, tousled blond-haired, mountain of a man with muscles that look like he could pop me if he got his arms around me and squeezed. He's fucking gorgeous.

His eyes run the length of me, a smirk coming

to his lush lips as he takes in my starch-covered form.

"Did you lose a fight with a bag of flour?" he asks, his voice all gravelly with amusement lacing his tone.

I cross my arms and glare at the man, feeling slightly defensive about my disheveled appearance.

"No, but unlike some people, I work hard for my money," I growl, annoyed that it took them this long to get here.

"Ma'am, you made a report to the watch operator, but they didn't take down what the actual problem is. We're sorry it took us so long to come around. It's been a crazy night." The voice comes from over the mountain man's shoulder, and when I look in that direction, I meet another glowing set of eyes. These ones are so blue they look like a tropical ocean on a summer day. Jesus, what is in the shifters' water? This man is not quite as tall as his teammate, but he's equally as muscular as the mountain man in front of me. They both fill out their dark blue watch uniforms like they were molded to their forms, but this one has long, black hair tied back into a ponytail at the nape of his neck with a few strands framing his face from where they have come loose.

Before I can answer, the blond man in front of me stiffens, and his eyes glow even brighter as he sniffs the air and scowls at me. "Why do I smell a shifter cub?" he growls and takes a menacing step forward. I watch with alarm as scales shimmer across his cheeks before they disappear again, and I hold my hands up in a nonthreatening way.

"Whoa, easy, tiger." I step back and wave them in. "It's why I called the night watch. I found a shifter cub near the dumpster when I arrived at work this morning. I tried to tell the woman on the phone, but she cut me off, telling me she had no available teams." I wave a hand, inviting them in, and the two men step into my kitchen, instantly shrinking the large space with their presence.

"I'm not a tiger," the first man growls at me, and I roll my eyes.

"Easy, Hunt, it's just an expression." The blue-eyed shifter puts a hand on his friend's shoulder before their attention turns to the little cub sleeping next to my oven. Their eyes soften, and some of the tension leaves their body.

"Are you telling us you found the cub?" the blue-eyed guy asks skeptically, and I shrug.

"Yeah, poor thing was cold and wet, and it was starving. I brought it in, dried it off, and fed it, and it's been sleeping ever since. Poor baby seems exhausted."

The two exchange a loaded glance.

"I was just about to call the watch again now that I've finished prep for the day." I wave my hand at the table covered in tiny marshmallow animals, and the two men turn their attention from the cub to my display of tiny edible creatures. The blue-eyed man's lips quirk up at the side.

"Crafting a little army to do your bidding?" He arches an eyebrow, nodding at my creations.

I blush a little at the suggestion. "It's in celebration for the shifter king and queens' retirement," I tell them sheepishly. Here I am, cashing in on something that's probably pretty important in their society.

"Yes, it's quite an occasion," he murmurs. "It's a nice thought, though there aren't any penguin shifters." He turns his attention on his teammate who has crouched down in front of the cub and put his hand on the little tiger, giving it a gentle shake.

Huh, no penguin shifters, but he didn't mention anything about the other three. Are there unicorn shifters? Now that would be something.

The little shifter yawns and stretches before they sniff the air and it comes instantly awake, its fur bristling as it snarls at the two men. It pushes past them and puts its body between me and the big men, its tail twitching back and forth while adorable threatening sounds come out of its mouth.

The blue-eyed man barks out a laugh, which warms something inside me. "What are you doing, cub? You don't need to protect the pretty lady from us," he assures it, still chuckling, but his words seem to have no effect. The tiger cub starts pacing back and forth between us, not taking its eyes off the two mountainous men.

"That's enough," the green-eyed man snaps, reaching down and picking the cub up by the scruff. The cub spits and scratches, but all it succeeds in doing is wearing itself out. "Now shift," the green-eyed man—Hunt, I think his friend called him—commands.

My mouth drops open as magic shimmers around the cub, and suddenly, there's a small boy in his place. He's possibly four or five, if I had to guess. He crosses his arms and glares at the two men, completely naked and unafraid.

"Leave my friend alone, you big bullies," he says in a high-pitched voice.

"Holy shit, is that..." The blue-eyed shifter gapes at the child in shock.

Hunt nods. "Yes, it's Prince Archer. Archie, your parents are going out of their minds with worry. How did you end up here?" he asks, turning a suspicious glare on me, but I don't cower under his stare, I just glare back at him.

The boy loses his glare, and his bottom lip starts to quiver. "I'm sorry, Hunter, don't be mad." The child obviously knows this man, which is a relief. "I snuck out of the castle so I could play with the kittens in the stable last night. A strange man was there. I didn't recognize him as one of the grooms, and he smelled funny, like moldy hay, not like a shifter. I told him he had to leave, but he just laughed and grabbed me."

"Witch," the blue-eyed shifter growls, and the two of them exchange a loaded look.

"He took me out of the castle grounds and tried to put me into the back of a van. I tried to fight him, but he was too big, so I shifted and scratched him. He dropped me, and when he tried to grab me again, I ran, and I just kept running until I couldn't run anymore."

"Holy shit, how did a little thing like you run so far? That has to be like five leagues." Blue eyes sounds both impressed and skeptical.

The little one wraps his arms around his body, shuddering with fear. I hurry to the cupboard and pull out a clean baker's top, but as I approach him to give it to him, Hunt growls, so I stop, not willing to upset this mountain man, and hold it out.

"For the boy."

He slowly reaches out and takes it from my hand before stepping closer to the child. "Here, put this over you." Hunt uses gentle hands to help him into the shirt. I'm not a tall person, only five-five, but the shirt swims on the child.

"I just kept going until I couldn't run anymore, and I found a space to hide, but it was raining, and I was cold and hungry, and when I saw the pretty lady, I couldn't stop crying." The boy bites his lip and stares down at his feet, looking ashamed.

"You have nothing to be ashamed about." Hunt crouches again and puts both hands on the boy's little arms, giving them an encouraging squeeze.

"You did the right thing, but how about we get you back to the castle and to your parents and grand-parents? Everyone is frantic and looking for you."

The little boy sags and collapses into the arms of the blond watchman who gathers him and stands up. Without another word, he turns and leaves my kitchen, not sparing me another glance.

"Thank you for everything you did for him." The blue-eyed man holds out his hand. "I'm sure the royal family will reward you for it."

I scowl at him. "I don't need a reward for doing the right thing. I'm just sorry the operator didn't care enough to listen to me so you could be here sooner." I take his hand, giving it a perfunctory shake, but I flinch back when a spark of something ignites between our hands. I look down at my palm, but there's nothing there, so I give it a little shake. It must have been static from all the starch in the air.

The shifter's eyes narrow slightly before he growls. "Yes, the operator will be suitably punished. No matter what is going on, your call should not have been blown off. Hell, the reason we were so busy was because we were looking for the boy."

"I'm just glad he's okay. Poor thing has been through so much. I would have asked questions, but he stayed in shifted form."

"Yes, shifter children need help from an alpha to shift back. It's why they are not allowed to wander on their own until they get control with their shifting around the age of twelve."

I'm almost positive that information is not common knowledge. I certainly didn't know it.

"Again, thank you." He nods and turns to leave, but not before snatching up a penguin and a tiger marshmallow. "You know what else would look cool as a marshmallow? Dragons and wolves." He gives me a wink and leaves, shoving the penguin into his mouth.

I gape at the now empty kitchen and nervously brush my hands over my apron, heaving out a breath of air. Now that they are gone, my nerves catch up with me, and I shakily lean against the prep table. They were fucking intimidating. Luckily for me, the child was able to tell them I wasn't involved in any of it, and they believed him. What did they call him? Prince Archer? Holy fuck, I had one of the royal kids in my kitchen. I'm probably lucky I'm not dead.

I'm still trying to swallow my nausea when Olivia sticks her head in and looks around. "Are they gone?" she asks nervously, and I glare at her.

"You knew they were here, and you left me alone with them?"

She shrugs sheepishly. "Yeah, sorry, but shifters scare the shit out of me."

I frown at her words. I'm sure I asked her about her feelings regarding shifters when I hired her. I can't have anyone working here who can't tolerate either species. She must see my look, because she quickly shakes her head.

"Oh no, I don't hate them or anything, but I could practically feel the menace flowing off those two and didn't want their attention on me. They were fucking scary dudes. Hot though. I peeked through when I heard voices, and they were some fine man meat." She chuckles, and I lose my annoyance. "I don't know how you stood there and looked them in the eye. I was virtually shaking in my boots."

I think about my reaction. Sure, they were intimidating, but I didn't feel any fear or menace. All I felt was their curiosity and suspicion, which turned to worry and relief when they saw the cub. Even when they were growling, I felt nervous but not terror.

"Oh well, hopefully that's the last of that," I tell her as the door chimes as another customer enters the store. "I'll finish up here and get the marshmallows into the display cabinet, then I'll clean up and help you with the breakfast rush."

"Sure thing, boss." She salutes me and goes out to serve, her friendly demeanor firmly back in place. It's one of the reasons I hired her. She always has a smile on her face and is really good with our customers. My other employee, Justin, isn't as good with the customers, but he makes a mean sandwich and is a whizz with the coffee machine.

He comes in a little later, closer to lunch when his skills are more in demand. For breakfast, we offer savory muffins and quiches, which we prepared last night, and bagels, which I bake twice a week. Thankfully that was yesterday morning's job, so I don't have to bake any this morning. They are all ready to go with a variety of smears on offer. It means we have a good flow of customers for breakfast, and it doesn't require a lot of work on my part except to fry up some bacon and eggs if people want a fresh bacon and egg bagel.

We aren't run off our feet this morning, and I have time to put the lunch rolls in the oven so they are ready in time. If I decide to add the marshmallows to my menu permanently, I'm probably going to hire someone else. It's a lot of work and gives me little time for the rest of the prep work. Thankfully, I thought ahead last night and prepared batches of muffin and cupcake batter that only needed to have the wet ingredients added, mixed, and then put into the oven this morning. I'll do the same this afternoon as well. It's going to be a long week, but hopefully it brings new customers into the bakery.

THREE

Brodie

We don't mess around once we have Archer secured. Hunter sets a fast pace toward our borders. Once we enter the forest that delineates the neutral zone from shifter grounds, he shifts, and I help Archie onto his back before climbing up behind him. Normally I would shift and run by myself, but I want to be here to make sure Archie doesn't fall.

Hunter flaps his giant wings, and we take to the air, Archie whooping with pure joy. I smile at the kid's reaction as the wind whips past us. Hunter's speed is unparalleled in the air. Archie always begs Hunter to take him flying every time we visit the castle, but his overprotective mother always says no. She's not here now, though, and I'm sure she will forgive us when we return her son to her safe and sound. Flying on the back of a dragon will be over-shadowed by the worrying fact that he was kidnapped.

Archie is the grandson of the current king and queens. They have three children themselves, and Archie is Princess Gracelin's son. Neither of the other royal children have found mates yet despite the mounting pressure from their parents.

Archie is lucky, Hunter's voice rumbles in my mind. *He could have disappeared without a trace like the other three children who are still missing. Someone is obviously targeting shifter children, but to go after the king's own grandson is bold.*

We suspected the witches were taking our children. They are the closest, and the vamps and fae are too far away. The other logical conclusion is a human. But why? I muse, my grip on Archie tightening with my worry. Thankfully he doesn't notice, just stretches his arms wide to pretend that he's flying.

I'm sure it means nothing good. It also bodes badly for shifter-witch relations, and goddess help the humans if it's them.

It's a terrible time for it. On the full moon, the new king or queen will be selected, and they are walking into a shit storm of epic proportions.

Do you think the timing is deliberate? he asks.

Without a doubt. What better time to stir up trouble when the shifter species is in a time of transition?

The castle comes into view, and Hunter spirals

down toward the large courtyard. Guards run out holding weapons, but I see them relax when they notice the deep purple dragon. Hunter is the only one of his race who is that color.

But the witches and shifters have always been on good terms. In fact, we've been at peace with all three other races for many years. I can't imagine that they would risk that after all races were almost annihilated by humans two hundred years ago.

So what? A rogue witch? He guesses as he puts his wings out to slow our descent and make the landing gentle.

I would assume so, but we'll leave that up to the king and his queens to determine. The witch queen will be here for the coronation of our new king or queen in a few weeks. I'm sure they will get to the bottom of it. Until then, we'll warn our people to tighten the security on their children and widen our search for the remaining missing ones. Dad will spin a story so as not to panic the shifter population.

I feel his renewed determination to find the other missing children. We've managed to keep the news from the general shifter population up until now, but we can't afford to do that any longer. Widespread panic isn't going to help either. This is really a bad time for any upheaval. The transition of a new king and queen is always a little rocky for the first year until they find their footing and get used to shifter ways.

I swing my leg off Hunter and slide down his body before turning around and gesturing to

Archie. He crosses his arms stubbornly, and his lip juts out in a pout. "No, I'm not getting down."

I chuckle. He looks so much like his uncle, one of my best friends, at the moment that it's comical. "Your mother will be here at any moment, and what do you think she will say when she sees you riding a dragon?" I ask, and his eyes widen before he quickly leaps.

Luckily I have quick reflexes and catch the small boy before he can damage himself. I lower him to the ground as Hunter shifts back into his human form. Thankfully our watch uniforms are spelled to change with us so he's not naked, because the castle doors fling open and the king and queens run out, followed by their two daughters.

"Archie!" Gracelin cries, pushing past everyone and snatching him out of my arms. Adam, her mate, joins them, wrapping his big arms around the two smaller figures. His bear's rumbling growl sounds both relieved and aggravated at the same time.

"Brodie, Hunter, where did you find him?" The king asks as his wives surround the family, fussing over the little boy. The rest of the guards fade away, leaving behind only General Bryson, the commander of the shifter army and Hunter's father. Bryson is a large man, and his oldest son Hunter is practically his twin, but King Lucas is slighter, not quite as tall, and he has a long, lean figure indicating he would excel at stealth just like his tiger. Bryson grips his son's shoulder in greeting but does not show overt affection when on duty in public view.

"Actually, we didn't find him. A human in the neutral zone did and tried to report him to the watch," I explain as the four of us make our way back into the castle, followed by the rest of the royal family. The only one not around is the king's son, but I know why, so I'm not particularly worried.

"A human?" The king frowns as he leads us through the extravagant castle that is their family home. Many of the rooms are only used for special occasions, but I can tell he's leading us toward his family space. Soon, they will move out of this castle for the next king or queen to take up residence. They have a family compound nearby they will move into. All outgoing royal families are gifted them from the goddess as part of their retirement package.

"*Tried* to report it?" Bryson growls, sounding annoyed. Not only is he the general of the shifter army, but he also is the night watch commander.

I sigh and turn my attention to my boss. "Gianna was manning the switchboard tonight. You know what she's like."

He grumbles and shakes his head. "That girl has gone too far. I never should have allowed her mother to convince me to hire her."

"What is she like?" the king asks, not hiding his annoyance, and Bryson runs an agitated hand through his hair as Hunter and I exchange a glance. Gianna is a man eater. I'm almost certain the only reason she took the job with the watch was so she could be around all the strongest shifters. She wants her pick of the crop and often lets her ambitions to snag a strong husband get in the way of doing her job properly. She's also not particularly fond of humans.

"Gianna told the human she had no teams to send, but the human female says she didn't even get a chance to tell her about the cub before she was cut off," I reply before Bryson can answer. The man is like a father to me, and I hate that he has to explain the behavior of one annoying shifter woman.

The king's tiger rumbles inside his chest, and Bryson's dragon joins in. I wouldn't want to be in Gianna's shoes.

"I will see to Gianna. She's going to be very sorry she didn't prioritize her job over her need for a husband," Bryson growls, and I wince. I don't like Gianna, but I've been on the end of Bryson's ire before, and it's not fun.

"No, send for her. I want her to explain to my face why she neglected to take an emergency call when the watch was on high alert for a missing child. Even if she didn't know all the details, she was still neglectful in her duties. The night watch is there to keep the neutral zone safe, and she failed," King Lucas demands, and Bryson lowers his head in acknowledgment of the order. He pulls out his phone and shoots off a message before turning his attention to Hunter and me.

"Tell us about the human. Are we sure she found Archie and wasn't the person who took him in the first place?" Hunter's father asks as we enter the royal family's living room. The king waves all the staff away, leaving us alone. We make ourselves comfortable, the tears staining Gracelin's cheeks making me feel thankful that we found her son in one piece. She's always been like a sister to me, and seeing her despair was heartbreaking.

"I'll kill her, and nobody will stop me," Adam rumbles, his fur bristling on his arms as he struggles with his shift. The three of them find a couch, and Gracelin puts a hand on her husband's arm, warning him to be careful. Archie rests his head peacefully against his mother's chest, but at his father's words, he sits bolt upright.

"No, leave Colbie alone. She was nice to me. I love her, and I want to marry her," he declares with hearts in his eyes, stabbing his father's chest with his little finger.

It breaks the tension in the room as we chuckle at his declaration. He's too young to realize shifters don't marry humans—or not often, anyway.

"No, Archie is right. The woman protected him. He told us he was snatched up from the stables when he snuck out of bed last night and went to play with the kittens. From how he described them, we think it might be a witch. He claimed they smelled like moldy hay," Hunter explains, leaning against one of the walls. I take my place next to him as the queens and Princess Gretchin find a place to sit. King Lucas and General Bryson also remain standing.

Archie squirms when his parents look at him with disappointment. He knows he fucked up, but he's definitely been punished enough. "Oh, Archie, you know you aren't supposed to wander around outside the castle on your own." His mother sounds so disappointed, I grimace. I know that tone well. I've heard it a number of times from my own mother when I was Archie's age.

Bryson and Lucas gently question him about his experience. Gracelin starts to cry again, and her sister squishes in next to her and holds her hand while Adam tries to whisper words of reassurance. I hide the smirk that wants to cross my lips at the sight of the big grizzly bear becoming a teddy around his wife.

Adam is a former watch member. When he mated Gracelin, he transferred to the shifter army so he could be home every night with his wife. He now leads his own team of men, but because we haven't been at war, they mostly train and patrol shifter territory.

"I'm so proud of you, son." He embraces Archie again, and I see a wide smile stretch across the boy's face as his chest puffs out. "You were very brave and did well to get away from the witch."

He really must have shaken the witch up, or maybe the witch isn't very powerful, because he should have easily been able to subdue a shifter child with his magic. Maybe that's why he smelled like moldy hay—most witches smell like fresh herbs or some kind of plant—or maybe it points to the other suspicion that is niggling inside my brain, which is that it could have been a human.

"And I rode on Hunter's back too," he announces proudly. Hunter winces and tries to melt into the wall as Gracelin's eyes narrow on him. Before she can voice a barrage of grievances, Queen Mia, Gretchin's mother, clears her throat, and we turn our attention to her. She shifts a couple of long black braids off her shoulder, her dark eyes alight with curiosity. She's wearing a red pantsuit that looks stunning against her dark skin. The king really is a lucky guy. The queens are all striking women, and not only are they gorgeous, but they are also kind and loving. I have gotten to know them well through my friendship with their son.

"Tell us more about the human woman. We need to show her our thanks. She obviously took care of our boy if he wants to marry her." Her lips twitch, but she smothers her amusement.

"The human owns a bakery in the neutral zone. She seemed kind enough," I tell them, thinking about the spark between us when we shook hands, then I remember the thing I shoved into my pocket. I pull out the little marshmallow tiger. It's slightly squished but doesn't look too worse for wear. I hold my hand out, showing them. "She's making these adorable marshmallow animals in celebration of your retirement," I tell them, stepping over and giving it to Archie, whose eyes light up at the treat.

"Colbie made me," he declares, snatching it from my hand and holding it like it's the most precious thing in the world. He runs a finger over the marshmallow head. "I will keep it forever," he declares, and Gracelin scrunches up her nose.

"No, you will not. You'll attract ants and critters into your room. Eat it now, and then we can find you some real food," she tells him. His bottom lip sticks out, and it's like his four grandparents hold their breath. I snicker at the reaction, but his curiosity must win out over his desire to keep his new friend's creation, because he stuffs it into his mouth and chews, his eyes going round with astonishment. "Tastes like oranges," he tells everyone, mumbling around the mallow. "It's really good."

"Don't talk with your mouth full," Queen Evelyn scolds, but there's no anger in her tone. Her hazel eyes sparkle with mirth as she watches him enjoy his treat.

"Did you say her name is Colbie?" Queen Layla asks, leaning forward. Her shoulder-length red hair falls forward with the movement, and I see the interest in her eyes.

"Yes, Colbie, and she's really pretty, with long black hair and pretty purple eyes. She's short like you, Mom, but she smells nice, like cupcakes, and she had a really nice voice." Archie sighs, and again, we all snicker at his lovesick actions. "She gave me milk and a whole plate of meat when I was in cub form and couldn't change back and eat cupcakes. She sang while she baked, and it was so nice, I went to sleep."

Gracelin's eyes soften at hearing how well her son was treated by the little human.

"Colbie's an unusual name. You don't think it's the same Colbie we were friends with as kids, do you?" Gretchin runs her hand over her nephew's tousled blond hair, smiling indulgently before turning to her mother. Gretchin keeps her hair cropped short against her head. She complains that her curls are too hard to manage when she's on patrol as part of one of the shifter army teams.

"Yes, I was thinking the same thing," Evelyn agrees as she turns to her co-queens. "Wasn't Malina Karridge's daughter called Colbie?"

"The dress designer?" Layla's eyebrows jump. "I think so, but when we stopped bringing the kids to our appointments, she stopped having her daughter there. I remember the four of them would sit under her design table and giggle the whole time she measured, fitted, and showed us samples. They would have tea parties, and it kept them out of our hair," she explains to the rest of us in the room.

"Yes, I remember she was a little younger than us but a sweet girl. She would bake us cookies to have with our tea. They were the yummiest things I'd ever tasted." Gretchin nudges her sister. "Do you remember?"

"Yes, she was such a shy little thing, always so nervous around Gryffin, but one day, she had a broken arm and wasn't able to pour the tea, and she started crying. Our brother almost had a panic attack. He took over, poured the tea from her little teapot, and assured her he would help with whatever she needed. I think he was a little smitten with the little girl." Gracelin laughs before frowning. "I had forgotten all about her. I feel guilty now."

Gracelin and Gretchin have an air of sadness about them. "Why did we stop going? I know you still use her," Gretchin asks her mother, but it's Gryffin's mother, Layla, who answers.

"You turned twelve and got control of your shifts. We didn't want you scaring the girl. Although her mother knew who we were, the girl didn't, and we didn't think it was fair to you three or her if you shifted in front of her and she was scared. You didn't seem to notice since you had plenty of your own school friends, and like you said, she was a little younger than you."

"Fine, but I would like to do something nice for her. She needs an award or something," Gracelin says, and I clear my throat, remembering what the intriguing woman said to me.

"I suggested the same thing, and she vehemently denied it. She was just glad Archie was safe," I explain, and there's a look of wonder on their faces. There aren't many people, shifter or human, who would turn down a reward from the king and queens. "I get the feeling she didn't want to draw attention."

"You know what would probably be a nice gesture?" Queen Mia muses thoughtfully. "If we supported her bakery and ordered some treats. That way, we'll show we are supportive of neutral zone businesses and encourage other shifters to visit."

"But in the past, you always suggested we avoid the neutral zone," Gretchin argues.

"We walk a fine line, Gretchin. We are the shifter king and queens, and despite me being a former human, we can't be seen as favoring the humans over shifters or vice versa, but I don't see any harm in it this time," King Lucas says to his daughter, going over to a side table and pulling the stopper out of a crystal bottle that holds amber liquid. He gestures to General Bryson and holds out a glass, but the general shakes his head. The king turns to Hunter and me and raises an eyebrow.

"We have to get back to command and sign out for the day, but thank you, sir," I tell him, and he nods in understanding. Despite being the king, we grew up as his son's best friends and have been bond mates since we turned seventeen. He is like another father to both Hunter and me.

He pours a glass for himself and Adam, handing his son-in-law his before turning his attention to his wives and daughters. "Can I order you some tea, ladies?" The five women have been whispering amongst themselves and quickly separate when he speaks to them.

"What, we don't get offered whiskey too?" Gretchin scowls at her father who winces sheepishly and pours her a glass, before passing it to her. He raises his eyebrows at the other women. Gracelin shakes her head.

"That would be lovely, thank you, dear," Queen Layla replies with a laugh. "You know, I believe I need a new dress for the coronation ceremony. I think I might just pop in and see Malina. It's been a while since we used her services."

Queen Mia claps her hands, her eyes sparkling. "What a wonderful idea. I believe we all could use new dresses. How about we all go?"

"Don't forget about us." Gretchin nudges her sister, who nods her head. "Yes, and I believe I would like to get a hot chocolate and maybe one or two tigers to float on top." She growls and pretends to scratch at Archie, who giggles and throws himself into his aunt's arms.

"And if I go too, I can see my future wife again, and maybe she will make me a hot chocolate too," he says, wrapping his little arms around Gretchin and hugging her tightly. When her eyes widen and she gasps for air, Adam untangles his son.

"Ladies, how about you leave the poor girl alone? She did this family a tremendous favor when she found our boy. Let's not go and ruin it," King Lucas warns, but they ignore him, and he huffs out an annoyed breath while Bryson doesn't even try to hide his amusement. Lucas scowls at him. "Shall I invite Ember and Sable over to conspire?" he suggests, and both Bryson and Hunter shudder and shake their heads. Hunt's mother and sister are just as energetic as the queens and princesses. Maybe a little more, to be honest, because they don't have to worry about keeping up appearances.

"We have to get going." Hunter pushes off the wall and nudges me with his elbow. "Come on, we need to check in with the rest of the team and clock out."

"If you see Gianna, make sure you let her know the king wants to see her, and if she doesn't come, escort her here yourselves," Bryson reminds us, and I nod while Hunter grimaces. He hates Gianna. She's made it very clear that she would like to mate our bonded group, but we have no interest in her. All our animals agree. She doesn't smell right to any of them, not to mention she doesn't carry our mark.

"And don't forget, you are all invited to our retirement party. It would be nice if you brought dates," Queen Mia calls after us.

"Or we could introduce you to some very lovely ladies," Evelyn suggests.

"Leave them be," Queen Layla scolds her co-wives. "They will find love when the time is right, and she will be perfect. You know how hard it is for bonded groups to find the one. The goddess will mark their mate when she deems them ready."

We hurry out of the room, their arguing voices fading behind us. I can't stop the yawn that leaves my mouth, and I rub my eyes. "God, I can't wait to get to bed. It's been a long ass night." I clap Hunter on the shoulder.

"It has been a long night, but thankfully a successful one. Want a ride back?" he offers, and I consider whether to shift and run and decide I'm too tired.

"Yeah, that would be great. The sooner I can get back, the sooner I can hit the hay."

He shifts, and I climb up. We soar across shifter land back toward the neutral zone. I am hoping soon, I can make my way back to the bakery to get coffee and take another look at the pretty human girl, but I keep that thought to myself. I have no business wanting a second look at her, but there was just something about her that piqued both my and my wolf's interest.

FOUR

Colbie

Over the next few days, the marshmallows prove to be a huge hit. We have twice as many customers coming in to get coffee, and all the tables in our café are full. I'm run off my feet and have doubled the batch of marshmallow creatures. I've added wolves and dragons after practicing late one night when the café was closed—not because that gorgeous watchman suggested it, but because it makes good business sense. I heard somewhere that shifters are all apex animals.

Thankfully we don't serve an evening meal and close our doors at five. Even then, though, I'm running on very little sleep, but I feel so proud when I see all those mugs of coffee and hot chocolate with little floating animals on top.

Both shifters and humans alike seem to find them amusing, and I have had requests for a variety of creatures, so many in fact that we put a suggestion board in the front for people to write their requests.

Justin has been working longer hours and has been a huge help to me. Despite not being the friendliest of people, he is picking up baking skills remarkably fast. Tuesday, I hired a shifter college student who came in asking if any work was available. Once I gained her parents' approval, I eagerly employed her to work the front counter with Olivia. Violet started off a little shy, but by the end of the week, she fit in like she's always been here.

I'm busy back in the kitchen when a breathless Violet slams open the door separating the front from the kitchen, and she rushes in and leans against the door with her hand over her heart.

"Oh my goodness. Watch Team One just walked in, and they are delicious. I didn't want them to smell my attraction," she tells me when I arch a questioning eyebrow at her.

"That's a thing?" I ask, scrunching my nose in surprise. "That must get old quickly if someone can smell your attraction."

She shrugs her shoulders. "Kind of saves time too. No fumbling, awkward rejections," she reasons.

"Huh, I guess it would." Being a shifter is way more complicated than I ever knew, but it would save time. I could have avoided a whole heap of embarrassing dates if I had those kinds of clues.

"Yeah. Honestly, it's not so bad unless you're in a crowded room full of people attracted to one another, and then it gets a little overwhelming. They sat down, so it's not going to take long before the café reeks. There are a lot of shifters in here today, all wanting to try the little marshmallows. You wouldn't believe the sweet tooth shifters have," she says, and I put down the cloth I was using to clean the prep bench.

"Do you want to stay back and finish doing those dishes while I serve? The smell isn't going to bother me," I suggest, not wanting to run my server off in her first week.

Violet is in her first year of college, but the schools are all on a two week holiday to celebrate the retirement and coronation.

She nibbles on her lip, her eyes sliding back to the door as she thinks about it. "Yeah, that would be great actually. I'm not one of those delusional females who thinks they have a chance with Watch Team One, even though they are gorgeous. I go to school with one of their brothers, and he's just as gorgeous. I avoid him like the plague so he can't scent how sexy I think he is." Her cheeks turn pink, and I chuckle.

"Have you ever considered that he might think you're just as gorgeous?" She's tall, like most shifters, and has this refined elegance about her. She has long, curly blonde hair that she ties back while at work, striking silver eyes that sparkle when she laughs, and a dimple on each cheek. Hell, I'm half in love with her myself, and I see Justin watching her with a little too much interest for a human toward a shifter. I'll keep an eye on him and warn him off if I think I need to.

Her mouth rounds, and she shakes her head. "No, of course not. I'm nowhere in his league. His family are all dragons, and his father is general to King Lucas. My family are all simple farmers. No, I know exactly where I sit in the pecking order, and I am fine with watching from afar."

I frown at her words, wondering if shifter society really is that elitist. I guess it makes sense depending on your animal and level of power, but I hate that this girl doesn't think she is worthy of more.

"Well then, he doesn't know what he's missing. You're a catch, gorgeous and kind, and I'd wife you up in a heartbeat if I were a male shifter," I tell her, and her giggles warm my heart as I check my apron to make sure I haven't made too big of a mess before heading to the front to help.

Wow, she wasn't wrong. The front is very busy, but Olivia and Justin seem to have a handle on preparation, so I take over Violet's job of waitressing. I pick up the tablet we use and look around the room. Most tables already seem to have their orders, but there is a large booth in the back full of men who can only be shifters. Each and every one of them is taller and broader than the average human male, and I recognize two of the men as the watchmen who came and got the tiger cub at the beginning of the week. I head in their direction. I can feel the gazes of the two familiar men on me, but I don't let it fluster me. Their intensity is heavy, but I've lived in the neutral zone my whole life, so shifter intensity is nothing new.

I get a good look at them myself. Unlike at the beginning of the week, none of them are in night watch uniforms. All wear a version of jeans and a T-shirt, and I almost want to reach up and make sure none of the drool pooling in my mouth has escaped. Holy shit, they can wear casual clothes like a dream. From what I can see under the table, their jeans mold to their legs like they were painted on, and their T-shirts do nothing to hide the fact that these guys work out a lot.

I plaster on a neutral smile—my customer service face—and stop beside the booth. "Hey, welcome to Glazed and Glorious. What can I get you today?" There are some amused smirks and childish snickers at the name. Yeah, I wasn't thinking with a teenage boy's mind when I named my bakery, but I feel like changing it now would just draw attention to the dirty connotations.

"This is her?" one of the men grumbles, and I turn my attention to him, raising an eyebrow at his tone. He has a shock of pure white hair that is longer on top but shaved close to his scalp around the sides. He pushes back his long white bangs and studies me with eyes so dark it's like looking in a mirror. The stubble on his face matches the color on his head, so I'm guessing it's natural, which is a little unusual. He has a punk vibe with a piercing in his eyebrow and through one of his lush lips which are pressed tightly together, and I can practically feel his disapproval.

"Yeah, this is Colbie." Huh, Archie must have told them my name. I wasn't even sure if he understood what I said when he was in animal form, but I guess he did. "She's the woman who found Archie when he went missing and rescued him," the blue-eyed hottie says before smiling at me. "I'm sorry we didn't introduce ourselves the other day. Seeing Archie in your kitchen was both a shock and a relief. I'm Brodie, and you know Hunter." He waves at the blond mountain man sitting next to him. His green eyes study me, but I don't feel any anger or aggression in his gaze, just curiosity. He nods his head in greeting. I turn up the customer service face slightly and give him a more genuine smile. I could tell he really cared about the cub.

"These are our other teammates, Liam and Jeremy, but we call him Gem." Liam is the grumbly one who stares at me with unblinking eyes, but I ignore the intimidation tactics and turn my attention to the final man in the booth. My breath hitches in surprise. His whiskey brown eyes have flames in them, and unlike the others who are all large, muscular men, this one, although just as tall, is leaner, like a runner or a swimmer, and has a head of unruly dark red curls. His features are slightly more feminine than the others, but they look good on him. His plush lips turn up in a smile as he reaches for my hand. I don't stop him as he leans over and places a kiss on the back of it. His lips are shockingly hot, and I tear my hand away then frown down at the spot he kissed. It stays warm for a moment before fading.

He smirks and winks. "It's a pleasure to meet you, Colbie, and we can't thank you enough for looking after Archie like you did," Gem says, and his voice has a musical quality to it.

Brodie chuckles. "Yes, you certainly made an impression. He went home and told his parents that he is going to marry you."

I chuckle at his words. "He was definitely a little cutie and very brave. I could do worse," I joke, shrugging my shoulders and smiling. "And seriously, it's what anyone would do if they found a lost child."

"No, actually, it isn't, though I find it suspicious that he wound up in your alley. It's a long way for a small cub to run. Are you sure that's where you found him?" Liam demands aggressively, and I step backwards as Brodie glares at his friend.

"Easy, Liam. Archie corroborated her story. You're just looking for trouble where it doesn't exist," Hunter cautions him, and Brodie rolls his eyes.

"What the fuck is wrong with you, man?"

Gem wears that ever-present smirk as he watches his friends argue. "He's pissed because Gianna lost her job for cutting off the call when Colbie called the watch. No more after-work booty calls for him. She's been asked to move out of the watch apartments." Gem looks like the turmoil amongst his friends is amusing him.

Hunter's mouth drops open in shock, and it's the first time he hasn't looked formidable. "You've been fucking Gianna?" He sounds surprised, like it's the first time he's hearing about it.

"What the fuck, man? Why would you do that? Our bond is supposed to agree on who we want to be with!" Brodie's blue eyes blaze with fury, and I step back a little.

"How about I give you all a few more moments to decide? I'll come back." I turn and flee, but I don't even think the shifters notice, so caught up in their own drama. There are a few coffees at the counter, so I take them to the tables they belong to before returning to the counter. They seem to have things under control, so I decide to check on Violet. That scene with the shifters was way too intense, and my stomach feels funny. It's weird, kind of like I feel jealous about a woman I've never even met having sex with a shifter I only literally met and who was kind of an asshole. How ridiculous. Maybe

I'm just nervous to be in the presence of four huge shifters.

"How's it going?" I ask her, slightly breathless, and she looks up from the bowl she is drying and tilts her head to the side quizzically.

"Are you okay? Your heart is racing."

I wave a hand, trying to make light of the situation. "I'm fine. It's been a long week. As good as this whole retirement and coronation stuff has been for business, I won't be sad to see it go back to normal. I'm exhausted."

"Yeah, it's ridiculous. All the shifters are edgy too, and a lot more fights have been occurring. I'm almost done here, though, since you just about finished everything yourself anyway."

"Yeah, I want to go see my mom this afternoon, so I was super organized today. I haven't seen her for about a week, and we live in the same building."

Her eyes light up. "Olivia was telling me your mom is Malina Karridge. She's my hero. She designs such beautiful clothes. I hope I have half the amount of her talent after I finish design school."

"You want to be a designer?" I ask, surprised. I don't think she mentioned that before, or maybe she did, and I've been so busy this week it kind of just slipped past me. She puts down the pot she was drying and folds the towel over the rail on the oven, nodding enthusiastically.

"Yeah, my family isn't poor, but we don't have

extra money for designer clothes, so when I saw something I liked and couldn't afford it, I taught myself to sew. I got a scholarship to Aramis University, and I'm studying both business and design classes. I read somewhere that's where your mom went."

Aramis University is located in the neutral zone and is attended by both humans and shifters. I attended some business classes there while I was doing my apprenticeship with a human baker in the human zone.

"Yeah, she did, and how she tells it, it was some of the most exciting times of her life. I'll have to introduce you to her when she's not so busy. She's fully booked at the moment because of all the shifter celebrations," I tell my new friend who squeals and jumps up and down, clapping. It makes me wonder what kind of shifter she is, but I'm not going to be rude and ask. She will tell me if she wants to, and it really doesn't matter to me. I hope she doesn't regret meeting my mom though. You know that saying, never meet your idols? My mom is a lot, and to be honest, she could probably do as much to destroy Violet's self-esteem as she could to boost it. She's not callous and mean, but she can be selfish and thoughtless.

"Oh, I wonder whom she's making dresses for. I read somewhere that she used to regularly outfit the queens. Does she still do that?"

I frown, thinking back to when I was little and

spent time hanging out in my mom's studio on the weekends.

"Um, I don't know, to be honest. I don't remember her outfitting queens, but I was a child and didn't really pay attention."

"Oh well, it's still exciting. Now tell me, is Watch Team One yummy or what?" she asks me, abruptly changing the subject, and it takes me a moment to get my thoughts into order. I don't want to admit that they are the reason I'm feeling slightly off-kilter.

"Yeah, they are gorgeous, but I already met two of them at the beginning of the week. I found a lost cub in the alley, and they eventually came and returned him to his family."

I didn't think her face could hold any more expression, but her eyes widen even further, and she waves her hands around in agitation. "You're the human who found Prince Archie? Holy crap, how did I not know this? There are so many rumors about what happened, but nobody knows the truth, and the royal family has been tight-lipped. I'm sure they tried to keep the fact that he was missing quiet too, but one of the night watch operators has a big mouth, and when she got fired, she blabbed it everywhere." Her brow creases in a frown.

My mind goes back to the conversation the men at the booth were having. "Are you talking about Gianna?"

Violet's nose scrunches up, and she purses her

lips like she tasted something sour. "Yes, you know her? Ugh, I go to school with her sister Liana, and she's a witch."

"Like a real witch?" I ask, and Violet chuckles, shaking her head.

"No, just a regular shifter bitch witch, but she's awful. She thinks she's better than anyone else and is going to find herself a powerful bond."

We fall silent as I work up the courage to ask what I desperately want to know. "Violet, do you mind if I ask a question?"

She shakes her head, smiling at me. "Normally you probably shouldn't if it's a shifter thing, but I want you to trust me as a friend and worker, so ask away."

"What's a bond?"

"Ah, yeah, okay. So a bond is a group of shifters who have been brought together by the goddess Aramis to share a mate. They are all marked with a matching tattoo above their heart on their seventeenth birthday. They then move into one of the parents' houses and learn to work as a team. It doesn't happen to all shifters, and there are some one-on-one matings, but for some reason, there aren't as many female children born as males, and bond mates sharing a mate makes it so no one misses out. I'd love to be fated to a bond, but I don't think I'll be so lucky." I can hear the disappointment in her tone, even as my eyes widen at the thought of having a relationship with more than one man. Hell, I can't even keep the attention of one, let alone multiple.

"The females don't get a tattoo?" I ask.

"Only when the goddess thinks she and her fated bond are ready. It can happen at any time for females, which is why Gianna keeps hoping she will be blessed with Watch Team One's symbol. It hasn't happened yet, though, and now that she's been reprimanded by the king, she's certainly not going to be welcome at any royal functions for a while."

"Thank you for sharing. I won't tell anyone," I promise her, and she smiles at me.

"I know you won't. You're a good person, Colbie Karridge, I can feel it."

"Listen, do you think you could take that team's order? They were arguing, so I gave them a few more moments, but I really want to go visit my mom." I pull the apron over my head and pray that Violet doesn't notice how nervous and unsettled I feel after seeing those shifters. It's weird, they are all gorgeous and most of them have been nothing but cordial, but there's still something that puts me on edge. I really don't want to go back and have the black-eyed growly man grill me about my involvement with Archie. Nope, it will be better if I steer clear. I do feel a little guilty knowing they are going to smell Violet's attraction, but if it's a shifter thing, then I'm sure they are used to it.

She swallows nervously but nods her agreement as I hang up my apron and grab my bag. "Yeah, okay, but you owe me. If Talon ever comes in, you're going to have to serve him for me." I'm assuming that's the brother she spoke of earlier.

"Agreed," I promise. "Please tell Olivia and Justin where I went. I'll probably be back later to do some prep, but tell them to lock up when you all leave."

Tomorrow is the day of the retirement party. There will be a parade through the streets of the shifter zone that is being televised, as is the party, so I'm hoping it might be quieter tomorrow. Then, at the point when the full moon is high in the sky, the next shifter king or queen will be chosen by magic. I will be well and truly tucked up in my bed by then, but I wish the human who gets chosen much luck.

Hunter

"You fucked Gianna?" Brodie growls at our bond mate. "I thought we all decided to avoid her."

"Fuck, man, I told you how my dragon feels about her. I can't believe you would do that to us," I scold our brother in all but blood, unable to stop the smoke from drifting out of my nostrils with my annoyance.

Liam is one angry messy ball of emotions, and my chest aches in the spot where our bond resides. I rub a hand over it. Most of the time, I can block out their emotions, but extreme ones seem to push their way through, even if I don't want them to. I know he's sick of waiting for our mate to turn up, but to fuck someone my dragon wants to decapitate, especially after I told him how I feel? That's kind of spitting on our bond.

"Whom I fuck is none of your business," he snaps, not looking at either of us. The damn phoenix just crosses his arms and smirks, watching our interaction with amusement. Liam glares at him for telling us.

"You could have kept your fucking mouth shut."

The phoenix shakes his head. "No, I couldn't, because since you gave her hope, she's been hovering around everywhere we go. Hell, I'm surprised she hasn't turned up here." He looks around the café like he's searching for Gianna, but I know him better than he thinks. The little human intrigued him, and I'm almost certain he's looking for her instead, which will just piss Liam off further. I wouldn't say he's anti-human, but he avoids having anything to do with them. We're just lucky that as the top team in the night watch, sanctioned by General Bryson, that we don't have to have a human on it. We need to be able to move quickly, and humans just can't keep up with our animals.

Liam's eyes light up, and he looks around the room, hoping to see Gianna. I can't stop the grumble that comes from my chest. Seems like she got her hooks into our bond mate. This is going to cause issues with our bond, because the rest of us won't even look at her. We know our mate is out there, and we will wait until Aramis decides it's time for us to know who she is.

Before Brodie and I can scold him any further, a shifter girl approaches our table. I recognize her, though I can't remember her name. I quickly glance at her name tag—Violet. She goes to school with my brother, and he has a massive crush on her, but he has recently formed his own bond group, and I advised him to take the same caution. You don't want to be responsible for a girl's heartbreak. I can see why he's interested though. She's a pretty little thing.

"Hi, are you guys ready to order?" she asks nervously and holds up the tablet, waiting for our orders.

"Where did Colbie go?" Brodie asks.

Her nerves drop away, and she puts her hands on her hips and glares at us. "She had to duck out, but did you know you painted a target on her back? Colbie doesn't deserve all the shit Gianna is spreading about her. She's a good person."

"Huh? What do you mean?" I ask, not sure what she's talking about, and I can tell that Gem and Brodie don't either, but Liam shifts uncomfortably on his seat.

"Well, since Gianna got raked over the coals by the king and General Bryson and lost her job, Gianna has been telling everyone that the human lied, and she didn't tell her about the shifter cub. She claims she had to prioritize the calls because everyone was out searching for the cub, and Colbie was just a silly human who was complaining about something unimportant. Gianna has even gone so far as suggesting that she was the one who kidnapped Prince Archer and then pretended to rescue him to get in the royal family's good books."

Our gazes swing to Liam. We glare at him when he nods his head. "She was really upset when she lost her job and had to move out of the night watch apartments. She claims the human was lying and that she didn't cut her off. She said she didn't mention a thing about the lost cub, just that she needed the night watch to check out the alley because she heard a funny noise. Stupid human needs to learn to stay in her own lane," he growls, and my dragon pushes forward, wanting to take a bite out of our bond mate. I wrestle him back, but not before scales flutter across my lower arms. Liam eyes me warily, knowing he's playing with fire— literally.

"That's bullshit and not true," Brodie explodes. "Archie told us the truth. That could be dangerous for Colbie. You know how shifters can get. Maybe we need to warn the general so he can put a security team on her for a while until things die down. Everyone will be on edge until the next king or queen has been found."

"Gianna has been banned from the neutral zone for six months anyway. I have to go back to the shifter lands to see her," Liam grumbles, completely oblivious, or maybe stubbornly determined to ignore our feelings on the matter.

"Good riddance is all I can say," Gem mutters before turning his attention to the menu and telling the girl what he wants for lunch. "I'll also have one of those adorable hot chocolates with bear marshmallows please. I'll enjoy drowning them." Liam glares at him, but Gem ignores him while the girl enters his order into the tablet.

The rest of us place our own orders, and Violet scurries off to take care of them. "You need to stop seeing Gianna. It's only going to cause problems when we find our mate," I tell him, my dragon very upset with our friend's selfishness right now. He keeps pushing to shift and fry his ass—not that we could, because our bond makes them immune to my fire.

There's a stubborn set to his lips, and he crosses his arms. "I don't want to, and you can't make me."

"Look, we get it. We've been waiting for our mate for a while, but Aramis must have a plan for us. Giving Gianna hope is not doing anyone any favors. You're just breaking her heart. You know we can't mate with her," I remind my stubborn friend.

"Unless she ends up with our mark," Liam argues belligerently.

"The likelihood of that is slim. My dragon can't stand her," I tell him.

"Neither can my wolf," Brodie adds, and when

Liam looks at Gem, he shakes his head. His usual smirk is gone, and he looks sad for our friend.

Liam slumps down in the booth, looking defeated. "My bear is getting unruly. He doesn't particularly like Gianna as a person either, but he does like fucking her, and he wants someone to care for. He doesn't really care who it is anymore," Liam admits quietly, and Gem holds out his hand. Liam takes it, and Brodie and I watch as phoenix flames appear, helping to soothe Liam's bear. Phoenix shifters are healers, both of the body and soul, so hopefully that will ease the bear a little so Liam can start making better decisions.

We watch as some of the tension in Liam's body eases, and he breathes out a large sigh. "Thanks. I'm sorry. He's really riding me hard. It's becoming tricky to hold him back. Maybe I should take a leave of absence for a while. Move back home away from temptation."

"Don't be too hasty. You know the goddess often blesses more shifters than normal during a coronation year. Hopefully by the time a new king or queen has been crowned, we will also have been blessed with our mate," Gem reasons, and some hope comes back into Liam's dejected eyes.

"At least we don't have to worry about being tapped as a mate for the next king or queen. Being in a bond saves us from that," Brodie remarks. "I don't envy all those single shifters waiting on tenterhooks to see if they are going to end up being selected as a possible mate for the new royal."

"I feel sorry for the new royal. It must be hard enough to figure out how to coexist with an animal without the added pressure of picking a mate, let alone more than one."

The others murmur their agreement as Violet returns to the table with our drinks.

I asked Gryffin once when we were younger how his dad picked his three moms, and he said his dad just knew. Apparently he had a connection with the three of them he didn't have with the other potentials, although he did have to date them all to give them a chance. How confusing that must be for a recent human.

I smile at the sight of the two little dragon marshmallows floating in my coffee. Brodie gets a goofy grin and scoops up one of the wolves in his with a spoon and studies it closer before sticking it in his mouth. His eyebrows jump. "Oh, they are minty," he exclaims. "I told her to make wolves and dragons," he says, his mouth full of marshmallow, and Gem gags.

"Jesus, Brodie, where are your manners? No wonder the goddess hasn't deemed us fit to grant us a mate yet." The phoenix shudders and stirs his hot chocolate, being unnecessarily rough with the bears floating on top and grinning wickedly when they start to melt and drown.

"Ridiculous," Liam grumbles, taking a sip of his

black coffee, nothing floating in his. I'm pretty sure he's just being a stubborn asshole. He has the sweetest tooth of us all and would usually have multiple marshmallows covering the top of his.

"Your lunches won't be long. Justin is just frying the bacon for the BLTs," Violet tells us.

"When do you think Colbie will get back?" Brodie asks, and the girl's eyebrows jump in surprise. He quickly realizes his mistake in showing too much interest in a human. "Ah, we need to ask her a couple of questions regarding the other night," he explains, and the girl nods, but I can see she doesn't believe him.

"She will be in tomorrow, but we aren't expecting it to be busy because of the parade and the party, so she will probably close early, and we are closed on Sunday because of the holiday, so Monday will be the next time she's back in the café."

Brodie winces. "We will be involved in the parade and party tomorrow. We're pulling security for the parade, and our bond has been invited as guests to the party. That's okay, we will come in on Monday and talk to her."

Violet walks away, and Liam growls at Brodie. "What the fuck are you playing at? You think I'm bad for showing interest in Gianna, but that's not as bad as sniffing around a human."

Liam is right. Brodie should forget about the human. Sure, she was pretty, and she wasn't easily intimidated when we collected Archie, but she's not for us, even if she smells delicious, like cupcakes and cream cheese frosting. My dragon would like to give her a lick to see if she tastes as good as she smells, but we won't. That's only a road to heartbreak for all of us.

"Gods, you're such an asshole." Brodie flips Liam off, and Gem watches eagerly, like he's waiting for them to brawl in the café. Our phoenix is mischievous and likes to stir up trouble.

"But he's right." I agree with Liam, even though it hurts to admit it. "Colbie is human and isn't for us."

Brodie's aggravation drains away, and his whole body slumps. "I know, but my wolf likes her. He wants to roll around and cover himself with her scent."

"Huh." Gem sounds surprised. "That is unusual. Humans usually don't smell like anything to me, but you're right, she does smell nice, like cupcakes."

"And frosting," I add, my dragon licking his lips.

"It doesn't matter, she could smell like the best thing ever, and we still couldn't do anything about it. If I have to forget Gianna, who is at least a shifter, then you need to forget about the pretty human baker."

Brodie smirks, but Liam hasn't even realized he admitted he found the human attractive.

We fall into an uneasy silence, all lost in our

own thoughts as Violet returns with our sandwiches. We all ordered chicken schnitzel and cheese BLTs, and the rolls that are placed in front of us need two hands to eat so the filling doesn't fall out. Violet tells us to enjoy the food before serving another group who just walked in, and we eat our meal in companionable silence. I watch as humans and shifters come and go. Some stay and eat in the café, while some just get takeaway orders, but all have excellent things to say about the bakery and its food.

"Why haven't we ever eaten here before? This is fucking delicious," Gem asks, taking a sip of his soda, half of his sandwich already gone.

"Probably because it's human owned. We tend to favor shifter establishments because we are supporting our people," I reply, acknowledging our slight prejudice, but it's not about shifters being better than humans or anything, just that we're shifters so we should support our shifter brethren.

"Well, clearly we're idiots," Brodie says after swallowing his mouthful. "I wonder if they will deliver to the night watch tower in the evenings?"

"I'm sorry, but we aren't open for evening meals," Violet says, hearing his comment as she hurries back and forth from the counter to the tables. "We close at five."

Brodie groans his disappointment.

"But you can order earlier, and we can deliver to you. You would just need to keep it in the fridge until you're ready to eat it," she suggests, and he perks right up. "The menu is on our website."

She disappears into the back with the dirty dishes, and Brodie takes out his phone. I can see him googling the bakery. I'd bet my last dollar that he is trying to find out more information about the owner. I can't wait for Gryffin to return from wherever he went. Bryson said he asked to go into witch territory to look for Archer, frantic about his nephew missing, but Gryffin has also had a personal preoccupation for the last couple of years, and he uses these trips for another reason. We've told him to give it up, but he refuses to.

He should return soon though. We messaged him that Archer had been found, I just hope he got it, because cell phones are notoriously unreliable between kingdoms. Something about the magical borders disrupts the signals.

Hopefully he can help talk some sense into Liam. His bear has always responded well to Gryffin's tiger. Between Gryffin and Gem, they will balance our bond mate, and not a moment too soon, because the next few weeks are going to be busy with all the royal engagements, and I'm sure by the end of it, both Gianna and the pretty little human will be off everyone's minds.

Suddenly, our phones all start to ring with a specific tone—that's the night watch alarm. We're all on alert as I pull it out of my pocket and look at the screen. "Fuck." A wave of adrenaline washes through me at the message. "A group of ferals have been sighted."

The four of us stand up. Gem tosses a handful of bills on the table to cover our meal and tip, and then the four of us hurry out of the restaurant.

"It's been a few months since we had a feral problem," Liam comments as we run toward night watch headquarters.

"And a group of ferals is something we've never dealt with. Usually they are solitary creatures." Gem sounds devastated. He hates the part of our job where we have to put a feral shifter down. He's a healer at heart, so killing a feral who didn't ask to be that way always destroys him.

"If only we could trace a feral back to the shifter that tried to turn them, then we could punish the real culprit." Brodie's face is stone cold. The cheerful, joking man is gone, and in his place is someone who is prepared for what we might face, but he still hates it.

Ferals are the worst part of being in the night watch. They usually escape to the neutral or human zones, and we have to put them down. Very rarely do they stay in the shifter zone, where they are dealt with by the shifter armed forces. They know being a feral is a death sentence. Although they start off fairly rational, the mental deterioration happens quickly, making them aggressive and dangerous. They don't have the king's magic to balance them. It is an ongoing bone of contention for the shifter community and the only issue that causes the royal family grief. It obviously needs to be addressed again, but with the royal handover, the new king or queen is going to have to be brought up to speed swiftly. Thankfully the outgoing royals will be able to advise, because it isn't a decision that should be made by someone who's uninformed.

SIX

Colbie

I leave through the back door of my bakery, the urge to avoid the gorgeous shifters fierce inside me, but as I pass the door to the book-shop across the alley, the screen bangs open, and Brock appears. Brock isn't a super tall man, maybe five-ten, but he is fit, though his muscles aren't anything on the watch team's. Maybe it's a shifter thing, and all of them are fit and have incredible bodies because they shift into animals and run or fly everywhere.

I look down my curvy body, sucking in my slight pouch from tasting my own creations. Damn it, I need to add some exercise to my daily routine, not just the walk between my apartment and business.

"Colbie," he hisses, his chestnut hair all awry

like he's been running his hand through it. His black-rimmed glasses are slightly askew as well. This is the most frazzled I've ever seen him. Usually he is immaculately put together, the epitome of cool, calm, and collected. His partner, Niles, is usually the flighty scatter-brained one. "Girl, I have been trying to pin you down for days. Why did I see some of Watch Team One leaving your kitchen on Monday morning with a child in their arms?" He puts a hand against his chest, looking aghast. "Were you the human involved in finding Prince Archie? It's all anyone is talking about. So much juicy gossip, not to mention the sacking of the night watch operator for dereliction of duty, but who knows what's true and what's false. Now dish," he demands, putting his hands on his hips, and I sigh. There's no way I'm walking away without telling him what happened.

"Yeah, when I arrived early Monday morning, I found him huddled up under some of your boxes near the dumpster. Poor thing was soaking wet from the drizzle and terrified."

He gasps and leans against the wall like this news is so shocking he needs the wall to hold him up. "Oh my goddess. Where do you think he came from?" His eyes narrow, and I see a calculating look in his gaze. This man lives and breathes gossip, both of them do, and I'm pretty sure he thinks he has a line straight from the source's mouth, which is so much better than all the ideal gossip he has already heard.

"I'm not sure if that's something that is public knowledge, so it's probably best if I don't repeat what I heard. I'm sure you understand." I start to edge my way down the alley to the street. I know this man, he will grill me until he has wrung every last drop of gossip from my mouth, and I really don't want to be responsible for adding to the rumors that are apparently floating around the shifter side.

"What are you doing with the door open, love?" I hear Niles call out to his mate. Crap, if I stop now, I'm never going to get away, and they will wear me down until I tell them everything they want to know.

"I'm just talking to Colbie about the other day," Brock calls back, and I pick up my pace.

"Colbie's there? What does she know?" Niles's voice gets louder as he comes closer.

Out the corner of my eye, I see the tall blond man appear next to his partner, but I just wave, walking faster down the alley, away from the two men.

"Got to go, my mom is expecting me." I hurry around the corner and onto the street, heaving out a sigh of relief. I have no doubt they will try even harder to pin me down to get the gossip, but I'm probably safe for the rest of the weekend. They will be enthralled with all the pageantry for the next couple of days, at least until the new king or queen has been revealed. Hopefully that will be enough to get them to forget about the whole Archie thing.

The streets are way more crowded than I was expecting, and I bump into a woman who glares at me and snaps, "Watch where you're going."

I hold up my hands and apologize, but she doesn't even stop. I groan as I take in the number of humans flooding our streets, each and every one of them praying and hoping they are going to be the next shifter king or queen.

The parade will start in the shifter zone tomorrow, winding its way through there so shifters can give their thanks to the current king and queens before heading to the neutral zone. The retirement party will then be held in the Aramis Arms, the fanciest hotel in the area. At the zenith of the full moon that night, the goddess Aramis will appear to send out the magic which will pick the next king or queen. It is supposed to mark the chosen human with the goddess's symbol. King Lucas's appeared down one side of his face, but it's different for each of the chosen.

I hear excited chatter and speculation all around me, but I'm not interested in it one bit. I have no delusions of grandeur like a lot of these people seem to have. I'll leave them to their dreams of being king or queen and having magic, I am happy just the way I am. The thought of being responsible for a whole race is fucking terrifying, and having magic and being able to shift? Pass. The idea of all my bones breaking and reforming into something new makes me want to hurl—although I'm not sure if that's how it works exactly. When Archie shifted, I didn't hear any bones cracking, so maybe it's not so violent, and he didn't seem to be in any pain, but it still isn't for me.

It takes me longer than normal to walk the distance between the bakery and our apartment building, but I refuse to get annoyed. Instead, I just smile and stay out of the crowd's way. I hate confrontation, and the vibe in the air feels like we're one sharp word or elbow strike away from an all-out brawl. All this tension in the neutral zone is weird. It's an area that prides itself on being exactly what it claims to be.

I catch sight of a night watch team patrolling the area, and the crowd gives them a wide berth. Maybe there needs to be a few more available. I watch as a small scuffle breaks out and they step in to break it up. Instead of hanging around to gawk, I keep my head down and move quicker in the direction I need to go.

Finally, I get to the block our apartment is on.

"Mom, where are you?" I call out as I enter her studio through the back alley. Mom's studio sits on the bottom floor of our apartment building. Above it are two stories with two apartments on each level. I live on the top level in one of the apartments, and Mom lives in the one directly above her studio. She convinced the landlord to put in a set of stairs leading directly to the downstairs retail space. We've lived here as long as I can remember. I only recently moved into my own apartment the last two years. Prior to that, I lived with Mom while I went to university and took pastry classes. Mom's and my relationship has been contentious over the years. I love her, but I am not sad to live separately. She is a difficult woman to please.

"I'm with a client," she sings back, and I wince. Shit, I'm going to get it now. I fill the kettle and turn it on before pulling out her fancy set of china she saves for her clients. If I'm going to annoy her while she's with someone, then the least I can do is make everyone a cup of tea, though they may prefer glasses of champagne, so I grab a fancy bottle out of the fridge and some flutes. I can hear more than two voices, so I go for four just in case. While I wait for the kettle to boil, I plaster on my customer service smile and move out into the studio.

My mom is a gorgeous, statuesque woman, a former fashion model turned designer. I get my long black hair from her, but unlike her six foot frame, I max out at five-five. She says it's my paternal grandmother's fault. She was a small woman, and apparently, I get my boobs and hips from her too—not that I ever met her. Both of my father's parents died before I was born, and my father only blew into my mother's life long enough to make me and cause some deep-seated damage to my mom's psyche before blowing out again. Her parents tell me she was a different person before him and she loves me, but my father's departure made her feel inadequate, and now she strives to be the best at everything and expects the same from me.

She has three women with her. They look kind of familiar to me, but I'm not sure why. "Hi, would any of you like a glass of champagne or a cup of tea?" I offer, and my mother's steely glare softens a little.

"Your Majesties, I'm not sure if you remember my daughter, Colbie. Colbie, this is Queen Layla, Queen Mia, and Queen Evelyn."

I freeze in shock at my mother's words before quickly dipping into a curtsy. "Your Majesties." When I look up, my mom is beaming. Well, at least I did something right.

"Pfft, none of that. You are not a shifter. Just call us by our names, like your mother does." One of the women approaches me. She's about the same height as me but slim with blonde hair. She reaches out and puts her hands on my upper arms, giving them a squeeze. "Thank you for making sure our grandson was looked after. We are forever in your debt." She pulls me into a hug, and her perfume engulfs me like a warm embrace, slightly spicy. Before I can get my stunned self to react, she pulls away. "I'm Evie, and that's Mia." She points to the tall black woman who has the same kind of figure as my mom, like a former fashion model but with undeniable shifter strength. My mom is in the middle, showing her some fabric samples. "And that's Layla." This woman looks like a goddess. She's slightly taller than the others but has curves in all the right places, and her mid-length red hair has a slight curl in it. She's fucking gorgeous, and I may have a slight crush on her. To be honest, I have never paid much attention to the royal family before. I'm a human, so I am not under their rule.

"You made quite an impression on our boy. He has declared you are the love of his life." Layla's voice is husky, and all three women chuckle at her words. When I look at my mom, her eyes are just about bugging out of her head.

"You did what?" She forgets about the samples in her hands and looks at me with a panicked expression.

"When I went to work on Monday, I found a tiger cub huddled under some boxes near the dumpster in our alley," I explain. "I took him inside, called the night watch, and looked after him."

Three rumbling growls reverberate around the room, and my mom takes a step back from the three women, a hand going to her chest in surprise.

"Yes, we heard all about how badly you were treated by the watch operator. She has been dealt with," Mia says darkly.

My mom gapes at me, and I shrug. "I only did what any decent human being would have done." I don't need any praise for doing the right thing.

"Please pour us all a glass of champagne—don't forget yourself and your mother—then come and join us," Evie suggests, waving at the bottle and glasses in my hand.

My gaze slides to my mom, and she gives me a small nod before holding the samples up once more.

"I recently got these fabrics on a trip to the witch kingdom. They are spelled specifically for shifters, so you don't have to worry about ruining them if you shift," she explains, holding out the swatches for the three women.

I pour all three queens glasses of champagne as they discuss their requirements with my mother. "We don't want to overshadow the new queen," Layla explains. "The previous one did that to us, and it made us feel small."

"She was a horrid bitch. She didn't want to give her power up at all, but all the extra magic drains from them as soon as the goddess does her thing. She kept her shifter form, but her extra abilities went straight into Lucas when he was chosen," Mia says, giving Mom and me an unprecedented glimpse of the whole process. "If she couldn't upstage us with magic, then she wanted to upstage us in appearance."

"But if you've been queens for the past forty years, you must have been babies when you were selected." I speak before thinking and then wince at my mom's glare. All three women break into peals of laughter.

"Oh, sweetie, you're good for our self-esteem. Shifters age very slowly. All three of us were in our twenties when we were marked as potential mates for Lucas," Mia explains, taking a sip of her champagne as she studies the samples Mom handed her. Holy shit, that means they are in their sixties but don't look older than their late thirties.

"And so you basically competed with a whole heap of other women to catch his eye?" My mouth gets the better of me, and again, I'm subjected to one of my mother's glares. I wince. "I'm sorry. Forget I asked. It was rude," I apologize, but Layla waves my apology away.

"We trust you won't share this information with others. The royal family will forever be in your debt, so we are happy to answer your curiosity. Aramis marked a number of potential shifters that would be compatible with Lucas. They all presented themselves to the palace, and he got to know each of them. He wasn't forced to pick a specific number or any really, but man and animal need to be in agreement. The three of us clicked with him instantly as well as with each other."

"You're all in a sexual relationship?" I ask, and this time, my mom doesn't just glare, she snaps at me.

"Colbie, that's enough!"

Evie laughs and reassures her. "It's fine, Malina, we invited the questions. No, but when you're in a four-way relationship, boundaries become a thing of the past. It helps that we all get along like sisters."

I wrinkle my nose. "There would be nothing worse than sharing a mate with someone you hated."

"You have no idea. One of the potentials was a former high school rival of mine, and I thank the goddess every day that she was one of the first to be dismissed." Evie shudders.

"What about the marks on the ones who are not chosen?" my mom asks, and I gape at her. She blushes sheepishly. "What? I'm invested now."

"They fade, and only the marks on the chosen ones remain." Layla lifts her dress shirt and shows me a mark on her hip that looks like a tiger.

"Are you all tiger shifters?" I ask. "Archie is one too. Is that a family thing?"

"A shifter child will take after one of their parents. Lucas is an orange tiger, which is what we were all marked with. Mia is a black panther, Evelyn is a lioness, and I am a white tiger," Layla answers, and my eyes widen with all the new information.

"All cats," I murmur, and they nod.

"Yes, I think that's why we probably all clicked so well with him. Archie takes after his mother, Gracelin, who takes after her father instead of a lioness like me," Evie tells me.

Something she says triggers a memory in my mind. "Gracelin... That name is familiar. Didn't I used to have a friend named Gracelin?" I look at my mom, and her eyes widened slightly.

"You remember that? I thought for sure you had forgotten them. You were maybe seven or eight when they used to come around." My mom sounds surprised.

"We used to bring our children when we would visit your mother. You would all sit under that very table and have tea parties." Mia points at Mom's workspace where she has a couple of machines set up as well as cutting mats.

"I used to bake for them," I murmur, more memories assaulting me. "I was so sad when they stopped coming."

"Yes, you cried for days," my mom says, smiling sadly. "I had to send you to my parents whenever the queens were due to arrive because you were inconsolable for days after each visit, but eventually, you forgot."

I think about my visit to my grandparents in the human sector. They are two of my favorite people. Granny and I would flip through her extensive collection of recipe books, and I would get to pick something new each time. It's no wonder I forgot my friends, because I found my soul mate—baking.

I shake off my memories and find the queens looking at me with guilt. "Shifters gain the ability to shift back at will around the age of twelve. We were worried they would show you their new skills and frighten you, so we stopped bringing them."

There's a weird kind of lump in my throat when I think about those three children. Gracelin, Gretchin, and what was the boy's name? Try as I might, I can't remember it, although I remember the way being near him made me feel, like I was safe and loved. Weird, right? They were my first friends, and since them, I haven't really tried to make any kind of lasting friendships. I wonder if deep down I did remember the hurt I felt when they stopped coming and decided I wasn't ever going to feel that way again.

"Well, I'm just happy I could help one of my old friends with her son. I'm going to leave this here" —feeling all kinds of weird and awkward, I place the remaining champagne off to the side so I don't risk getting it on Mom's fabrics— "and head up to my apartment. It was nice meeting you again after so many years, and congratulations on your retirement. I hope you get to do all the fun things that being royal may have hindered in the past."

I don't wait for a response and bolt for the foyer with the elevator, which will take me to my level. I pull my keycard out of my pocket and tap it over the sensor, telling the elevator where I need to go.

I half expect my mom to run after me and yell at me for some reason, but she doesn't, and I heave a sigh of relief when the doors shut. I close my eyes and rest my head against the elevator wall as it moves up two levels to my floor. What a clusterfuck. How fucking awkward am I, and I just made myself look like a fool in front of the current queens. Thankfully I probably won't ever see them again, so I just need to forget it ever happened, though whether my mother will ever allow me to or not will be another story.

CHAPTER

SEVEN

Colbie

Saturday morning, the streets in the neutral zone are even more hectic than the day before. Luckily for me, though, the curfew was still in affect when I walked to work, so I didn't have to dodge mobs of edgy humans. As I look out the window and gape at the masses, I realize the trip back to my apartment after we close is going to be a nightmare.

We get a steady influx of people wanting take-away coffees, but no one wants to give up their spot on the parade route long enough to sit for a meal, so I let the others go early. I can handle the take-aways on my own, and I know the three of them want to join the festivities.

The parade route doesn't go past my bakery, but I know when it starts because my steady influx of customers dwindles to nothing. Sighing, I put up the closed sign and lock the front door early, then I return to the kitchen and make a new batch of bagels for Monday's breakfast rush. Next, I prep some of the muffin and cupcake batters, measuring and mixing all the dry ingredients into portions for the different flavors. I'll add the wet ingredients just before I bake them. I put lids on all the containers to keep any possible rodents or insects out and place them aside on the prep table, then I clean the coffee machine and wipe all surfaces down before hanging up my apron.

Flicking off the light, I pull the door closed behind me. The light is on inside the Romance Nest, and since I have a couple of free hours, I decide to pick up a new book to read. Maybe I'll soak in my bath and enjoy a glass of wine as well. It's been a long time since I wasn't too tired to enjoy something like that. Hopefully with the parade today, Brock and Niles have forgotten all about my run-in with the watch at the beginning of the week.

Smiling with the decision, I push through the front door of the bookstore. The bell tinkles, letting Brock or Niles know someone is in their store. The place is deserted, but I hear noise downstairs. They are probably watching the broadcast of the parade. If I wanted to watch it, that's how I would do it. There is no way I would squeeze myself into a crowd of people just to get a glimpse of the king and queens. Heck, I got my own private glimpse of the beautiful women yesterday.

I breathe in deeply and look around. There is just something about the smell of paper and ink that warms the soul. Now what do I want to read? Normally if I pick up a book, it will be a thriller or an action and adventure tale, but for some reason, I drift toward the paranormal romance section. I know it's a popular genre, and Brock told me it's his biggest seller, but the section sure is huge. I stare at it, feeling somewhat intimidated.

"Colbie?" I turn around to find Niles and Brock both watching me with small smirks. "Not watching the parade on this momentous occasion?" Niles asks, pushing a lock of blond hair behind his ear, his brown eyes shining with excitement.

I wrinkle my nose. "Pass. I'm sure I'll hear all about it over the next few weeks from my customers. It doesn't affect me, so I'm going to take advantage of a quiet day for some me time."

Niles nods, a look of understanding crossing his face, but Brock practically bounces next to him with unrestrained joy. "But it's a once in a lifetime event. Surely you must have had the thought that the new king or queen could be you?"

I frown, thinking about his words. "Um, no. I can be completely honest and say it has never once crossed my mind that I would be the unlucky human to be selected by the goddess."

His eyebrows jump. "Really? You think the chosen human is unlucky?"

"Yeah, there's no way I'd ever want that job. I pity the next human, whoever it is. I'm not sure I'm built to deal with that kind of upheaval. I would probably have a meltdown."

"Huh." Niles's eyes narrow. "I guess I hadn't thought about it like that. I mean, the likelihood is slim, so I wouldn't worry about it. Now, let's pick a steamy romance for you to keep your mind off everything." He steps up and runs his fingers over the bookshelf. "So what's your poison? Vamps? Witches? Fae? What about some hunky shifters?" He pulls out a book and waves a hand like a game show host. "Now this has a cornucopia of shifter mates."

"Mates? As in more than one?" I ask, and Brock chuckles.

"Yes, darling. Some lucky shifters get to share a mate between them," Niles teases, even though I know he and Brock are a couple and perfectly happy, but I remember Violet said something similar. "Could you imagine having the attention of multiple men all focused on making every one of your desires come true?" He practically swoons, and Brock watches him with affection.

"Yes, this is definitely the kind of distraction you need today, I insist." Niles drags me over to the counter and pops the book into a bag. I take out my phone to pay for it, but he waves it away. "No, this is our gift to you. All I ask is that you come by when you finish it and let me know what you thought, okay?"

I'm still feeling somewhat steamrolled as the two of them escort me to the door and practically push me out, but I guess I am distracting them from the parade coverage. I tell them goodbye, but they've already closed and locked their door. I guess they are not going to risk being interrupted again.

I walk down the now deserted streets toward my apartment, taking a different path than normal because the parade goes along a small section of my usual route. I can hear the roar of the crowd in the distance, and I grimace. Ugh, too many people all in one place for me.

I pick up some takeaway from a small Chinese restaurant which I'm sure is hoping to catch the after parade crowd, and then I grab a bottle of wine from the supermarket. The checkout clerk looks bored out of her mind. I'm her first customer since the parade started. She grumbles about having to work and missing it. I give her a fake smile of sympathy because I'm pretty sure that's what she's looking for, but as I leave the shop, I see her pick up her phone and hear the parade broadcast from its small screen. Well, at least she isn't missing it completely.

Finally, I get home. The lights in Mom's shop are off, and I consider stopping and seeing if she wants to share my bottle of wine, but then I remember her sending me a message saying she was invited to the retirement party, so she's either in the middle of getting ready or has already left for the event. The queens must have issued her an invite yesterday, because she hadn't mentioned being invited before, and she definitely would have mentioned it.

The elevator doors open on my level, and I tap my keycard against the sensor on my door and push it open. As I step through the doorway, I notice a fancy envelope on the floor like it was slipped under the door. I bend down to pick it up before going into the kitchen and putting my purchases on the island counter. The envelope is definitely made from good quality paper, and it has my name written on the front in elaborate calligraphy. On the back is a wax seal, and when I look closer, I see the royal standard stamped into the wax. Pursing my lips, I break the seal and pull out the card. It's an invite to the retirement party. A small note flutters out, and I read it.

It was lovely seeing you yesterday. We would all love it if you could attend our retirement party. Maybe you can reconnect with our children.

It's signed by all three queens.

For the smallest moment, I consider finding a

dress and going, but then the smell of my takeaway drifts to my nose, and I look down at my book and bottle of wine.

It was a nice gesture, but it's not really how I want to spend my day. I place the invite off to the side and head into the bathroom to run a bath. I'm really not the rubbing elbows with royalty kind, unlike my mother. A bubble bath, a rosé, and a good book are much more in my wheelhouse.

I splash some bubble bath that my mom gave me into the water. The scent of freesias fills my bathroom, and I smile. It's my mom's signature scent, one that has always brought me both comfort and heartache over the years.

When I was smaller, Mom was loving and kind and wonderful, teaching me to sew at her work desk and encouraging me to express myself creatively, but as I became older, her expectations of me have made my life difficult. It seems like nothing I do is ever quite good enough.

There's also my lack of desire to be a social butterfly like her. She has a thriving social calendar, and I'm glad it keeps her mostly out of my hair. If only she would stop nagging me to have one too. Up until now, all my focus has been on creating a thriving business so that at least she might be proud of that. Now that my business is settled and booming, perhaps I'll take her advice and have a look at one of those dating apps. I'm not having any luck meeting men at work. They don't even register me as a person behind the counter, which is kind of a kick to the self-esteem.

While the bath fills, I pour myself a large glass of wine and prepare a bowl of rice and beef with broccoli. As I eat, I cave to my curiosity and switch the television on, changing the channel to the one dedicated to everything royal for the next few weeks. There are a couple of royal commentators discussing key points of King Lucas's rule with a background of the parade route. The streets in front of the hotel where the retirement party is being held are chock-full of cheering humans, while the street directly in front is lined with limousines dropping off the wealthy and influential people who all managed to score an invite to the retirement party. I watch with interest as the commentators break off the subject they are talking about to announce the arrival of the vampire king and his consorts. Like King Lucas, the vampire king has three wives. All of them are as gorgeous as the shifter queens, but they have this kind of cold grace to them. They almost float across the ground, like statues come to life. There are no emotions on their faces, just blank stares. All four of them stop to pose for the cameras, which focus on them, and the vamp king winks at the camera and flashes a fang-filled smile. The crowd screams like he's a pop star or a famous actor before they continue on their way, and I tune back into whatever the commentators are saying.

"Just like the kingdom of Aramis, the other kingdoms have the same kind of royalty succession. Next year, it will be King Victor's retirement year, and some lucky human from Eryx will be crowned the next vamp king or queen," the male commentator explains.

The female commentator screws up her nose. "I don't envy them one bit. Imagine needing to drink blood to survive." She gags slightly, which I think is super rude. The male commentator obviously agrees, because he scowls at her before plastering on a mischievous smile.

"I don't know... Rumor has it there is something inherently sexual about blood exchanges. Sounds like a fun time to me." The female stares at him with disgust, but he ignores her and tries his best to get the broadcast back on track. I'm sure the network does not want to make enemies of the vampire kingdom, and he's working hard to deal with her faux pas.

"Let's go to a quick commercial break before the next exciting guest arrives." He smiles brightly at the camera, and a commercial comes on.

I use the remote to turn the TV off, absently wondering if that woman is going to have a job come Monday morning. I recognize them as the hosts of the popular morning program in Aramis, so maybe she will be okay.

I place my bowl in the sink and return to find my bath at the perfect height and temperature.

Stripping, I sink into warm water and groan, closing my eyes and resting my head on the padded cushion. For a few moments, I just revel in the feeling of relaxation. It's been a long time since I really let myself unwind and breathe. I free my mind of all my worries and let my mind drift over inconsequential things. Small little snippets of memories float to the surface of my brain—a tea party under my mom's cutting table, giggling with three other children, a young boy with unusual silver and black hair and dark sapphire blue eyes helping me pour my teapot when my arm was broken, a small dark girl with a shock of curly black hair telling me that my cookies are the best she ever tasted, and a girl with blonde pigtails with pretty purple ribbons tied in them wrapping her arms around me, telling me that I smelled good and that she loved me.

My eyes pop open, and water sloshes over the edge as I sit up. "Whoa." I guess seeing the queens yesterday brought my memories to the surface. I smile as a feeling of happiness washes over me. I loved my friends so much. I guess my brain was trying to protect me by forgetting them. I now remember how I felt when Mom told me they wouldn't be coming to visit again. I press my hand against my chest as the feeling of absolute sadness batters my soul. No wonder I latched onto baking. I felt like my heart was ripped out of my chest. It's not surprising that I decided to avoid any solid friendship after that.

Brushing away the hurt and loneliness, I dry off my hands and reach for the book sitting on the little tray across my bath. Yes, it's indulgent, but having somewhere to put my glass of wine and phone is so handy. My phone buzzes with an incoming message, and I look at the screen, seeing it's from my mother. I make the decision to ignore it. I'm sure I will receive an earful of her ire tomorrow, but parties are not my scene. I'm sure the queens won't even notice that I am not in attendance.

Taking a large sip of wine, I open my book, ready to delve into a life other than mine. I'm certain this female main character's life will be exponentially more interesting.

CHAPTER

EIGHT

Liam

I tug at the collar of my dress shirt and curse the fact that I had to wear a tie to this event. I love Gryffin's parents, and I am happy for them in the wake of their retirement, but his mothers insisted we had to dress up after the parade, and I really could have done without it.

I'm hiding in a corner of the ballroom behind a large potted plant, staying away from all the fawning dignitaries and celebrities. My teammates are angry with me, and I don't really blame them, but Gianna was very persuasive, and I'm tired of waiting for our mate. Who knows when she's going to appear? I bet she doesn't expect us to be monks before we even meet her.

I peer through the foliage, and I see Hunter and Brodie standing with the general, his wife, and

Hunter's twin brother and sister, Ember and Talon. They are both in their first year of college, and they are good kids. I'm pretty sure Talon wants to join the night watch like his brother, and he has been working hard to prove himself. Hunter said a bond mark has recently appeared on his body, which is a little later than usual since most appear at seventeen, and he is two years past that. I wonder if the general will insist on his bond moving in with them, or if he will leave to live at one of the other parents' place. They are all laughing at something, and I consider joining them, but I chicken out in the end. I'm sure Hunter has told them about what happened with Gianna, and I don't want to feel their disappointment.

Gianna was supposed to attend this event with me, but I was firmly instructed not to bring her after her major fuck up with the human girl. I can still hear her voice screeching at me through my cell phone speaker when she called to ask me what time I was picking her up, and I had to break the news to her. I don't think the guys have to worry about Gianna again anytime soon. Oh well, she was getting a little clingy anyway, even though I made it clear we could be nothing more than casual bed buddies. She was pushing for more and asking for group dates with the rest of my bond, even though one of them is missing.

I look around the ballroom, searching for the standout figure of Prince Gryffin, son of King

Lucas and Queen Layla and my other bond mate. I'm surprised he's not here. Surely he wouldn't miss his parents' retirement party. Archer was found a week ago, so why hasn't he returned?

"What are you doing hiding back here?" I jump as Gem appears from nowhere. Damn phoenix using his powers of invisibility in his human form. The mythical shifters are able to do that, unlike us everyday shifters.

"Meh, avoiding those two." I nod in Hunter and Brodie's direction. "I don't need a lecture about where I stick my dick." He passes me a beer, and I nod my thanks. "I was looking for Gryff, and I can't see him."

Gem's eyes blaze, and he growls, sounding like my own bear. "The bastard hasn't returned from his wild goose chase."

I sigh, and my gaze moves to my best friend's parents who, while they put on brave faces, are also worried about their son not being at their retirement party.

"He promised his mothers he would be back," I murmur, and Gem scoffs.

"I don't know why he keeps looking. Our sixth, whoever he is, does not want to be found. How do we even know that what the witch told Gryffin was true? What shifter wouldn't come forward when a bond mark shows up on their body? The witch was just trying to stir up trouble, and now Gryffin spends as much time roaming, looking for our sixth, as he does at home. Our bond is not as strong as it should be, and I bet that's part of the reason the goddess hasn't revealed our mate to us." Gem is pretty easygoing most of the time, except when it comes to this very subject. He and Gryffin have been dancing around each other for years, and I think he's jealous about how much time Gryffin spends looking for a mythical sixth member of our bond. They just need to fuck and make nice.

A commotion by the entrance to the ballroom draws our attention.

"Ah, there he is, the prodigal son deigns to make an appearance." I point my beer in that direction. Our bond mate looks immaculate in his black tux, his black streaked silver hair brushing his shoulders. He's smiling as he greets his parents, but I can feel the tension in our bond. He obviously wasn't successful.

Gem dumps his empty glass on a server's tray as they walk past us and grabs another, tossing it back. He eyes the prince like he's a tasty morsel of meat he wants to take a bite out of. I roll my eyes. Hunter, Brodie, and I are all straight and strictly into females, but Gryffin and Gem are fluid, not leaning to either side. It's become awkward as fuck. Gem watches him obsessively, and Gryffin seems oblivious, wrapped up in a reading a witch gave him a couple of years ago telling him we wouldn't meet our mate until the sixth member of our bond was found. He's taken it upon himself to search for this unknown member, but I don't believe they exist. Being marked for a bond is a privilege, and no shifter I know would not come forward and admit to being marked. If we don't sort out our issues, our bond is going to be permanently broken.

I watch as Brodie and Hunter make their way over to our bond mate, welcoming him home with hugs and whispered conversation. I grimace. I probably haven't helped our problems with the whole Gianna thing, but fuck, my bear is becoming unruly and aggressive. It isn't often a born shifter goes feral, but it has happened, and I'm worried that might be my future if our mate doesn't appear soon.

I sigh. "Come on, we better go say hi. I want to find out where he's been all week. He should have returned as soon as he got the message that Archer was fine," I grumble. "We needed his help with those damn ferals yesterday."

The lust drains from Gem's eyes and is replaced by sadness. We caught up with the feral pack and took them out. They were lost to the madness of being bitten without the king's magic to stabilize them. Four wolves had to be put down. It's why unsanctioned turning is outlawed. Once turned, the king's magic can't even fix the problem, though they have tried. We even tried to imprison them in the hope we could find a solution to the madness, but that made it worse.

When we returned home, Gem disappeared for

the rest of the night, wallowing in his grief. Nothing the three of us said could get him to come out of his room. I hate not being able to comfort my bond mate, and his residual sadness leaked through the bond, making us all miserable. Thankfully it doesn't happen too often because I'm not sure if Gem would survive.

Brodie and Hunter must be filling Gryffin in on what happened as we approach, because his gaze shifts to Gem, and I can see the compassion in his eyes. He opens his arms and engulfs our phoenix in his embrace, hugging him tightly. We watch as Gem sags against him, shuddering with emotion as Gryff whispers words we can't hear into his ear. I know they will be the same thing as what we all tried yesterday, but it's more effective coming from our unofficial leader.

I exchange a knowing glance with the other two as Gryffin pulls back, turning to face me while keeping one arm around our phoenix. "I hear you've been stirring up trouble," he says to me, cocking an eyebrow.

I glare at the two tattletales who just shrug unrepentantly. "Look, you might like to pretend you're a monk and ignore what is right in front of you, but my bear has needs, and seriously, you have the nerve to have a go at me. Where have you been all week? We needed you yesterday, and you were off on a wild fucking goose chase. Archer has been safe since Monday. Did you get lost on your way home?" I snap, unwilling to deal with his crap.

"I was checking out a mythical town on the border between us and the witches' kingdom," Gryffin tells me, and I see Gem stiffen slightly.

"You're still trying to find this mythical sixth member. It's bullshit, man. You should be here, working with the bond you do have, not ditching us all on a pipedream." I can't stop the rumble of my bear in my chest. He is angry and pacing inside me like he wants to gut Gryffin.

Before Gryffin can answer, Brodie clears his throat. "I mean, it's not a bad idea. Maybe one just recently manifested and was marked as a part of our bond."

"Ever the fucking peacemaker," I mutter, rolling my eyes.

Unlike regular shifters, mythical shifters don't have the ability to shift into their creature's form at birth. It's because mythical shifters often have extra magic that would be unruly in a child. Hunter's and Gem's animals manifested at seventeen. Could you imagine baby dragons and phoenixes flying around, wreaking havoc and setting shit on fire?

I scoff. "There has never been a bond group with an age gap like that, and you know it. You're grasping at straws," I argue. "Maybe you are just going to have to face the fact that a sixth doesn't exist, or if they did, maybe they died in an accident before being marked. Give it up, Gryffin, and focus on the bond you have right in front of you, because we are falling apart." I don't wait for any of them to reply before I leave.

My bear growls inside my chest as I make my way through the shifters and humans on the dance floor. He is both pissed and sad, and I feel the hair on my arms ripple as I struggle to keep from shifting. It's a full moon tonight, as is required for the ceremony, and instead of being out in the woods and shifting like we normally do, we're stuck in here, wrapped up in confining suits and playing nice. We want nothing more than to shed the uncomfortable clothes and run, and it's making us miserable.

"Liam, hey, Liam, wait up," Brodie calls, but I don't stop. Instead, I make a beeline to the balcony doors for some much needed fresh air. Maybe if I get outside, I can stop some of the panic inside me.

The cold air slaps me in the face, and I breathe deeply as I step out onto the deserted balcony. The nights are getting colder, and the leaves are starting to change color in the forest. Winter is definitely on its way. The urge to shift and run hits me hard, and I reach out to grab hold of the railing to steady myself, my knuckles turning white with the exertion.

"Hey, are you okay, man?" Brodie puts a hand on my shoulder, and I shake my head.

"No, I'm really not. I'm so pissed at Gryffin. How can he be so blind and stubborn? He is so obsessed with that damn reading that he ignores everything he has in front of him. Anyone with half a brain can see he and Gem are hot for each other, but he's like a fucking ostrich sticking his head in the sand. This obsession with finding this illusive sixth is going to break us. My bear will not survive if our bond breaks. I'm already struggling," I admit, breathing hard. I concentrate on the view. The Aramis Arms backs up to the shifter border and the forest that delineates the two zones. I can feel the full moon calling to me, but I don't look up. Shifters don't need to shift on the full moon, but it's more comfortable for us if we do.

Brodie sighs heavily, his hand tightening on my shoulder. "I know. It's tricky. I think in Gryff's brain, he would be betraying our mate if he and Gem started anything before she is marked."

"That's just stupid." I whirl around to face him. Brodie's normally laughing blue eyes show concern, and I hate that I'm the cause of that. "Plenty of bonds are in relationships with each other before they find their mate. The goddess wouldn't put people together if it wasn't meant to be. Our mate will love them even if they are in a relationship with each other as well." I'm not only angry, I'm also slightly jealous. I'm not interested in either of them like that, but I want someone to love.

"Yeah, I know. Look, let's just get through the next couple of weeks. Once the new king or queen is secure, we can sit down as a bond group and talk about it. We can't ignore it any longer. I can see you're struggling with your bear, and my wolf is pissed as well. They have to have it out once and for all and clear the fucking air, and we have to convince Gryffin to give up on his quest. Maybe we can talk to Lucas and Layla about it, and they can intervene, but I don't want to add more to their plate just yet."

I nod, and my bear settles slightly, knowing our bond mate is right.

A gong sounds out in the ballroom, and I hear the roof start to open.

"Shit, it's time. Come on, let's go watch history in the making." He releases my shoulder, and I take one last deep breath before we rejoin the crowd inside the ballroom.

We make our way over to our bond group, which is close to the front. Gryffin wants to watch his parents' ceremony. He narrows his eyes on me, and I glare back at him, but he turns his attention upwards, and I do the same. The roof of the ball-room slides open, showing the moon at its zenith. The air begins to buzz with magic as the four royals step up onto the platform and kneel. The crowd falls silent as the goddess Aramis appears in front of them. As one, we all sink to our knees and bow our heads in reverence to the goddess who gave us life.

"Stand, my children." Her voice reverberates around the room. When we return to our feet, I try to see through the magic to make out what she looks like, but her glow makes it impossible to see any features, even with my heightened sight.

"Lucas, Layla, Mia, and Evelyn, you have been just and kind rulers, and I thank you for your service, but it is time for some new blood. Once I send my magic out, the countdown to the new ruler's appearance will begin. You four will continue to advise until their mates are found, they are crowned, and have selected their new council."

There's some uncomfortable murmuring in the crowd, and I smile. I had forgotten the council was also at risk tonight. The new king or queen always gets to select their new advisory council. In the past, it has remained virtually unchanged, with former kings and queens and their family members, but it is at the discretion of the new ruler. Lucas refused adding the previous queen and her mates to the council because she was a bitter old twat who was jealous and made his mates feel small. She must be at least a hundred by now, which isn't that old for a shifter since, on average, we live to about three hundred. She lives somewhere in the country toward the borderlands near the witches, banished there by Lucas, which was somewhat of a scandal and unprecedented. She really did not like giving up her magic, or so I've been told.

"Please remove the crowns," the goddess asks, and the four rulers use both hands to lift the symbols of their reign into the air. The goddess waves a hand, and magic swirls around the four frozen people. I see Lucas sag slightly before he straightens and stands tall. Apparently having the magic removed from you is both painful and freeing. The magic swirls around, and the crowns begin to fall apart, becoming one with the swirling magic. A portion breaks off and shoots up into the sky through the open roof in search of the new chosen king or queen, while the remaining magic whirls furiously, growing so large, the king and queens need to step back off the dais.

The crowd murmurs loudly, and I look at Gem, our resident genius bookworm. "What's happening?"

He doesn't take his eyes off the spectacle. "This is when we find out how many mates the new king or queen will have."

"It's pre-decided?" Brodie asks, frowning. "I thought the ruler got to choose."

"They do get to choose the individuals, but not the number—that is determined by magic." He waves a hand, shushing us, so I turn my attention back to the platform.

The magic finally settles, and in its place is one large crown—the ruler's crown. It's hard to tell whether it's more masculine or feminine, which I heard was a good indicator of whether a male or female was chosen, but what happens next has the crowd gasping and surprised chatter breaking out despite the goddess's presence.

Floating on either side of the large crown are

six smaller ones, three on each side. "Holy crap, six consorts," Gem mutters. "There has never been a king or queen with that many consorts."

The magic fades, the goddess waves a hand, and all seven crowns rest on busts surrounded by glass. The magic surrounding her person clears, and we finally get a look at the goddess. She's tall, probably seven feet, with a body made for sin, all curves and long legs and lush, flowing gold hair. Her face is so perfect, it's almost hard to look at. She has a smile on her face, which I would say borders on mischievous. "Ah, six consorts. Yes, that seems like a perfect number for my new chosen. I'm really going to enjoy watching this play out. It's going to be very interesting," she murmurs almost to herself before facing us and raising her hands.

"Please join me in thanking your king and queens." Magic shoots out of her fingertips, and fireworks explode in the air as the crowd bursts into applause. "I will be watching closely. Remember, I am never too far away," she reminds the crowd, but she turns to look at our bond group, and I feel like she's staring directly into my soul for a moment before her gaze slides away and she fades as quickly as she first appeared.

The band starts up again, and the applause dies, so I tune into the speculation.

"There has never been so many consorts," a man behind us murmurs.

"No, usually it's three," his female companion replies. "What does this mean?"

"It can't be anything good," the man says, and I feel a pang of dread. Great, just what we need, shifters speculating.

"I wonder when they will start appearing?" I turn around to look at the couple discreetly. The woman is craning her neck like they will start appearing at any moment.

"Pfft, everyone knows the marks don't start appearing until the king or queen has stepped across the threshold of the castle." Gem glares at the people. "I really do pity the poor chosen. I'm almost certain there will be double the amount of marked consorts for them to choose from. The goddess wouldn't be so cruel as to give her a small amount to select from. It's going to be a circus here while they try to woo them."

"I wonder if we can get an assignment that takes us far away," Gryffin murmurs. I know he doesn't care about being picked as a possible consort, still determined to search for that elusive sixth. Damn him.

"What's to say none of us are going to be marked?" I spit out, being argumentative because he pissed me off.

"Members of bond groups are never marked because we already have a predetermined mate, and it would mean tearing the group apart," Hunter reminds me.

"Well, that really is unfortunate, isn't it?" I mutter, and Brodie elbows me.

"I need to go check on my parents," Gryffin says stiffly before leaving us.

"Damn it, Liam. Let's get through the next couple of weeks, and then we will sit down and talk to him. Maybe we can find a way to finally get him to give up this wild goose chase. Maybe the witch queen can help us when she arrives for the coronation, whether to confirm or deny the reading and help us track them," Gem suggests and follows Gryffin.

A wave of guilt washes through me, and I feel awful. I hate picking fights with Gryffin, but I can't seem to help it.

"Now that that's over, let's shift and go for a run. Maybe your bear will feel better after," Brodie suggests, and I grasp the idea like it's a lifeline.

"Yes, thank you," I agree, and I don't even wait to say goodbye to anyone. I make my way through the ballroom, ignoring people I know, with only one thing on my mind—shifting and running, hoping like hell it will even out my mood, or maybe our bond group will end up broken anyway.

Colbie

I spend a good portion of my evening reading, especially because the bakery will be closed tomorrow due to the retirement celebration. I am not sad about a forced holiday, but I was still up early, and I can barely keep my eyes open by the time ten o'clock comes around. I am definitely not a night owl. I put a recipe card into the page I'm on and place it on my bedside table. Turning off all the lights in the house, I grab a glass of water and turn in. I lie in bed, thinking about what I might do tomorrow since I haven't had a day off in a while. I think I'll go visit my grandparents in the human zone. I'm almost positive they are not caught up in all the king and queen hype.

Happy with my decision, I close my eyes and feel my tired body relax, drifting off to sleep, but my sleep is not restful. I toss and turn, my dreams filled with snarling animals, jealous women, and magic. At one stage, I jolted awake, feeling pain in my wrists from being kidnapped and shackled by some unnamed assailant.

I'm breathing heavily, and I rub my wrists, trying to ease the discomfort. Holy crap, the pain from my dream traveled into real life! That was some very lucid dreaming. I glare at the book on my bedside table. I'm almost certain it's responsible for the ridiculous thoughts in my head.

I get up and go to my bathroom cabinet, pulling out a bottle of sleeping pills I was prescribed when I first started my bakery and had trouble adjusting my circadian rhythm to the required hours. I pop two into my mouth before washing them down with the glass of water and climbing back into my bed. The rest of my night better be dream free.

The pills work, and I wake up feeling better than I had. Although the dreams were not as vivid, I remember a voice talking to me. It was muffled and unclear, and I guess not all that important if I can't even remember what they were saying to me, but that's the way of dreams. The only ones you do remember vividly are the ones that scare the crap out of you.

I push my hair back from my face and grimace. I definitely need to wash it today. I keep it tied back in a ponytail or a braid while at work, but I like to wear it down on my random days off, and greasy is not a good look.

Throwing the covers back, I head to the bathroom and turn on the shower, stripping off the tank top I wore to bed and sliding my panties down my legs. Both bits of cloth end up in the laundry basket. Stepping under the steaming stream, I close my eyes and tip my head back. I let the water run over my hair before reaching up and lifting it from my neck. My hair is thick, so if I just stand here, only the top gets wet. Once it's drenched, I reach for the shampoo and lather it into my hair before rinsing it off and repeating with the conditioner. I let that sit for a while and wash my body using my loofah gloves, groaning at how good it feels to scrub my skin raw.

Seriously, there is nothing better than a good exfoliation. Finally, I rinse my hair and turn off the faucet. Stepping out, I wrap my hair in a towel before drying myself off. I reach out to drag a hand across the foggy mirror and freeze. What the fuck is around my wrist? I snatch my hand back and look down at the gold mark around it. It looks like someone grabbed my wrist too hard and squeezed. I hurry to my bedside table and get my reading glasses. I don't wear them as much as I should, but last night, my eyes got tired, and the words started to blur. Putting them on, I study the mark on my wrist. Holy shit, it looks like faded, gold crescent shapes with a pretty scroll to link it together.

My stomach rolls, and I grab my bathroom sink for stability. No, this can't be right. I lift my other hand to rub the marks and squeal when I notice it, too, has the same markings. My heart skips a beat as I realize where I have seen a tattoo like this before—not crescents, but phases of the moon. King Lucas has a similar tattoo down the side of his face. His is a lot more masculine than mine, and he doesn't have pretty filigree linking the phases.

"No, no, no." I think back to last night and try to remember what time I had that dream. Did I look at the clock? No, I didn't pick up my phone. This can't be what I think it is. I rub harder before picking up the soap and scrubbing the marks. They don't budge. Tears stream down my face as I stare at the marks in horror. I can't be marked as the next queen of the shifters.

I'm not cut out for it. I hate confrontation, and I'm not good with people. Those shifters are going to walk all over me. Nope, it's not going to happen. I'm going to hide the marks, and they can keep looking. Nobody knows about the marks but me, and if I don't tell anyone, no one is going to be any wiser. I bet if I make a trip to the witch kingdom, there would be a spell that would help me hide the marks. I need to apply for a travel pass immediately. It takes at least a week for it to be approved.

In shock, I dry off and get dressed. I could hide in my house all day, but I bet my mother is going to come find me to ask why I didn't go to the party and tell me all the gossip from last night. If she sees the marks, she's going to ask questions, and she has always been able to see through my lies. It took the fun out of being a teenager.

Where should I go? I don't want to go to the bakery, I don't want to be anywhere in the neutral zone today. People will be on the lookout for someone with unusual markings, but if I disappear completely, it will be suspicious. Maybe I'll tell Olivia, Justin, and Violet that my grandmother is ill, and I have to go visit, then I can take a couple of extra days to come up with a solution. I can have them tattooed over in black, no one would question them then. The goddess's marks are always golden.

Happy with my decision, I quickly pack a bag. When I look out the bedroom window, the day looks sunny and bright, so I pull a sundress out of my wardrobe and slide it on. I don't often get to wear anything but leggings and shirts, so when I do get a chance to change it up, I grab it with both hands. I throw in my swimsuit as well, even though the water is bound to be cold, but maybe I can get a tan while I'm there. The sun isn't going to be around much longer with winter closing in on us. Their place is in a seaside community near the port, and there are some nice beaches and coves. I'll just treat it as a mini vacation and pretend the marks aren't even there. I'm sure once the goddess realizes I'm not interested, she will remark someone else, or at least that's what I desperately hope.

Glaring at the offending marks on my wrists, I dig through my extensive jewelry box. Today, I am super thankful that my mother is a designer and loves to buy me costume jewelry despite the fact that I never really wear it. There are all sorts of gorgeous items in my box, and I never had the heart to get rid of any of it.

I finally find the items I was thinking of—a set of jeweled cuffs that my mother gave me after one of her trips to the fae kingdom. They make unusual jewelry, and she told me that these were wedding cuffs that fae gift to their partners after the ceremony. I kind of scoffed at that, because who wants to have ownership cuffs, but she told me all partners wear them, and it's considered a sign of complete devotion. Those who are married and refuse to wear them are believed to have a relationship that will fail. It's a weird custom as far as I'm concerned, but they are freaking pretty. The cuffs are made from a shiny silver metal that has elaborate designs stamped into them, as well as embedded moonstone gems. The fae who sold them to her told her the moonstone was for protection and helped ease stress and anxiety. Holy crap, do I need it to work now.

I slip them on, and they cover the marks perfectly. Nobody will ever notice they are there, and I'm certainly not going to tell anyone.

I dry my hair using a blow-dryer and leave it hanging loose, then I grab my bag, my phone, and my keycard and hurry out of my building. I cross my fingers that my mother isn't in our foyer as I leave. I'm sure she will still be in bed after last night, and that's if she even made it home. I wouldn't put it past her to have a wonderful affair with a dashing shifter she met at the party.

Public transport is running again and the only way out of the neutral zone for those of us who don't have electric scooters. I hop on the bus at the stop closest to my apartment and take a seat. There is a smattering of humans on it, all of them looking slightly downcast after the big day of celebrations yesterday. I send Olivia, Justin, and Violet a message, letting them know I have a family emergency, and pray I don't get struck down for lying.

All three send back replies of sympathy and assurance, and I feel even worse. I slump down in my seat in the back of the bus and tune into a particularly loud couple of girls.

"I thought for sure I would be selected as the next queen of the shifters." She holds her arms out like she's examining them and lifts her top to study her stomach. I snort under my breath at the sheer audacity. I can't believe there are people who think like that. It's fucking bold. "But I don't have any new marks on my body this morning."

The other girl looks out the window and sighs. "Do you really think it happens like they say it does, or is it just a marketing ploy to keep the humans in line? Like maybe they select who they want and tattoo them quickly to make it look like they are the chosen one." The girl's conspiracy theory is solid and something I used to wonder about. Unfortunately, the marks on my wrists suggest I was dead wrong.

"Surely if someone had been selected, it would be all over social media this morning." The first girl holds up her phone. "But there's nothing. I've been searching all platforms, and there isn't even a whisper of someone being chosen."

"Maybe they haven't noticed yet or haven't realized the significance?" The second girl turns back to look at her friend. "Or maybe it hasn't happened yet, and we still have a chance." They squeal and bounce up and down, and I turn my attention to the window, rolling my eyes.

Don't hold your breath, I think and desperately wish I could transfer the marks from my wrists to one of theirs. I'm sure either of them would make a better queen than me because they actually want it.

The bus winds its way slowly through the neutral zone before passing into the human one and speeding up, merging into the traffic. Early Sunday morning traffic isn't too bad, and it doesn't take long before we arrive at the capital city. My grandparents live in a cozy little suburb on the far side of the city. Their suburb is beach side, and the sea marks the border of the kingdom of Aramis. Across the sea is the fae kingdom, and the only viable way to and from there is via boat, though trade and tourism between the two kingdoms is booming.

I stay on the bus as it makes its way through the city. It takes at least another hour, but I'm happy watching the human world go by—anything to distract me from my real problems.

When we arrive at the stop I need, I hop off, taking my overnight bag with me. It's a short walk from the bus stop to my grandparents' place. I smell the ocean the moment I get off the bus, and the wind whips briskly around my legs, making my dress flutter. I push down on the material as the bus pulls away and start the short walk to my destination. The sun is shining despite the wind, and I can hear the waves rolling onto the shore. I can't see the ocean from here, since there is a row of houses blocking the view, but my grandparents can see it from their backyard and have a little path that leads down to the beach.

I pick up my pace and soon find myself at the gate to my grandparents' cottage. The white picket fence looks like it could use a fresh coat of paint, but the flowers in the garden beds are lovely. I can tell they are coming to the end of the cycle and will soon die off to hibernate for winter. I'm surprised neither of my grandparents are out here in the garden, since it's one of their favorite places to be, but when I look at my phone, I realize it's almost lunch, so I bet they are on the back patio having coffee and something to eat.

I push through the fence, and instead of going to the front door, I walk around to the backyard.

Sure enough, I hear voices, and I smile as warmth rushes through me, pushing away the abject panic that has been at the forefront of my mind all morning. I've missed them.

"Colbie, honey, is that you?" I hear my granny call, and I realize I stopped, and I'm just staring up at the enclosed porch.

"Hi, Granny and Grampy, I thought I'd come stay for a few days."

"Hey, my pretty girl." My grampy opens the screen door at the top of the stairs and waves me up. "Well, don't just stand there, come give me a hug." He holds up his hands, and I hurry up the stairs and throw myself into his arms. I've never felt safer than when I'm being hugged by my grandpa.

"I missed you, my girl," he says, placing a kiss on the top of my head before letting go.

We move into the enclosed porch, and my grammy sweeps me into a hug as well. She's tall, like my mom, and smells like freesias as well. Both her and Mom wear the same perfume.

She pulls back and looks at me carefully. I wince internally, hoping she can't see that anything is bothering me, but my granny is astute. I'm pretty sure she knows everything. Instead of saying anything, though, she nods. "Let's pour you a cuppa, and you can tell us what's going on."

She waves a hand at one of the spare chairs, and I drop my bag to the side before sliding into it.

She places a cup and saucer in front of me and pours me tea from the pot.

"That was good timing. Granny just filled the pot," my grandpa says as he places a sandwich on the plate in front of me. "And you know she always makes too many of these."

I snatch up the chicken salad sandwich and groan as I bite into it. My granny's chicken salad is delicious. I stole the recipe to use in my store, and it's one of my most popular lunch items.

"This is so good," I mumble around a mouthful of bread, chicken, and mayo. Granny frowns at me, but Grampy just laughs.

"What brings you to town? I see you have a bag. Are you staying for a couple of days?" he asks, and I nod after swallowing.

"Yeah, it's a declared holiday today with the retirement of the shifter king and queens, so I decided to take a couple of extra days. My staff can handle the bakery," I answer, and the two of them exchange a glance.

"Yes, we watched a bit of it on TV last night," Granny says. "The queens looked gorgeous, and King Lucas is so handsome," she gushes.

"It won't be long until there's a new king or queen. I'm sure the announcement will come any moment. It's kind of exciting. I remember when Lucas was crowned and picked his mates. If you thought the retirement party was fancy, then you should see the coronation. It's wild," Grampy remi-nisces. "I wonder who it will be."

I avoid looking down at the cuffs on my wrists and shrug my shoulders. "Doesn't really matter to me."

"Aww, sweetie, it should. It's history in the making." He chuckles. "Hopefully they are as good as King Lucas was. The one previous to him, Queen Rowena, started off okay, but by the end of her reign, she managed to piss off the witches, fae, and vampires. It's a surprise we didn't end up at war again. There were rumbles of it when her retirement thankfully came around, and Lucas and his queens managed to smooth everything over."

"It helps that the fae, witches, and vampires all had their own successions after. New blood all around, and we avoided a catastrophe." My granny shudders. "I don't like to think of what would have happened to the human population if the four mystical ones went to war again."

"Probably drafted to the cause," I grumble, but I'm happy the subject has moved on from the current royal succession.

"Well, eat up. I'll go put some fresh sheets on the spare bed. We have dinner and cards at the senior hall this evening if you want to come with us," Granny suggests as she gets up from the table, taking her and Grampy's empty plates with them.

"Thanks, but I'm kind of tired, so I think I'll go for a walk along the beach and call it an early night.

I'll just grab something from the boardwalk for dinner," I tell her, and she nods before disappearing into the house.

"Are you okay, Colbs? You're quieter than normal." Grampy looks at me with concern. I don't meet his eyes because I know if I do, he'll see and push.

"Yeah, just really tired. It's been a long few years of getting the bakery established," I lie and feel a wave of guilt, not ready to talk about what's bothering me.

He reaches over and gives my hand a squeeze. There are age spots on the back of his hand, and the guilt turns to sadness, knowing that these two aren't going to be around forever.

"You deserve the break. You work too hard. Being the boss means you should be able to delegate. You need to trust that your employees have your back. You're a good judge of character and wouldn't have hired people you couldn't trust."

My grampy used to have his own business, a hardware shop, prior to retiring and selling it, and both Mom and I learned so much from him that we applied it to our own businesses.

"You're right, and I do trust them. That doesn't mean it's not hard letting go though," I admit, and he chuckles before picking up his cup and taking a sip of tea.

"You'll learn."

Colbie

I chat with them both a little longer, but they have to get ready for their night out, so after dumping my bag in the spare bedroom I always use, I wave goodbye and walk down the street. I'm going to check out the little shops along the boardwalk before walking along the beach to my favorite cove. It has this amazing rock I can sit on and look out at the ocean as I contemplate life. I take a blanket and the book I was reading last night.

I am doing everything in my power to pretend the marks under my cuffs aren't there, but it isn't working. It's constantly in the back of my mind, like a specter haunting my every thought. How am I going to get out of this? I wonder if the fae or the witches can help me. Would one of them have a spell strong enough to override a goddess's magic?

Probably not. I'd most likely need help from another goddess, but the idea of appealing to one of the others is terrifying.

I fiddle with a cuff as I make my way through the little shops on the boardwalk. There are clothing and bookshops, a new age shop with crystals and self-help books, and my personal childhood favorite, the candy store. I stand at the window and watch as the man pours molten hot candy onto a table before adding flavor and color, then it gets pulled on machines, changing its color, before it eventually gets rolled, cut, and wrapped in colorful paper wrappers.

I head in to get a sample of the fresh taffy. It's coconut and delicious, but instead, I buy a huge bag of mixed taffy. There isn't a flavor I don't love, and it's too hard to pick, so mixed is the perfect solution.

I pop a piece into my mouth and keep walking. I consider grabbing something more substantial to eat, but I'm not all that hungry. Instead, I buy a frozen cola slushie and walk down the steps onto the beach. It's afternoon, and the wind has kicked up even more, chasing away any possible beachgoers. There's only me with the gulls and sand whipping across the shore.

The waves crash against the shoreline, and the sound goes a long way in drowning out all my thoughts. I kick off my sandals and place them in the bag with the taffy, my book, and phone. I wrap a towel around my neck, and I start moving. There is something so calming about just putting one foot in front of the other, not worrying about where you are or where you have to be. It's freeing.

I'm thankful for my sunglasses, because they protect my eyes from the blowing sand. Most people would think I'm crazy enjoying the beach like this, but it's my favorite way.

The sound of a dog barking hits my ears, and I look up. Farther down the beach, I see three dogs racing around, chasing a ball thrown by someone. I can't make out if it's a male or female because they are too far away. It doesn't bother me though, and I'm sure by the time I get to them, they will have had enough and left.

I look out at the ocean, and I see clouds starting to build up, growing darker. The storm is still a while off, so I have time to finish my walk before I have to head home. I love watching storms from my grandparents' enclosed porch. I wrap myself in a blanket, and Granny brings me tea and cookies while I count the flashes of lightning and the claps of thunder.

My mind returns to my problems, and I grimace. Ugh, I came for a walk to forget all my issues. I wonder if there has ever been an occasion where another human who was selected didn't want the job. Maybe I'll do a computer search or head to the library and look through some history books. I feel a tear trickle down my face, and I quickly wipe it away, but more join it. Fuck, what am I going to do? My stomach rolls, and my heart pounds. I can't be the shifter queen. I have to get out of this.

A dog barks again, and I look up. The woman and the dogs must have turned and started walking in my direction, because they are a lot closer now. In fact, all three of them ignore the last throw of the ball and come barreling toward me. I chuckle as the three little poodles surround my legs, wagging their tails furiously and pawing at me for cuddles. I crouch down and scratch their ears. They are adorable. I always wanted a pet, but my mother would never let me have one because she didn't want fur all over her fabric. I tried to argue that poodles don't shed, but she still wouldn't let me have one, and now as an adult, my hours are so unsociable it wouldn't be fair for any creature I decided to bring home.

"Oh my goodness, aren't you adorable and sandy... So sandy," I say to the three dogs.

"Yeah, it's a nightmare to get the sand out of their coats, but they love it." I look up as the woman approaches me, and my mouth drops open. She's gorgeous. Her beautiful blonde hair whips around her face in the wind, her hazel eyes sparkle with joy, and her lush lips are turned up in a grin.

"Sorry about them. They are man whores who will do anything to get a pretty girl's attention." One of the dogs yips at her, and she chuckles. I stand as she picks up the ball and throws it again. The three dogs take off after it, and we watch them as they tackle each other, trying to get to the ball first.

"They look like a handful," I murmur to her, and she grins at me.

"They are the loves of my life, but yes, they can be a lot to handle. Luckily I'm good at juggling. Are you okay? I couldn't help but notice you looked a little sad," the woman says as she turns her attention back to me.

"Ah, yeah, I just got some unexpected and unwanted news this morning, and I'm trying to figure out what to do about it," I reply, surprised by my honesty. *What the hell, Colbie? Why are you telling a stranger about your problems?*

She frowns at me, and her eyes slide to the cuffs on my wrists. I wonder if she thinks I'm trying to hide cutting scars or something. It really is slightly unusual to be wearing these on the beach.

"Those are fae wedding cuffs. Are you being forced into something you don't want?" she asks, and I consider denying it, but instead, I shrug.

"Kind of." I'm never going to see the woman again, so there's no real need to lie to her.

She purses her lips and sits down, patting the sand next to her. "You know, I've always been of the opinion that we are never given more than we can handle." I consider whether I should just keep walking, but there's something about this woman that makes me feel comfortable. Maybe I can talk about my problems without actually telling her the whole truth.

I sit next to her as her dogs come racing back. The red one has the ball, and he drops it at her feet before lying down and putting his head on his paws, his tongue hanging out as he pants. The black and white poodles do the same. The white one places his head on the red one's back, and the black one rests his head on the woman's feet. She reaches out and runs her hand through his fur.

"But what if I don't want to do what I'm being forced to? What if I'm no good at it?" I've always had these insecurities, even growing up. Huh, I guess I have a lot more issues than I thought—abandonment and inadequacy. I'm sure it comes from Dad leaving and my mom's attitude toward me. Add in the recently remembered friends abandoning me, and it's no wonder I became withdrawn and doubted myself.

She looks out at the ocean. "So is the problem that you are being forced to do something you don't want to do, or are you worried you are going to fail at what you are being asked to do?"

I think about it for a moment and shake my head. "I don't see how I can do something I have no understanding of. That's the problem. I'm being asked to do something I don't know anything about, and what if I fail? What if I do so badly that it has far-reaching consequences?"

The woman turns to look at me, her hazel eyes

serious. "It's okay to ask for help, you know. I'm sure you aren't expected to do whatever it is on your own. You need a support system, someone who will have your back no matter what." She reaches out to stroke a hand over each of her dogs. "Kind of like my guys. I know no matter what happens, they will be right by my side." The black one licks the back of her hand before all three of them tackle her, almost like they planned it. She bursts into laughter as she falls backward, and they lick her.

I can't help but smile. I think our situations are different though, and I'm not sure a dog will help me rule a kingdom. I shake my head. "I just think there is someone else out there more suitable for the job."

She sighs and stands up, brushing the sand off her pants. The wind has died down, and the sea has settled, but a rumble of thunder can be heard on the horizon as the clouds darken even further.

"Colbie, take another few days and think it over. I have no doubt that once you stop doubting yourself, you are going to do amazing things. Come on, boys." She picks up the ball and tosses it down the beach. The dogs chase after it, and they suddenly disappear like they walked into thin air.

My mouth drops open in shock, and I scramble to my feet, looking from where the dogs disappeared to the woman who laughs.

The woman I just realized I never gave my name to turns and winks at me. "I have all the faith in the world for you. You just need to believe in it and trust that I have put all the support you need in place."

I gape in surprise as the woman follows her dogs and also disappears in the blink of an eye, her voice carrying on the wind. "You have a week before I make you go, Colbie."

Holy fuck. I think I may have just been visited by the goddess, and from her words, there is no way I am getting out of this.

My heart races, and my breathing picks up as I start to panic. I feel tears well in my eyes at the realization that there's no getting out of this.

I start to run down the beach, my movements jerky in the deep sand, my tote bag flapping against my side with each step. I get to the end of the cove and scramble over the large boulders that jut out into the ocean like a handful of marbles rolled by a giant. The sounds of the ocean and the coming storm become a background blur in my panic. My thoughts are chaotic as I still try to think of a way out of this, but deep down, I know it's futile. There's no where I can escape to where the goddess won't find me—not even one of the other kingdoms.

I reach the next secluded cove, one where I'm even less likely to see anyone, and collapse onto my favorite rock. It's flat and perfect for sunbathing on a sunny day. This cove backs up to a forest that is private land. There's a cottage up in the woods, but

I'm not sure I've ever seen anyone there, so maybe it's a holiday home.

I bury my face in my hands and start to sob, letting out all the fears and emotions that have been building since this morning. If that really was the goddess who visited, because who else could it be, then there is no getting out of this. Everything I've ever worked for is about to go up in smoke. My stomach rolls when I think about my bakery. I'm pretty sure they are not going to allow the shifter queen to work a normal job. Hell, what does being the queen even involve? The thought of ruling over a society I know nothing about is terrifying, and I haven't even considered the rest that comes along with being the queen of the shifters.

Magic is something I have never even really thought about. I'm human, and I was never going to be anything else. I was happy with my lot in life. Now, all of that is going to change. My entire being is going to change. I'm going to be gifted with magic that will allow me to shift into an animal form.

I wipe at my cheeks and look up as another crack of thunder booms across the bay. The storm arrived a lot sooner than I expected it to. The sky is dark and ominous, and I can see the sheet of rain racing toward me as a couple of drops land on my cheeks. A bolt of lightning streaks across the sky, striking the ocean far out. Fuck, there is no way I'm going to make it home without getting soaked. What was I thinking?

Oh, that's right, I wasn't. I was operating on fear and emotions. I scramble to my feet and look for shelter, but there is none—only the beach, the boulders, and the woods.

There is also the cottage in the woods. I guess that's as good a place as any. It has a porch I can shelter under until the rain eases. I grab my tote and start to scramble over the last couple of boulders before I hit the sand, then I run up the beach toward the woods and the cottage nestled amongst them. The sky opens up, and I groan as it pelts against my back as I run the remaining distance. The rain is cold against my skin as the sand gives way to gravel, and I'm able to move a little faster. My breath heaves out of my lungs as I reach the cottage and scramble up the steps and out of the rain. I turn around as another boom of thunder rolls across the sky, followed by another flash of lightning. The wind has picked up again, and I shiver as it blows against my wet clothes.

Well, this sucks. I lean against the railing and catch my breath, pushing the bedraggled tendrils of hair out of my face. I look down at my body. My sundress is plastered to my skin, and my tote bag is soggy. I groan and drop it on the floor before looking around the porch. There's a surfboard rack on the far end with a couple of boards sitting in it, as well as a wet suit tossed haphazardly across them, like the owner took it off and threw it there without any other thought. There are a couple of chairs, but they have cushions on them, and I don't want to get them wet. I consider removing them and sitting on the bare chair when I hear a voice behind me.

"Can I help you?"

I scream and whirl around, grabbing my chest in fright.

I stumble backward a little, staring at the man leaning in the doorframe of the cottage. He's tall, maybe six-two, and has the most amazing chestnut-colored eyes with flecks of gold in them. He pushes a lock of dirty blond hair back over his shoulder, which is almost as long as mine and has that *went swimming and let air dry* look about it. It's windswept and a little messy, but it suits him perfectly. His skin has a beautiful golden tan, like he sees the sun regularly, and I guess he does if he surfs. He has a cord around his neck holding a pendant made up of black and gold stones, and above his heart is a tattoo, but I don't stop to inspect it too closely. My eyes drop lower, and I lick my lips as I take in his naked chest and eight-pack slab of muscles. Holy shit. Unlike the shifters, he's long and lean, and his muscles have a sleekness to them rather than bulk. I reach the waistband of his gray sweatpants, and I realize what I'm doing, so I shake my head and bring my gaze back to his face. He has a small smirk on his full lips, and his own gaze slips lower. His expression heats when he sees my sundress plastered to my body, but then his gaze catches on the cuffs on my wrists and his eyes widen minutely. When his gaze returns to mine, he looks closer and obviously notices the remnants of my sob fest. I bet my eyes are red and my face is blotchy. I am not a pretty crier, so it's ugly sobs and snot all the way for me.

The smirk drops, and he pushes off the frame and steps forward, holding out a hand.

"Are you okay?" I can hear the concern in his voice, and I almost start to cry again, but I bite my lip as the wind picks up, blowing straight through my dress. The rain falls even harder, and I can't stop the shiver that racks my whole body.

"I'm sorry. I got caught in the rain, and I was just going to stand under here until it cleared enough for me to return home," I tell him as my teeth start to chatter.

He looks away from me and out at the storm and frowns. "I don't think this is going to ease anytime soon. Do you want to come inside? You can dry off and wait until it clears."

I bite my lip and look from him and out to the storm again. He's right, it looks like it settled in for the evening.

I shake my head. "I'll just call a rideshare and get out of your way. I'm sorry I disturbed you," I say as I feel my hair drip down my back, and I wince.

He chuckles. "I'm not sure anyone will let you in their car soaking wet."

Ugh, he has a point, but I don't know this guy, and for all I know, I will walk through his door and never walk back out. Before I can make a decision, I hear a plaintive meow, and a cat slinks between his legs, weaving in and out of them. A wide smile brightens his face, and I stare, stunned at how gorgeous he is. He bends down and picks up the fluffy gray and white thing and holds it up, rubbing his head against the cat's. "What do you think, Stormheart? Shall the pretty lady come in and get dry?" He talks to it in a baby voice, and I can't stop the snort of amusement that comes from my mouth. It's so freaking adorable and kooky.

He turns to me, tucking the cat under his arm, and the two of them look at me. I swear the cat narrows its eyes on me in warning, like it's saying don't you dare, but the guy still looks welcoming.

"I'm Nox, and this is Stormy. Come on. I'm not going to bite." He doesn't wait for a response, just heads back inside, leaving the door open.

I glance back at the storm and shrug. What do I have to lose? If he kills me, at least I won't have to worry about the shifters.

ELEVEN

Lennox

I don't bother to turn around, but I know the minute the female crosses over the threshold and into my space. I'm not sure if it's the magic that floats benignly around her marriage cuffs or if there is something else to this woman, but my own magic is going crazy despite my charm to conceal it. I'm almost certain she's human, but I'm not sure I made the right choice by inviting her in. What if she's also concealing her nature like I am, but my magic isn't telling me that she's dangerous so I have to trust it for now? I rub a hand over my chest where I can feel it. It's usually quiet and sullen, annoyed that I choose to hide my true nature, but today it almost seems excited.

I place Stormy down on the top of his cat tree,

and he circles a couple of times before settling down without taking his eyes off the girl.

"What's your name? Do you want to get out of those clothes? I can give you a towel and something dry to wear," I ask, turning around. Her dress is completely plastered to her figure, and my mouth waters at the sight of all her delicious curves. I need to get laid. It's been too long if I'm getting turned on by a poor female who looks like a drowned wolf. Instead, I focus on her stunning face. I can sense that she's upset about something, and there are visible signs she's been crying. Her pretty lavender eyes are red, and her plump bottom lip is cracked where she's been biting it. The girl is fucking gorgeous, and I feel my creature stir for the first time in ages, trying to see through my eyes, but with my charm on, he can't. I feel his annoyance at me, and he gives a halfhearted kick but settles down when it doesn't get him anywhere. He knows if he wants to be let out occasionally, he can't fight me. My stomach rolls with guilt at suppressing him, but it's the best for both of us.

"I'm Colbie, and yeah, that would be great. I'm freezing," she replies, hugging her arms around her body as she looks around my living area. I know she's probably not too impressed. I live a fairly simple life. My cottage consists of one main living and kitchen area, my bedroom, a bathroom, and the spare bedroom where I have my workspace. I have a couple of old, overstuffed sofas that Stormy and I use to watch TV or read and a bookcase full of all sorts of interesting books. I hope she doesn't look too closely, otherwise she's going to guess I'm not human. Most of them are texts I've gathered from all four kingdoms, but there are a few fiction books in there as well. I'm an eclectic reader, reading anything from crime fiction to romance, but my love of knowledge beats out everything else. When I was growing up before my animal emerged, I had dreams of working in the archives in the shifter capital. That all went up in flames when my animal emerged at seventeen. My heart broke when I also received a bond group mark, but there was no way I was going to search for it and make myself vulnerable to rejection when they discovered what I was. The ridicule I received from my peers in the village was bad enough. Instead, I slunk off and hid here in the human zone where no one suspects that I am anything but mundane.

I shake off my thoughts as I head into my bedroom and grab her a shirt and spare set of sweatpants. They'll be way too big on her, but there's a drawstring, so they should stay up. I don't have anything to offer her for underwear unless she wants a pair of mine. I groan. The thought of her in my clothes, let alone my underwear, is a little too enticing, and I adjust myself as my cock twitches in interest. She's going to think I'm some kind of deviant if I go out there like this. I can't hide anything in my sweatpants. It's hard enough with the size of my dick without it becoming erect. I wasn't expecting company when I got dressed this morning. I conjure up thoughts of being teased by the village teenagers, and my hard-on quickly deflates. Scrubbing my hand through my hair, I return to the living area, holding the dry things out to Colbie.

I find her exactly where I left her. Stormy is still staring at her suspiciously, but she just looks exhausted. "Here you go," I say, holding out the towel.

"I didn't move because I didn't want to drip all over your place," she explains, taking the towel and scrubbing it over her body to remove some of the dripping water.

"Pfft, it's nothing that doesn't clean up easily. My bedroom and bathroom are through there." I point to where I just came from. "You're welcome to use the shower if you want to warm up. How about I light a fire and make us coffee? That should help too," I suggest, moving away from her so she doesn't feel overwhelmed. The fire is already set, so I just have to throw a match on it. I crouch down in front of it, and I hear her walk in the direction of my bedroom. As she passes behind me, I get a whiff of her scent, which is what originally brought me outside. I didn't hear her over the sound of the storm, but the wind blew her scent inside, telling me she was there. She smells like cupcakes and frosting, and it makes me crave cake.

I hear her close the door to the bedroom as I strike a match on the side of the box. The flame bursts to life, and I throw it in the fireplace. It hits the starter blocks and catches them on fire. I watch as the flames spread across the blocks, a pretty red and blue, and feel the heat radiating off them as they set the wood alight. It doesn't take long, and the fire crackles gently, warming up the room. I hadn't noticed how cold it had gotten, my shifter biology making me naturally warm.

I stand up and turn, my gaze drifting to my closed bedroom door. My fascination with the little human outweighs my natural inclination to avoid anybody. Normally if someone had turned up on my deck, trying to escape the weather, I would have been an asshole and chased them off, but there's something about the gorgeous woman that intrigues me. She smells and feels like magic, which can't be true because she's definitely human. I'm assuming the magic is coming from the fae cuffs she's wearing, but she's like a puzzle I want to solve, and I can't help but be curious. I feel this strange need to get to know her, and I haven't felt that in a long time.

Sighing, I head into my small kitchen and turn my coffee machine on before checking the cupboard for something to eat. I don't have a lot, and I really need to do some shopping, but I've been putting it off. I do find a packet of chocolate chip cookies, though, so I pull them out. I hear the bedroom door open as I shove a pod into the machine and put a cup under it, pressing the button.

I turn around and inhale quickly at the sight of her in my clothes. My creature starts rolling inside my chest, and I rub over that spot, trying to ease the ache. Fuck, I never thought seeing someone in my clothes would cause such a reaction, especially a human somebody.

I always thought if I mated, it would be with a shifter, but when my animal emerged, and I was ridiculed, I quickly let go of that idea. I haven't really dated since I moved to the human zone, preferring to keep to myself. A relationship with a human was never going to work, because I would always be hiding something, unless I got the guts to tell them the truth. Children wouldn't be a possibility either, so I remain single.

This gorgeous creature is really making me reconsider how I feel. She smiles at me and holds up her wet clothes. "Do you have a dryer or somewhere I can hang these?" she asks, and I hurry over and take them out of her hands.

"My dryer is in the mud room out back. I'll just go put them in for you. It won't take long to get them dry, and I can bring you home if you want."

"That would be great, thank you," she replies, and I hurry to do just that. When I return, she's taken over making the coffee and is sitting on the sofa in front of the fire, with two cups on the table in front of her and a plate of cookies. She's nibbling on one, lost in thought as she stares into the flames. Her legs are tucked up under her, and she looks cozy and right sitting on my sofa.

I take a seat next to her and grab my cup. "I would have finished making these, thank you."

She turns away from the fire and smiles at me, shrugging her shoulders. "It's not a big deal. It's the least I can do for you since you're giving me shelter. The weather was fine when I left my grandparents' place. I really wasn't expecting the storm."

"You live with your grandparents?" I ask, jumping at the chance to learn more about this girl who suddenly appeared in my life like a breath of fresh air.

She shakes her head. "No, I'm just visiting. I needed a break, and they always welcome me with open arms," she says, the smile on her face telling me how much she loves her grandparents. I feel a pang of longing for my own parents, but I shake it off. Although they don't understand my reasons for hiding, they still support my choices, but I do miss them.

"Do you live farther in the city?" I ask, trying to hold my grimace in, but I don't think I succeed when she starts to laugh.

"Not a fan?" she asks, blowing on her hot coffee before taking a sip.

"It's too noisy and smelly, and there are too

many cars and not enough trees," I grumble, not getting upset at her amusement.

"Yeah, you aren't wrong, but no, I live in the neutral zone."

I freeze in the process of taking a sip of my own coffee. "Really?" I'm kind of surprised. Maybe that's why she smells of magic, because she comes into contact with shifters regularly.

"Yeah, I grew up there. My mother has a business, and now I do as well."

"Oh, what do you do?" I'm intrigued. I've avoided the neutral zone too. Being around shifters and not being willing to shift is painful, which is why I live in the human zone.

"I own a bakery café," she replies, taking a bite of one of the cookies.

"Now I feel a little embarrassed for offering you store-bought cookies." I grimace and look at the sad plate of offerings.

She giggles and shakes her head. "Don't be. Sometimes it's nice not eating something I had to bake. These aren't too bad for store-bought ones. You got the good ones, nice and chunky and full of chocolate," she assures me.

"And what do you do for fun?" I ask, picking up one of the cookies and looking at it closely, not even realizing there are different kinds. I take a bite and nod—she's right, they are good.

Her nose wrinkles adorably, and she shrugs. "Not much right now. I've been so focused on making my business successful, I stopped doing the things I used to love."

"Like what?" I press.

Her gaze drifts to a framed photo of me surfing above the fireplace. It's one of the reasons I bought this place, because I can step out the door and the water and waves are right there. Surfing feels like flying, and I love it.

"I used to love sewing, or anything crafty really. My mom's a dress designer, and she taught me to sew. I would make my dolls fancy dresses to wear, and when I used to visit my grandparents, I loved swimming. I always wanted to learn to surf, but I had no one to teach me—oh, and I'd love to learn to dive, but I'm scared of sharks."

I chuckle and lean back in my chair. "Sharks are probably more afraid of you than you are of them. I can teach you to surf if you want." My mouth snaps shut. I can't believe what just came out of my mouth. I haven't spent any real time with another person in a long time. My IT job allows me to work from home, and apart from trips to the grocery store, I'm a real loner by choice.

I almost take the offer back, but the way her eyes light up and she sits up straight has me clamping my lips shut. "You would?"

"Sure, we can start as soon as the storm clears if you want. Hopefully by the day after tomorrow."

Her face falls, and she slumps back again. "I'll probably have to go home on Wednesday. I have to get back to my bakery." She sounds so disappointed.

"Why can't you come out here once a week on your days off?"

She slumps even further and groans, tears welling in her eyes again. "I don't think there are going to be many of those to come."

I frown, not sure what she means, but her sadness from before returns.

"I should probably get going," she says and goes to stand up, but I feel a wave of panic and put my hand out. I don't want her to leave just yet.

"Do you want to stay and hang out with me? We could order some food and maybe watch a movie or play a game." I wave at the game console that's plugged into my TV. "I'm really enjoying your company," I mumble shyly, not wanting to look at her and see any pity in her eyes. Maybe I have starved myself of company for too long.

"Yeah, I'd like that. Let me just text my grandparents and tell them I'll be out for a little longer so they won't worry if I'm not there when they get home." She stands up and heads over to where she dropped her tote. She rummages in it and pulls out her phone, and her fingers fly across the screen.

My anxiety turns into excitement, and I jump up to find my tablet from my office space, bringing up the food delivery app. "What do you feel like eating?" I ask as I return to the living area. She's back on the sofa, curled up in front of the fire again, and I can't believe how right she looks.

"I don't care, something hot though," she replies.

"Spicy or just a hot meal?" I ask, and she shrugs. "Either. I don't mind, I'm not all that fussy."

I scroll through the options, stopping on one of my favorites. "What about Italian? We can order a couple of dishes and share." You can't go wrong with pasta, right?

Her eyes light up, and my heart thumps harder as she beams at me. "How did you know that carbs are the way to my heart? Surprise me, but can we get cheesy garlic bread? It's my favorite." I quickly put in an order and place my tablet on the side. I'll have to keep an eye on the delivery because they often get lost on the way to my house, though most of the regular drivers have been here before. I really don't cook for myself—why bother when there is an app right at your fingertips?

"Alright, done. Now movie or games?" I ask, turning on the television, excited to spend more time with Colbie.

"Hmm. What do you have?" she asks me, and I chuckle, waving my hand at the large amount of game cases.

"Most of them," I admit, and I see her brows furrow.

"Do you have Shifter Quest?" Again, my heart jumps for an entirely different reason, and my enthusiasm is replaced with worry. Does she know what I am?

"Ah, yeah?" I reply, and she blushes prettily.

"My staff was raving about it the other day, and I had never heard of it. I kind of want to know what the big deal is."

I almost huff out a huge sigh of relief but keep it in. "Sure, I'll load it, and we can get started while waiting on the food." I turn my back to her and grab the right game.

"Oh good, my friends were telling me about the different shifters you can play, and I desperately want to be the pegasus."

I drop the remote in my hand, and it clatters onto the floor, missing one of the rugs I have on the hardwood.

"Are you okay?" Colbie jumps up and hurries over, bending down to pick up the remote before handing it to me.

"Ah, yeah, sorry. It slipped out of my hand." I take it back from her before clearing the surprise from my face and turning to look at her.

"Why do you want to be a pegasus? Wouldn't one of the more apex shifters be better?"

She shakes her head. "They are so majestic and beautiful. Who cares if they can't breathe fire or have sharp teeth or claws? I bet they make up for it in other ways. Wouldn't it be awesome if there really were pegasus and unicorn shifters? I bet they would have other special kinds of powers." She sighs wistfully before shaking her head. "Sorry. That was silly."

"Huh, no, that isn't silly. So you don't know much about shifters and the different types?" I turn back to the machine and load the game, and I hear her return to her seat.

"Does any human? They are super secretive. I know there are wolves and tigers, I've seen them in the neutral zone, but that's pretty much it, though I was told the other day that there is no such thing as a penguin shifter."

I chuckle with amusement at the wonder in her voice before grabbing the second controller and returning to the sofa. "No, there isn't. Could you imagine it? I bet they would be as useless as pegasus and unicorn shifters," I mutter, and she elbows me, growling playfully.

"Hey, don't put down my soul creature." Sure enough, when we get to the character selection page, she scrolls through and finds the pegasus and unicorn. She has trouble deciding.

"The unicorn is so pretty with all those different color options, but I want wings like the pegasus," she grumbles and finally selects the winged horse in the end. "If only they came in different colors."

And just like that, I fall instantly in love with the little human, but it's followed by such heartbreaking regret because nothing will ever be able to happen between us.

TWELVE

Colbie

I spend the rest of the afternoon and late into the evening hanging out with Nox. It was not what I planned for my day, since I was totally going to wallow in my misery, but it turns out it was exactly what I needed. I was able to switch off all my worries and ignore all the drama in my life for a few hours in the company of a handsome, interesting man.

Shifter Quest was awesome. You would think it would make all the current drama in my life swirl around in my brain, but I was so busy doing quests and trying to level up that everything else became unimportant. I can see how people can become addicted to video games.

The two of us worked well together as a team. Our characters blended seamlessly with one another and the other avatars that were on our team, and together, we were able to push back the rebel forces and defend the castle and shifter nation. We didn't make it all the way to the end, but we were reluctant to give up, so I'm going to come back tomorrow and hang out a little while in the afternoon again after he's finished his work for the day.

The food was delicious, and the storm raged on outside, but eventually, I had to go home, so he offered to drive me. It was too wet and dangerous for me to scramble back over the boulders.

On the car ride home, we're both quiet, lost in our own thoughts, but it's not uncomfortable at all. He pulls up to my grandparents' place, and I really don't want to get out. Sighing, I unbuckle my seat belt and open the door.

"Thanks for the ride," I say as I climb out of the car, feeling a pang of loneliness. In a short period of time, I have become very attached to Nox. He's handsome, kind, funny, and a balm to my turmoiled soul.

"So I'll see you tomorrow after lunch?" he asks, and I feel slightly better. He seems as reluctant to part as I am.

"Yeah, I can't wait," I tell him, leaning against the doorframe of the car and peering back at him. His handsome face is illuminated by the interior light, and the gold flecks in his eyes are more prominent, almost swallowing the rest of the brown.

"Good, because I think with a few more missions, we might reach the boss level, and we can take out the bad guy," he gushes, and I smile at his nerdiness. He put on glasses to play the game, but he took them off again to drive. He looked super cute in them too. It kind of gave me some naughty schoolgirl and professor fantasies. I had to stop myself from squirming on the couch while sitting next to him. I was worried I said something out loud at one stage, because he inhaled deeply, stiffened, and gave me a weird look, but he didn't move away from me or comment, so I might have been imagining things.

"I can't wait. Hopefully the weather clears tomorrow, because I'll walk down the beach again. If not, I'll catch a rideshare. Can you give me your address so I know which way to send him."

"Oh, how about I come and get you instead, and we have a meal somewhere before going back to my place and playing games? There's this amazing little café up on the cliffs on the other side of my place at the lighthouse." Nox's cove ends in large cliffs that are inaccessible, and a lighthouse sits on top of them. It's a popular destination for both locals and tourists alike. My grandparents took me a couple of times when I was younger.

"I can't believe it's still there. I've been a few times when I used to visit my grandparents," I tell him as the wind swirls around me, and I shiver, wrapping my arms around myself.

"It closed down for a while but was recently purchased and renovated. They do good, wholesome home cooking, and it's really popular for dinner, but I should be able to get us a late lunch, early dinner reservation. Shall I pick you up at about three?" he suggests.

"I'd like that. I'll see you then." I reach out and give his hand a squeeze, and I get a jolt of static. He frowns as I pull away. "Shit, sorry," I apologize, and he shakes his head.

"No reason to apologize, it's not like you did it on purpose." He puts his truck into gear. "Go inside, it's starting to rain again. I don't want you getting sick and not being able to come out. I'll see you tomorrow."

I step back, slam the door shut, and look down at my hands. The stupid marks beneath my cuffs are tingling, and all of my previous worries flood back like a tidal wave. He drives off, and I wave as the lights of his truck disappear. The rainfall becomes steadier, so I hurry inside and sneak through the house quietly, not wanting to wake Granny and Grampy. The lamp on the bedside table of the bedroom I'm using is on, and I quickly strip off my sundress. I reluctantly replaced the clothes Nox lent me before I left. They smelled so good, like a warm churro, and it made my mouth water. I'm so glad nobody saw me sniffing them when I first put them on, because they would have thought I was crazy.

I throw on the tank top I use for pj's, unclasp the wedding cuffs from around my wrists, and place them on the bedside table. Sitting on the bed, I study the marks around my wrists. They seem to have gotten a little darker, the gold color looking more prominent. I have no idea how I am going to hide these for a long period of time. I can't wear the cuffs while I'm at work. I sigh and drop my hands into my lap.

The feeling of dread has returned as I climb between the sheets and shimmy down, shivering at how cold they feel. The storm has settled a little, since the thunder and lightning has blown past, leaving only rain behind. The gentle pitter-patter sound against the roof is soothing, but I toss and turn, and my thoughts return to the beach this afternoon.

I'm almost certain I got a visit from the shifter goddess Aramis. Who else could it have been? She made it sound like there was no getting out of this at all. As much as I want to run away from this whole situation, I don't think she's going to let me. She made it sound like she would come and get me if I didn't present myself to the shifters.

I heave out a sigh and roll over, pulling the blanket up over my head so only my face pokes out. I feel tears prickle in my eyes as I try to come up with some kind of solution, but I can't think of a single thing. She didn't even give me a chance to argue with her, just disappeared into thin air with her dogs. Who would have thought the shifter goddess would have poodles?

I don't get much sleep, and eventually, I come to the conclusion that I'm going to have to accept this is my destiny, but I'm going to take a couple of days to enjoy being free first. I need to make arrangements for my bakery, because I bet they are not going to allow me to continue working there, and I want to enjoy the company of a man whom I choose, not one the goddess has chosen for me. That's a whole other bone of contention—one I think that annoys me even more than being selected as the shifter queen. I'm going to have to choose complete strangers to be my mates, men who have been marked by the goddess, and I'm just supposed to say, "Hey, want to be my husband for the next forty years?"

Do shifters even have divorce? If I don't like them, do I get to try again? How am I expected to know, and how long do I get to choose? Maybe I can take my time, like I can get to know the men the goddess selected before I have to make a choice. How am I supposed to deal with three husbands? That's how many wives Lucas has. I mean, they seemed happy, and they looked like they got along, but what if the men I choose hate each other or get jealous? I wonder if there is an option to choose none. I can be the spinster queen. It's not like I need to produce an heir.

I finally fall into a fitful sleep full of growling,

pissed off shifters and the pretty brown and gold eyes of the human man I spent the day with.

When I wake up the following morning, my head hurts, and my eyes are sticky, like I've been crying in my sleep. Not even a hot shower makes me feel any better.

"You look like crap, Colbie girl," my grampy says as I enter the kitchen. He's sitting at the table with a cup of coffee in front of him and the newspaper in his hand. Granny is washing a few dishes at the sink, and she turns to look at me with a raised eyebrow.

"Ugh, I slept so badly. I need coffee," I mumble, and she grabs the pot off the warmer and pours me a cup. I wrinkle my nose, spoiled by having access to the coffee machine at work, but I thank her. The two of them chuckle at my dramatics.

"What did you get up to yesterday?" Grampy asks, putting his newspaper down as I take a seat next to him at the table.

"I went for a walk and got trapped in the rain. When I tried to take shelter under someone's porch, they invited me inside to warm up. I ended up playing video games and having dinner with him."

Grampy's eyebrows jump. "You went inside a strange man's house?" He sounds a little surprised. "You don't usually make rash decisions."

I shrug and look between them. "I don't know, there was something about him that made me feel comfortable."

Granny's eyes narrow, and she nods. "You've always been a good judge of character."

"I'm hanging out with him this afternoon too," I tell them, and Grampy purses his lips but doesn't argue with me. I appreciate that. Although they worry, they acknowledge that I'm an adult who can make my own decisions.

I lift up my coffee mug to take a sip, even if it's a little sludgy, and my granny gasps.

"What are those?" she asks, hurrying over to me and snatching the hand holding my coffee mug. Coffee sloshes over the side and down my hand, but thankfully, it's not too hot. I grimace as she runs her finger over the marks. Fuck, I forgot the cuffs.

Grampy jumps to his feet and grabs my other wrist as Granny releases the one holding my coffee mug. "Colbie girl, is there something you need to tell us?" he growls, shaking the hand in front of my face.

I put the mug down and snatch my hand back, then I sigh and close my eyes, trying to control the tears that want to burst free. When I open them, they are both staring at me with a mixture of worry and sadness.

"They appeared on my wrists on Saturday night," I tell them, and Granny gasps, pressing a hand against her chest in shock.

"You were chosen?" Grampy says flatly, and I nod, a tear rolling down my cheek.

"Yes, I'm the next shifter queen," I confirm, and

Granny lowers into one of the chairs and gapes at me, speechless.

Grampy doesn't say anything, he just scoops me up and holds me against his chest, hugging me tightly. The tears I've been holding back flood out, and I sob, surrounded by the warmth and strength of my grampy. Neither of them says anything, they just give me silent support during my meltdown, but eventually, I run out of tears and pull away, wiping my face. Granny passes me a box of tissues she must have retrieved while I was sobbing.

I sit down, blowing my nose, and Grampy retakes his own seat. "I know this isn't what you wanted in life, but if you want my two cents, you're going to be the best damn queen the shifters have ever had," he tells me confidently, and I feel a rush of warmth and support as Granny agrees.

"Of course she is. There is no one more compassionate, kind, and intelligent as our Colbie. Does your mother know?" she asks me, and I shake my head.

"I haven't told anyone. I was hoping there was a way out of it," I admit, and Granny gasps in surprise, but Grampy nods.

"I understand. I would probably feel the same way."

I tell them about my visit with the goddess on the beach and what she insinuated.

"So what are you going to do?" Granny asks, and I groan, placing my head on the table.

"I'm going to take a couple more days to adjust to this life-changing news, and then I'm going to make arrangements for my bakery and apartment before I present myself to the shifters, but I'll do it in my own goddamn time." I growl that last bit, and I feel a hand brush over the back of my head.

"You take as much time as you need. They can wait, and if they don't like it, tough," Grampy agrees, and I lift my head and raise an eyebrow. He laughs. "I mean, you are the queen, right?"

A small smile reaches my lips as he chuckles, and Granny nods her head.

"That's right, you're the one in charge. Don't let them walk all over you, because if you give them an inch, they will take a mile. Don't let your mother do it either. I'm sure she will insist you present yourself as soon as she finds out. She's such a stickler for rules, but stand your ground. You need to be ready for this, because your life is about to change dramatically. Take all the time you need. Be sure, and be ready."

"What if I don't like any of the men who have been chosen for me?" I ask quietly, sitting up and taking a sip of my coffee.

"I forgot that you would have your mates selected for you. That's bullshit." Grampy starts pacing back and forth across the kitchen. "No woman should be forced into an arranged marriage."

"Easy, Joseph. The goddess would not bless her

with mates that weren't compatible, and she gets to choose from those selected." She turns her attention back to me, ignoring her husband.

"Go with your heart, my girl, and if none of them are suitable, then don't pick any of them, but I'm certain the goddess will be looking out for you. Maybe talk to King Lucas about it. He will be there to advise you. He's been through exactly the same thing as you, so lean on him."

I heave out a sigh. "Okay, but can we just forget about it for another day or two? Today I'm going to hang out with my new friend again and pretend that my life isn't going to change completely. If the weather is good tomorrow, Nox is going to give me a surfing lesson. I'm just going to pretend to be regular, boring human Colbie for a little longer, then on Wednesday, I'll return to the neutral zone and make arrangements for my bakery. I don't know how I'm going to find a baker at such short notice. Olivia, Justin, and Violet are great, but they are not going to be able to manage on their own."

Granny's eyes light up, and she and Grampy exchange a glance.

He nods, chuckling. "How about Jenny and I help out? After all, you stole most of your recipes from her," he teases, and I sit up straight, hope welling inside me.

"You would do that?" I ask, and Granny nods eagerly.

"I would love to. Retirement is great and everything, but both of us are bored. There's only so much gardening you can do, and I'd rather pay someone to paint the fence than do it myself. Running the bakery would be exciting and exactly what we need—at least until you can hire someone you trust."

"Yes, yes, a hundred times yes. That would be amazing, thank you. You can have my apartment too, so you don't have to travel back and forth everyday if you want."

"That would be nice, like a mini vacation," Granny says, and I wrinkle my nose.

"Not much of a vacation when you're getting up at four in the morning."

Gramp groans. "Ugh, I forgot you have such early hours."

Granny laughs and shushes him. "It will be fine. If we are both going to go in, we won't need to be there so early because there are two of us doing the work." He cheers up, and I laugh, feeling a little lighter now that I know my baby is going to be looked after by someone I trust.

"How about we spend the morning going over the recipes I use, since they are not all Granny's?" I suggest, sticking my tongue out at Grampy, and he laughs. "I'll need to give you a lesson on our new marshmallow treats too."

"Pfft, what is so hard about marshmallow? That was one of the first ones I taught you," Granny scoffs.

I open my phone and show her the photos of the animals, and her eyes widen with surprise. "It's not the actual recipe, but what I do with it that matters," I explain. "I might make a video of myself, making them step by step so you have a guide."

"Look at those. They are amazing!" Grampy exclaims, and I can hear the admiration in his voice. "Think of all the different things we could do!" He sounds excited.

I tell him about the white board in the shop that people leave suggestions on, and he starts to search the kingdom-wide network, which is a computer network that links the four kingdoms, allowing us to share information and ideas.

The three of us spend the morning going over my recipes and writing a list of all the things we produce for both breakfast and lunch. They are practically giddy with the idea of playing in my café. My grandparents are where my love of food came from. I have to keep distracting my grampy when he keeps going off on tangents, trying to come up with wild and wacky ideas. I'm pretty sure my customers are in for a fun experience over the next couple of months, but at least my baby will be in safe hands.

THIRTEEN

Colbie

Nox picks me up in the afternoon. My grandparents can't help but be nosy and hang around out front gardening, so I can't avoid introducing him to them. He takes it in stride, though, shaking Grampy's hand and telling Granny how fantastic her garden looks. It goes a long way, and Granny gives me an impressed wink as we walk away.

I chuckle as we get into the truck, and he looks at me questioningly as we drive away.

"What?" he asks, smiling, and I pat his leg reassuringly.

"You certainly know how to make a good impression. You've obviously done the meet the parents thing before."

His smile drops, and he frowns. "Actually, not

really. I've never really dated that much."

My mouth drops open in shock as I stare at him. He has to be at least the same age as me, maybe twenty-five or twenty-six, and he's fucking gorgeous. Women would have to be blind not to want to date him, and even then, with how good he smells, I'm sure that wouldn't be a problem.

"Why the fuck not?" My polite filter fails me as I try to wrap my head around it, but then something occurs to me. Maybe he's a hit it and quit it type, and he never got as far as the meet the parents stage. That makes more sense, and my stomach rolls at the thought. I don't want to be another notch on his bedpost, but I'm not going to be able to start anything long term with him either. This is just temporary, and I guess a quick fling is exactly what I need. I let the hurt recede and decide to embrace this for what it is—a nice distraction from my life.

"I was an awkward kid and a late bloomer, and a little too nerdy for the kids in the town I grew up in. They were all into sports and the outdoors, and I preferred my books and computers. Then, when I finally had a growth spurt and filled out, I gained a reputation as a weirdo." His cheeks blush red at his words, and I can hear the hurt in his tone no matter how casual he tries to sound.

"Eventually, I couldn't take the taunting anymore, and I moved here. I have developed a love of the outdoors and surfing, but I like my solitude, though occasionally I do get lonely. My mom got me Stormheart to keep me company because she was worried about me. She keeps telling me people aren't meant to be alone."

"She's right. I don't have a lot of friends, but I think I'd be lost without my mom or the people I work with."

"Well, maybe you can be my friend, at least for the time you're here." He sounds sad when he says this, like he knows our friendship has an expiration date. He probably thinks it's because I will return to my life in the neutral zone, but little does he know, that's about to change completely too.

I put my cuffs back on when I got ready earlier, and I fiddle with one as I murmur my agreement. "Of course, and maybe you can come visit me in the neutral zone occasionally," I say, but I can tell from his reaction that's not going to happen. We're silent as we continue the drive to the lighthouse. The silence isn't awkward so much as I think we're probably both lost in our own thoughts.

When we arrive, I mentally shake myself and turn to face him. "Let's not let thoughts of the future or the past ruin today. Let's live in the moment and enjoy what time we have together, okay?"

The heaviness in his eyes lightens, and he nods and holds out his hand. "Agreed," he says as I take it and shake it, a spark of static jolting us, but instead of pulling away, he holds on tight, looking down at my hand and nodding to the cuffs.

"Are you promised to someone? Those are fae mating cuffs, right?"

His hand is steady and warm in mine, but my heart races at his words. I hope he doesn't want me to take them off so he can get a closer look.

I pull my hand from his and unbuckle my seat belt, not looking him in the eye. "No, they are just a pretty trinket my mother picked up on a shopping trip to the kingdom of Shayla. She liked the moonstones in them and said they would protect me."

"They feel kind of magical," he murmurs distractedly as he watches me, his gaze not leaving the cuffs.

"You can feel magic in them?" I snap, wondering if I made a mistake in assuming he is human. A human wouldn't be able to feel magic. I can't feel any magic in them, and I'm using them strictly because they cover my marks. Shit, maybe my marks feel magical, and he can feel that? I didn't ask my grandparents if they felt magical to them.

He blanches and quickly shakes his head. "No, of course not, but they look kind of magical, right?" he says sheepishly before also undoing his seat belt and hurrying out of the truck.

I frown but follow him out of the vehicle. He puts his hand against my back as he guides me into the restaurant. There's no weird static charge this time, but the breeze brings his scent to my nose, and my stomach rumbles. I have no idea what cologne he's wearing, but the manufacturers surely knew their stuff when they made it smell like cinnamon and sugar. It's mouthwatering, and I have a craving for cinnamon donuts.

The hostess shows us to our table and hands us menus before giving us a moment to look over them. The silence is a little awkward as I look over the menu, and Nox shifts uncomfortably in his seat before huffing out a sigh.

"Did I ruin this? Can we forget the last few minutes happened?" he asks, and I sag a little.

"Don't worry about it. I was being oversensitive. I didn't want to think my mother had done anything to them," I lie, but it is plausible. "She's always harassing me to get out and date. I wouldn't put it past her to do something sneaky like give me magical cuffs."

"Oh, I think fae are fairly honorable when it comes to those things. I doubt she would have been able to find someone to put a spell on them. They are kind of sacred to the fae culture. I'm actually surprised she got anyone to sell them to her."

My eyebrows jump, but I smile. "My mother can be very persuasive. You seem to know a bit about them…"

He blushes adorably and looks down at his menu like he's embarrassed. "Magic fascinates me. I've done a lot of research on the four different supernatural races. I also do a lot of work for different magical species, so it was sensible to learn all I can about them."

He told me yesterday that he creates websites and security programs for a living. It's why he can work from home.

"I've never really thought about the other races. Sure, we're taught about shifters in school because that's who we share a kingdom with, but it's limited, and they are fairly secretive about a lot of things." Which I'm cursing now, because I'll be going into this queen thing blind. Aramis better be right when she said she gave me the tools and advisors I'll need to get through this, otherwise I'll be gunning for her, goddess or not. I should probably spend the next few days studying up on all my supernatural knowledge.

"I have some books you can borrow if you're interested," Nox offers, smiling, and I purse my lips.

"You know, I might just take you up on that. I like to expand my knowledge." I also desperately need all the help I can get. I'm certain the queen of the shifters will have to have some kind of contact with other species. Hell, for all I know, the supernaturals intermingle regularly. I know that humans are allowed to travel within all of the kingdoms.

After that, conversation flows naturally. The food is delicious, and I indulge in a couple of glasses of wine. I do not understand how this man hasn't dated more. He's witty and charming and an excellent conversationalist. He is the full fucking package, and I am so disappointed I can't spend more than a few days in his life. Whoever he ends up with is going to have a loving and devoted husband, and I kind of hate the fictional woman.

After dinner, we head back to his place to continue our game. We stop at a local bakery and pick up some dessert to have later. I study their offerings with interest. I lean toward cupcakes and muffins because they are easy and popular, but I have been thinking about expanding my range, and looking to see what is popular in other places helps me make decisions about that.

"See something you like?" Nox's breath brushes over my ear as he steps up behind me to study the display case. I kind of feel like there might be a double meaning to his words, but I choose to focus on the pastries in front of me instead of the delicious snack behind me. There are a number of different kinds of cheesecake, a chocolate coffee torte, and four different kinds of pie.

"You can't go wrong with any kind of pie," I reply, my voice breathier than I intended. His body is warm against my back as his hands rest on my hips, and he places his chin on my shoulder as he makes his own decision.

"I'm partial to a piece of pie myself," he replies, his grip tightening ever so slightly on my hips. "Should we get a couple of slices and share? I think I have some ice cream back home as well."

"Sounds good," I reply, squirming as my nipples harden when his words tickle my ear. I grit my teeth and hold as still as possible, even though I'd like to sink back into his heat and grind against him. I'm not sure if he's being friendly or flirty, and I can't see his face to read his expression.

The server bags up our order, and we also get a couple of coffees to go. The rain is drizzling again as we make our way back to Nox's cabin in the woods.

"I don't think I'm going to get my surfing lesson," I grumble, staring at the ocean in front of his place when we arrive. The waves are still crashing onto the shore, and even I can tell there's no way you could surf them.

Nox joins me, his hands full of coffee and pie, and he gives me a hip bump. "Be patient. You never know what tomorrow will bring. A shift in the winds and the swell might be perfect. Come on, let's put these in the fridge for later and load the game."

I turn away from the gorgeous view and follow another gorgeous sight into his house. Nox is wearing jeans that hug his ass spectacularly, and I am not sad to see him walk away from me in the least. He walks through the door, and I follow him but squeal in shock when a furry creature leaps at me, hissing and clawing at my legs. Luckily I'm wearing jeans, otherwise Stormheart would have done some damage.

"Stormy, no," Nox scolds, hurrying to put down his bundle as I try to nudge the attacking cat away from me. "I am so sorry. I don't know what has come over him." He hurries back and lifts the cat away from me. He glares at me over Nox's shoulder as he carries him to his cat tree, scolding him for his behavior. I feel such loathing and judgment from the animal. It's weird, I've never had a pet, but this doesn't bode well for me being a queen to the shifters if I can't even get a domestic cat to like me.

"No harm done. I guess I am intruding in his space. He usually gets you all to himself." Nox quickly dumped our pie and coffees on a small table inside the door, so I grab them and carry them over to the kitchen, popping the pie in the fridge for later then grabbing our coffees. I take a sip from mine. It's a caramel latte and just the right amount of sweetness I needed. Nox finishes soothing his cat, and I hand him his own hazelnut latte. He takes it before turning his attention to loading our game.

I toe off my shoes and take a seat on the sofa, bringing my legs up underneath me and just watching him. His body is pure poetry in motion, elegant and graceful as he moves around his home.

"See something you like?" His amused voice jolts me out of my slight trance, and I feel my cheeks heat with embarrassment at being caught.

"You're pretty to watch, what can I say." I shrug, owning my weird ways.

He winks at me. "You aren't so bad yourself." Nox passes me a controller and kicks off his own shoes before joining me on the couch. It's fairly large, but he sits right next to me so our sides are touching. I can feel the heat of his body through my clothes, and I can't help the shudder that rolls through me. He seems to run hot, and I can imagine what his naked skin would feel like against mine—toasty warm.

He must see it and mistake it for being cold. "Are you cold? Do you need me to light the fire? I don't feel the cold very often, so I don't usually bother lighting it."

"No, it's fine. I'm okay," I reply, but he reaches for a folded blanket at the end of the sofa and shakes it out before placing it over my legs.

"Well, I wouldn't want you getting sick or using the excuse of being cold for letting our team down," he teases me.

"You just worry about keeping up with me," I retort, and we turn our attention to the game.

I'm not sure how much time has passed, but eventually, I need to get up and use the bathroom. It's dark outside now, and the only light in the cabin is from the screen. I pause the game in the middle of a fight scene, unable to wait any longer.

He looks at me, his brows wrinkled with confusion. "What's wrong? We almost had them."

"Ugh, I need to pee, I'm sorry." I throw the blanket off, but I get tangled and end up falling into his lap. My breasts press against his chest, and my lips are only inches from his.

We stare at each other for a second. I think we're both shocked into stillness, but then it's like we both come to the same decision and close the gap between us. Our lips clash together as his hands circle my body and tug me into a better position. I groan, partly because my bladder aches, but mostly because he can kiss like the devil. His tongue tangles with mine, slowly and sensually, and he drags his teeth across my bottom lip before nipping. As much as I want to enjoy this kiss, I have to pull away, because I will literally wet my pants.

We're breathing heavily, and his eyes are foggy with lust when I push myself off him. "As much as I want to continue this, I really need to pee." I grimace and try to make my way through the dimly lit cabin.

A light flicks on, and when I turn back to look, he's standing next to a lamp, adjusting himself. I make it to the bedroom quickly now that I can see, and I can't stop the smirk that crosses my lips as I make my way into the bathroom. I'm pretty thrilled to see he was as affected by that kiss as I was.

I quickly do my business then flush and wash my hands. I stare at myself in the mirror, noting my eyes are hooded and my cheeks are flushed. I just hope we can continue what we started. Damn my bladder for interrupting.

When I return to the living area, he is in the kitchen arranging our pie slices on some plates. There's a tub of ice cream next to it, and he points to it with a spoon. "Do you want ice cream with your pie?"

I feel disappointed that he's not still on the

couch. I was hoping we could continue what we started. I bite my lip and remember how his teeth felt on it, and then I decide to be bold.

I stride over to him, take the tub of ice cream, and shove it back in the freezer, then I take the two plates with the pie on them and put them in the fridge before turning my attention back to him. He's leaning against the counter with his arms crossed, watching me with a small smirk on his face.

"I don't know about you, but I suddenly have a craving for something else," I tell him before palming his head and drawing him down to kiss me.

FOURTEEN

Colbie

Nox doesn't even hesitate. He reaches under me and lifts me by my thighs, molding my body to his as I circle my arms around his neck. I wrap my legs around his waist as his mouth plunders mine. His kiss is hot and doesn't let up as his tongue tangles with mine, demanding my submission. He owns me with this kiss, and I am so fucking here for it. I can't stop the low moan that leaves my mouth as my core grinds against the hard ridge of his cock in his jeans.

He pulls away suddenly, and we stare at each other. I'm breathless, and my heart is racing a million miles an hour. I put a finger to my lips. It's swollen, and there's slight chaffing from his facial stubble.

"Tell me if you would prefer pie, because if not,

I'm going to take you back to my bedroom and fuck you like there's no tomorrow," he says, his voice low and gravelly. He's just as effected by this as I am.

"What pie?" I mutter before dragging his mouth back to mine. He nips and licks my mouth like he's making love to me with his tongue. I feel us move, and before long, we're in his bedroom. He lowers me to my feet, and I shudder as I slide down his body before my feet touch the floor.

He grabs the back of his shirt and pulls it over his head, tossing it off to the side before he grabs the hem of mine and does the same. I reach for the button on his jeans and quickly thumb it open before pulling the zipper down and pushing on the waistband. He helps me, pulling them off his feet and tossing them to the side.

I look my fill, my body throbbing with need as I reach out and run both hands down all that glorious expanse of skin. He grabs my hands when I get to his stomach and chuckles, pinning them behind my back.

"Not yet, sweetheart, otherwise this will be over before we even get started. It's been a long time, and I want to make sure I worship your beautiful body first."

He keeps my hands pinned as he backs me toward the bed, his mouth brushing kisses across the tops of my breasts, which are still covered by my bra. He moves both my hands to one of his before skillfully flicking open the catch of my bra.

"Wow, hot and talented," I tease as he releases my arms and drags my bra straps down before that also joins the clothes that have been tossed aside.

"I might not have a lot of experience, but I make up for it in enthusiasm," he says, and I freeze.

"Have you done this before?" I ask hesitantly, and he chuckles.

"A few times. I had a wild phase when I first left my village and spent a few months trying to fuck my problems away with a wide selection of the population." Ah, so I was right about him being a hit it and quit it kind of guy. "But that was years ago. What I meant is I haven't had a lot of experience having sex with someone I actually give a damn about."

He looks me in the eye, and I see vulnerability in his gaze. I reach up and cup his cheek, running my thumb across his lip. "I know how you feel, but you're doing just fine."

His hands slide up my body, caressing my skin, the rough calluses on his thumbs creating a delicious friction. He caresses my breasts, his gaze dropping down to watch what he's doing, and he groans as he leans forward and takes one of my nipples in his mouth. He sucks, and my knees weaken. I stumble, but he holds me up as his tongue flicks across my nipple, circling it before he bites down gently. I hiss at the slight sting of pain, but then he soothes it with his tongue, and I'm putty in his hands.

He moves his mouth to my other breast, placing

kisses along the way as he lifts me and drops me back onto his bed. I bounce, but he reaches for the button of my jeans, and before I even get my bearings, he strips them off, and I'm lying naked apart from the cuffs on my wrists.

"Stunning," he murmurs as he strips off his briefs, and it's my turn to stare. Oh my fucking god.

"Nope, no way. That thing isn't going to fit," I stammer, waving at the cock that slapped against his stomach when he removed his pants. I thought he felt big when I was grinding against his jeans, but this is extreme. It has to be nine or ten inches and thick.

He chuckles and palms it, giving it a squeeze, and I watch as a bead of precum appears on the tip. My mouth waters, and I get the urge to lean forward and lick it up. "Don't worry, princess, I'll make sure you're ready for it before I fill your sweet pussy."

Oh my god, the man is a dirty talker. He climbs onto the bed and crawls toward me like a large cat stalking its prey. He pushes my knees apart and trails a smattering of kisses up the inside of one thigh before diving right in and sweeping his tongue through my folds, causing me to shudder in pleasure.

I groan and flop back on the bed, giving over to the overwhelming need to let him have his way. I might die—death by cock—but what a way to go.

Licking me with long, sure strokes, he alternates

between fucking my needy hole and circling my throbbing bud. I thrash my head back and forth, gripping the sheets as extreme pleasure rockets through my body, driving me closer and closer to the edge. My brain short-circuits as he shoves my thighs wide and sinks two fingers into my throbbing cunt, curling them against the spongy inner wall and caressing my G-spot. I hurtle over the edge into the most mind-blowing orgasm I have ever had.

I'm vaguely aware that I'm screaming and say a little prayer of thanks that Nox doesn't have any close neighbors.

I'm boneless and panting when he finally lifts his head. His mouth glimmers in the low light as he prowls up my body, cupping my breasts as he slowly tongues one swollen nipple before doing the same to the other. I thread my hands through his hair and tug him up, dying to feel his monster cock between my legs, even if I am nervous.

He drops a kiss between my breasts before turning his attention to my mouth. I can taste myself on him as he licks and nips, giving my mouth the same kind of attention he gave my pussy.

Reaching between us, I slide my hand up and down his thick, long length, and he moans, his head dropping as I thumb the dribble of precum leaking from his tip and spread it around the head of his cock. I notch him at my entrance, wrap my legs around him, and dig my heels into his taut ass, encouraging him. He thrusts slowly, sinking in slightly, and I moan as my pussy stretches wide, wrapping around him. I breathe heavily as he retreats and pushes again, sinking a little deeper with each thrust as he works himself into my tight channel until he's finally seated. He pauses as my heart pounds and my cunt aches as she acclimates to his size. There is a small bite of pain, but that eventually fades, leaving me full and empty all at the same time.

"More," I rasp out as I dig my heels into his ass. His breath is coming quickly too, but he listens and slowly drags his cock out before thrusting hard. My back arches off the bed, and I clutch his shoulders as he slides in, every inch of his cock dragging against my sensitive walls. He presses kisses against my shoulder, and I feel the scrape of his teeth, and all I can do is hold on as he impales me with rapid strokes. My body winds tighter and tighter with every plunge of his dick, his hands braced on the bed as he owns my body. I dig my nails into his back as he grabs one of my knees and hitches it higher, getting a better angle, and all it takes is two more strokes before my body explodes into ecstasy. My cunt grips him hard as he continues to thrust through my orgasm before he throws his head back and shouts, pumping me full of his cum.

He collapses onto me, his weight comforting as we let the sensations of our orgasms ride through our shaking, spent limbs. My legs ache, but I don't push him off. Instead, I run gentle hands up and down his sweaty back as he nuzzles into my neck, placing tiny kisses all over it while muttering words of praise. My soul aches at his words and the thought that this may be my only chance at real happiness. He rolls off me before gathering me in his arms and pulling me against him, running his fingers through my hair as I place my hand over his chest and snuggle in.

My breathing finally eases, and I lift my head from his chest and run my finger over the tattoo inked above his heart. It kind of looks like a tree with a heart on the trunk, and then there are six branches with symbols at the end of each branch. I try to get a closer look, but we never turned the light on, and the only thing illuminating the room is the light from the living area, so it isn't a lot.

Nox flinches at my touch before sliding his hand between mine and his skin, covering the tattoo.

"Sorry, it tickles," he mumbles, and I rest my head against his chest again.

"What does it mean?" I ask, and he's quiet for a moment.

"It's a symbol of a previous life best forgotten," he says flatly, and I decide to let it go. It's obviously a topic he doesn't want to talk about.

I'm so tired that I feel my eyes flutter closed, and he pulls me closer and presses a kiss to my forehead. As I fall into a deep sleep, I hear him murmur, "Unlike this, which I will never forget."

There's a warm, heavy body wrapped around mine when I wake the following morning. My body aches deliciously, and a smile creeps across my lips when I think about exactly why it does. Holy hell, Nox is talented in bed, and the stamina! I've never had sex with another man who could keep going like he could. I'm going to feel him for days.

I open my eyes and find him wrapped around me, his face slack with sleep. There's a small frown between his eyebrows, and I reach out to smooth it with my finger. He grumbles and swats my hand away before huffing and rolling over. I giggle quietly before sitting up and finding a shirt to throw on over my naked body. I grimace at the thought of putting on yesterday's panties, so instead, I grab a pair of Nox's shorts that are on a chair in the corner of the room. I pull them up and head out into the living area to make some coffee.

The bedroom was dark, the blackout blinds pulled across the windows, but the sun is shining through the windows at the front of the house. The bad weather has passed us by, and the ocean is glassy and calm. The waves rolling in form beautiful sets that look like they may be perfect for surfing.

Smiling, I stretch, but a sharp pain in my finger and a hiss has me yelping.

I stick my bleeding finger in my mouth and glare at the fucking cat. He's sitting on the top of his cat tree, his tail flicking back and forth aggressively, and there's a rumbling sound of hostility coming from him. I must have stretched too close to his perch, and he got me when he swiped at me.

"Asshole." I glare at him. "See if I feed you now." I stick my tongue out at him and head for the kitchen. The coffee machine is one of those pod ones, and I fill it with water before searching the cupboards for the pods. I get it running, and my finger is still bleeding, so I go in search of a bandage to wrap around it. I can't find any. He must keep them in his bathroom, and I don't want to go into his room and wake him up, so I wrap a tissue around it for now.

When my mug fills, I add creamer and sugar and wander out to the patio. I lean against the railing, one of my cuffs banging against it loudly. I was able to distract Nox last night, and I never ended up removing them. I'm not sure how I'm going to continue to hide the marks if we go surfing though. Maybe he will think they are tattoos. Heck, he has one on his chest, so he's no stranger to them, but he is somewhat of an expert on supernatural races. Maybe he has a long-sleeved rash guard I can wear that will hide them.

Before I can worry any more, a warm hand

slides under my shirt, and I'm tugged back against a hard body as kisses are placed on my neck. I tip my head to the side and sink back against him as he murmurs in my ear.

"Good morning, did you sleep well?" he asks, and I moan as his hand slips up and cups my breast.

"So well," I reply, turning my head so he can kiss me. It's lazy and slow, and just when I'm thinking fuck the coffee and the waves, he pulls away.

"Now that is a good morning greeting." He grins at me before reaching for my coffee and raising an eyebrow. "May I?"

I nod and pass him the cup. He takes a sip, groaning as he swallows, and my core clenches, but before I can tug him back inside, he notices the tissue wrapped around my finger, and his lips purse in concern.

"What happened?" he asks, passing me my coffee and picking up my injured hand.

"Stormy obviously isn't a morning cat, or maybe it's just me," I reply ruefully.

"Stormy did this?" He sounds surprised, and I nod. He unwraps the tissue, and thankfully, it's finally stopped bleeding. There's a long, deep scratch that caught the cuticle of my nail before digging into the back of my middle finger. It's actually quite an impressive scratch. He was really out for blood.

"I am so sorry. I don't know what has gotten into him," he apologizes, scrunching up the tissue.

"Maybe he's hungry. We did get distracted last night," I say, kindly making an excuse for the horrible creature.

"He has an automatic feeder, and have you seen him? It's not like he's starving." He moves back inside, and I follow him.

He heads toward the cat tree where Stormy is still standing guard, watching over his domain. He picks up the giant animal, and I watch as he snuggles his face into him while scolding him like he's reprimanding a toddler.

I'm not sure what breed of cat he is, but he's bigger than any I've seen before. He bats at Nox's face playfully, not a claw in sight, before Nox carries him under his arm into the kitchen and prepares him a can of wet food. He places it in a little ceramic bowl with the word "Stormy" on it before setting it on the ground. Stormy ignores me as I approach and tucks into his food. I take a seat at the breakfast bar as Nox grabs a mug and fills it with coffee before offering to refill mine. I nod, and then we both add cream and sugar before he joins me.

"You up for surfing today?" Nox asks, and I groan and stretch, the aches in my body not easing in the least.

"I don't know, my body is pretty achy," I tell him, and his smile turns into a wide, smug grin that tells me he knows exactly what I'm talking about.

"Maybe I'll just sit on the beach and watch. I don't even have a swimsuit here," I remind him, and he shrugs.

"I'm pretty sure I have a spare rash guard somewhere that my sister left behind when she and her mat—family visited."

He jumps up and hurries into the spare room as I think about what he just said. That's the first time he's mentioned his family. I look around the room, searching for evidence of a family, but there aren't any photos except for the one above the fireplace. I guess he must not be as close to them as I am to Mom, Granny, and Grampy, but then again, I don't have any pictures of them in my apartment either, so maybe I'm overthinking things.

"She didn't bother taking them home because there's no ocean near our village." I frown again as he mentions his village. I didn't actually know there were any villages in the human zone. I mean, it makes sense, but I thought all the humans lived in the city. I guess that was kind of silly of me to assume. "Ah, here it is, and a pair of shorts for you too."

He returns with a big smile, holding out a red, long-sleeved rash guard and a pair of black board-shorts. "These should fit you. She's a little taller than you, but that shouldn't matter. I have her wet suit outside in the rack with mine, and you can use that as well."

I take the offered clothes and look down at

them, unable to come up with any other excuse now. I need to put my money where my mouth is.

"Well, come on then, let's get moving. We need to take advantage of the waves while they are good. Luckily for us, this is a private beach, so no one else can use it, but it doesn't stop anyone from paddling around the point to tackle the waves. I'm actually surprised there's no one out there yet. Usually on a day like today, a lot of locals join me."

He doesn't wait for a response, just gives me a quick kiss on the lips and hurries outside, calling, "Get changed, and I'll make sure the boards are waxed."

The door closes behind him, and I finish the rest of my coffee, eyeing his half full cup. I guess surfing superseded coffee for him. Hopping off the stool, I head to the bedroom to get changed. I feel something before I see it, and I quickly jump to the side just as Stormy leaps from behind the counter, his claws extended, and tries to go for my leg. He misses, and I'm tempted to kick him because seriously, what is his problem, but instead, I pick up the pace and close the door in his face when he tries to follow me.

"Ha, suck on that, you evil Satan spawn," I grumble as I strip off my borrowed clothes to put on the other borrowed ones. They smell like fresh laundry as I pull the rash guard over my neck. The arms get stuck on my cuffs, and I have to ease them over. Grimacing, I remove the cuffs and place them on the end of the bed before tugging the sleeves over my marks. I can't surf in them, and I don't want the saltwater to ruin or damage them. Luckily the sleeves cover the marks, so I don't have to worry about Nox seeing them and asking about them.

I tug on the shorts, which are very tight, but thankfully they have an elastic waist which stretches over my butt and thighs. I'm a little worried I'm going to split them, but hopefully if I can get the wet suit on, it shouldn't matter if I do. Obviously his sister is taller and skinnier and he was just too polite to say anything.

I crack the door open and peer out. The little furry fucker is nowhere to be seen, so I make a mad dash across the room to the door and let myself out. I slam it behind me, and Nox looks up from where he's rubbing wax onto a board and raises an eyebrow.

"You okay?" he asks, and I lean on the door and blow out a sigh of relief.

"Yeah, to be honest, your cat hates me, and he's an asshole, so I thought it might be prudent not to get in his way."

His eyes widen in surprise as I step away from the door. He looks between me and it and goes to take a step, but then he shakes his head like he's thinking better of it. "Stormy hasn't really had a lot of socialization apart from me. He's probably jeal-ous. I'm sorry," he says sweetly as he wraps his arms around me and gives me a kiss, resting his forehead on mine. I lean into the hug as I stare into his gorgeous eyes. I can see the sincerity in his gaze, and I'm not going to hold his cat's behavior against him.

I sigh dramatically. "Fine, but I expect to be a surfing expert by the time we're finished. You better be one hell of a teacher." I lean in and press my lips to his, but he pulls away and puts a finger against them.

"None of that, or we are never going to get into the water. Stop distracting me, woman." He returns to waxing the surfboard, and I take a seat and enjoy the view.

He tosses the block of wax back onto the shelf once he's satisfied with the job he's done. Nox turns to meet my eyes and smirks before stripping off his shirt and shorts, leaving him only in briefs. He waggles his eyebrows suggestively, and I giggle as he grabs his wet suit and pulls it up over his body, grabbing the zipper and dragging it up. The gold flecks in his eyes seem to glisten slightly.

"Come on, let's get you suited up." He holds out a hand, and I jump up and let him help me into the spare wet suit before he grabs both boards, and then we head down the stairs and to the beach.

FIFTEEN

Gryffin

"It's been three days. Why hasn't anyone come forward already?" I watch as my father paces back and forth across the throne room, wringing his hands in agitation. My three mothers watch in concern from their thrones, and I see apprehension on all their faces.

"Did something go wrong with the spell?" I ask my frazzled father. I've never seen him this agitated before unless we're dealing with feral wolves, which is a heartbreaking process for him.

When I arrived at work this morning, Bryson informed me that we both received a summons from my parents and had to go to the palace immediately. I left the rest of my team behind. We were all on standby, waiting for the new ruler to emerge so they could be escorted to the palace under guard for their security.

"Has anyone called any tips into the tip line?" Layla, my biological mother, asks, looking at both Bryson and me.

Bryson frowns. "There have been a lot of calls, but when teams were sent out, they all turned out to be fake. We have been run off our feet dealing with wannabe royals, and I'm beginning to get annoyed," he grumbles, running a hand through his hair, smoke drifting out of his nostrils. His dragon is close to the surface with his fragile hold on his temper.

My father throws his arms up in the air and sinks down onto the steps leading up to the thrones. He stares at the glass encasing the new crown and the six matching crowns, and he shakes his head. "I don't know what to do. The people are starting to whisper."

Mia gets up and moves over to sit beside him, sweeping her dress to the side. All four of them are dressed to impress in case the new royal appears at any moment. She puts her arm around my dad and presses a kiss to his cheek. He grabs her hand and gives it a squeeze. "Darling, don't you remember how you felt when you were selected? I bet they are completely overwhelmed. Let's give them the benefit of the doubt. They are probably organizing their affairs before they present themselves to the palace."

My dad slumps. It's very unkinglike, and I feel a pang of sympathy for him. He's probably worried they are not going to appear, and he will have to spend another forty years ruling the shifters. It's not a particularly hard job, but they can be petty and exhausting at times.

"Cheer up, Dad. It will all be over before you know it, and you'll be wishing you were back in the thick of the action when the moms are nagging you to do something," I joke, and all three of my moms glare at me, but it does get my dad to smile.

"I wouldn't joke if I were you, Gryffin." Evie stands up and marches down the stairs, and I wince, knowing I'm in trouble. She approaches me, and I look down at her. She is the shortest of my mothers, not quite reaching the top of my shoulders, but she is no less fierce than the others. "There is a long forgotten law that if, for some reason, the chosen is injured or dies without any heirs, the crown switches to the oldest heir of the previous ruler to rule out the remainder of the forty years."

My mouth drops open in shock at this bombshell. "No fucking way." I look around the room, hoping someone will tell me this is her idea of a joke, but I can tell by their faces that it isn't.

Mom sighs, also standing up and smoothing out her dress. "It's never happened before, but it is a backup plan. Let's not get ahead of ourselves though. I say we're getting worked up over nothing.

Let's give it a few more days before we start getting into crisis mode."

"We need to go about our days like nothing has changed and show our people we aren't worried," Mia agrees. "Our new royal will appear when the time is right for them."

"That's right. We are in the middle of moving all our things to our new house and having the master palace suite renovated for the new incoming royal. Since they will have six mates, some major changes needed to happen." Mom gestures to the other six crowns, and Evie grimaces.

"Ugh, six mates. That poor person. Seriously, it was bad enough when there were three of us. All the bitching and infighting was awful." My little blonde mother wraps her arms around my waist and leans in to me. I pat her back soothingly.

"I'm just glad none of us will be marked. I can't imagine competing with a group of others to catch the eye of a potential mate," I tell them as she pulls away.

My dad snorts derisively. "You have no idea. Be very glad that you are in a bond group and your perfect mate will appear one day." He looks at his wives. "You three might have thought you had it bad, but try being the person who has to pick on top of learning that you are now ruling over a new group of people you know very little about, and add the new magic and shifting into that. It's a complete mindfuck." He stands up and stretches, pulling Mia up with him. "We need to make sure the bar is stocked. I'm almost positive I drank it dry during my first couple of weeks."

"Well, at least the new royal has the four of you to advise them," Bryson points out. "They couldn't be in better hands."

"Unlike me who had no one. That awful bitch refused to mentor me and instead disappeared to sulk in her new home. I refuse to do that to whoever is going to take my place." I watch my father visibly get his shit together after his small, private break down. "Gryffin, I'd like your team to be stationed here for the first couple of weeks. The new royal will need bodyguards until they can get a handle on their shift and how to protect themselves. Hopefully once their mates are chosen, there won't be any need for protection detail, because they will fight for their mate just like your mothers do for me." His three wives gather around him, and I smile as my mothers fuss over him. They have always been like this in private. In public, they show the shifter people a strong, confident team, but they save their affection for family only.

My father's words send a pang of dread through me. If I'm trapped in the castle doing royal duties for the next few weeks, I won't be able to continue the search for our sixth bond mate, which means I need to excuse myself now. I have been told of a small village at the very end of the shifter kingdom that I never knew about. I'm starting to lose hope. Maybe my bond mates are right, and I am on a wild goose chase. They insist the witch's reading was wrong. Why else wouldn't our bond mate present themselves to the matching office?

When shifters receive a bond mark, they are required to present themselves to the bond office in the city so their mark can be noted down and they can be matched with others who share that mark. Not all shifters get them though, but the ones who do are usually thrilled and excited to be in a bond, because it makes them a mini pack that is no longer beholden to the alpha of their village.

Shifters don't live in species packs. Each town, city, or village has a head alpha all of the residents are beholden to no matter what kind of animal you present as. It is an elected position, and usually the strongest shifter in the village is chosen, but that is not always the case. Sometimes popularity or fear can play a big part in who gets elected.

I hide my annoyance. "As long as that is okay with General Bryson." I look at my boss, praying he will not agree with my father and appoint another team, but I know that's pretty futile. They are best friends, and if the king wants his son, then the king will get his son—both their sons actually, not that Hunter will care.

Bryson gives a quick nod.

"Alright, you're both dismissed. Keep us updated, and as soon as the royal appears, you are all to present yourselves to the palace," my father orders.

I give my mothers a kiss on the cheek, and we take our leave. Bryson shifts, and I ride his dragon back to night watch headquarters.

When we arrive and he shifts back, we part. "Stay close. I'm sure I'll have another false lead for you to follow soon," he grumbles and stomps off to the communications room to monitor the tip line. I head back to our apartment, trying to figure out how I can make the trip to the village of Zalfari.

I use my palm print to open the door and hurry toward my bedroom. If I can get out quickly before anyone notices, I might have time to make it to the village and back before the new royal even appears. They are taking their sweet time, so hopefully they hold out a little longer. I don't want to even acknowledge the fact that I might end up as king if no human comes forward. It isn't something I want in the least, and I don't know what would happen to my bond mates if that occurred. Would they be default kings too? Would we be forced to pick a mate? No, I don't even want to think about it.

I hurry into my room to pack. It should only take me a day, two tops, to get to Zalfari, poke around, and then run back. If I told Hunter where I was going, he would probably offer to fly me, but I don't want to see the disappointment on his face, and I most certainly won't ask Gem. He thinks I'm insane, and I know he's angry with me.

"You're back?" the phoenix I'm thinking about says flatly as he leans against the doorframe of my room. His burgundy curls are all awry, and he's only wearing a pair of low-slung sweatpants. I feel a shot of lust go straight to my groin at the sight of his delicious flesh, but I lock that shit down tight. My desire for my bond mate makes me feel guilty, like I'm cheating on our future mate by wanting to know what his mouth tastes like and how it would feel to slide my cock into his tight heat.

Instead, I ignore him as I throw a couple of things into a bag I can easily carry in my tiger's mouth. "What did Papa Lucas want?" he asks, unable to tamp down his curiosity. Gem is so fucking nosy.

"He's worried that the new royal hasn't presented themselves yet, and he put us on alert. He assigned our team to be their security until they can get up to speed," I murmur, looking around to see if I forgot anything.

"That makes sense," Gem says, pushing off the frame and entering my room. I become very aware of him in my space. He smells like a campfire, all smoke and ash and whiskey, just like his creature, and my cock throbs against my uniform pants, but I resist the urge to adjust it.

He approaches me from behind and peers over my shoulder, his body hot against my back. His phoenix radiates heat, even in his human form. "What are you packing for? Don't you have a whole heap of things at the palace, or have your parents cleaned out our rooms already? I guess they probably have and moved them over to the new estate."

The five of us lived at the palace with my parents when we first formed our bond many years ago. We had our own suite, but we moved into the apartment here at the night watch headquarters once we graduated from college and decided we wanted to do this with our lives. I'm sure my parents are packing up our suite to make way for the new royal, but I know they have a suite for us in their new residence too, so it will probably all just go there.

I sigh and don't answer him, and I feel him stiffen behind me. "No! Don't tell me you're heading out on another wild goose chase again!" he growls, and I hear the anger in his tone.

I turn around to face him, and his eyes flame with anger. They always have a flame in them, but when his emotions are extreme, it's like the flames take over his eyes. His hair floats with his magic as well. Fuck, he is one of the most stunning creatures I've ever seen, and it's taking all my willpower not to pounce on him.

"I won't lie to you, Gem," I say quietly, and he shakes his head and throws up his hands as he paces back and forth across my room.

"Fuck, Gryff. You have to let this go. Can't you see what this is doing to us? Are you so selfish and single-minded in your pursuit of some charlatan's prediction that you can't see what it's doing to us?" he rants. "You are so blind, you can't see that Liam is turning into a man whore of epic proportions and attracting the wrong kind of female. He'll mate one by accident, and we'll be stuck with her. Hunter and Brodie are so focused on work as a distraction that they take every one of the feral calls and put themselves at risk. You don't see any of it! You don't see that this is destroying our bond!" He stops in front of me and grabs my top. "And me, fucking see me," he declares before slamming his mouth to mine.

I freeze in place as he swipes his tongue across my lips, asking for entrance, and when I open my mouth to say something, he slips his tongue inside, and I am lost to the taste of him. I groan as he plunders my mouth. He tastes like fire and whiskey and sin. My hands drift around him, and I haul his body against mine. He's almost as tall as I am, but his body is not as bulky as mine. He rolls his hips, grinding his hard cock against my own rapidly hardening length. My heart beats like it wants to pound out of my chest. I've dreamed of this for years, but I have resisted out of respect for our future mate. Instead, I've tried to fight and hide my attraction. I could see he felt the same way, but as long as I held him at arm's length, I didn't know what I was missing out on. Now I'm afraid I'm going to crave him like a drug.

He pulls away, leaving me breathless and dizzy.

"See me," he begs, and I shake my head, clearing the lust from my mind and catching my breath.

"The problem is that I do see you, and if I let myself, I'll lose myself in you. Is that fair for our mate when she comes along? As much as I want this, I also want our future mate's approval before we go any further, because if I let myself have you, I'll become addicted, and if she doesn't want that and I have to let you go, then I don't know if I will recover," I tell him, my words spewing out of me in a rush of emotions. I lean my forehead against his, looking into his eyes so he can see the truth in mine.

The fire in his eyes dies, and I see the moment he understands, because he sighs heavily, presses another gentle kiss to my lips, and walks away.

I don't watch him go, because I might cave and chase after him, but I do think about what he said. I make a silent promise to him that if I don't find anything at this next village, I will give up my search for good.

SIXTEEN

Gem

I'm so fucking angry and sad as I walk away from Gryffin, fire keeps erupting all over my skin as my phoenix tries to soothe me. I'm so pissed at Gryffin and his obsession with this fictional sixth member, I'm tempted to find the witch who suggested it to him and kill her, but I'm also so fucking sad that he doesn't want to give the two of us a chance. I've wanted him for as long as I've known him.

Unlike Brodie, Liam, and Gryff, Hunter and I have only had our animals since we were seventeen. Mythicals don't shift until their seventeenth birthday. I always knew I would be a phoenix. My father is one as well, but my mother is a wolf, so when I didn't shift as a baby, they knew what I was. Dragons like Hunter are born from eggs, and both of his parent are dragons, so they knew what he would be too. I grew up in a large mythical village in the central shifter zone. Hunter is from the same village, but because his father is a general in the army, he grew up in the palace. I knew of him but had never met him until his parents brought him to our village so he could have his first shift. There are a lot of dragons in our village, and all of the buildings are fireproof. Both of us had our first shifts within weeks of each other and practiced control of our fire together.

It took a couple of months, but we both gained excellent control of our fire, so my father was working on my other magical gifts when Hunter and I both received bond marks. We were thrilled to discover our marks matched. Together, we made our way to the city to register our marks, only to discover that both his childhood friends, Brodie and Gryffin, were a bond match as well as another, Liam.

I just about swallowed my tongue when he introduced me to his best friend, Prince Gryffin. He was gorgeous, but also nice, nothing like I imagined a royal to be. We all moved into a suite in the palace to develop our bond relationship, and I quickly fell in love with the prince. I would see him watching me out of the corner of my eye, and I knew my attraction wasn't one-sided, but he never made a move, and our bond group was pursued by female shifters hoping to be our mate. I watched as he had flings with both males and females alike, nothing more than a one-night stand. In fact, we were all rather promiscuous for a while before Gryffin's moms sat us down and lectured us about how our mate would feel to be with a bunch of playboys when she was finally marked. We straightened up after that, but I always hoped something more would happen between us. Hell, we were already bonded, so neither of us was going anywhere.

Somewhere deep down, I knew his mothers' talk had struck a nerve with him, and I was going to be sidelined forever, wanting what I couldn't have, and he just confirmed it in a heartbreaking way. I don't think the goddess would gift us a mate who wouldn't accept us in a relationship, but I do also understand on some level—the reasonable, clear-headed Gem level, not the horny, pining for Gryff Gem level. No, that Gem wants to burn the world.

Instead of doing considerable damage to our home, I head downstairs to the night watch head-quarters and decide to take my frustration out in our training room. Maybe there will be someone there I can spar with.

The hallways are clear as I make my way to the elevator, smashing the button to call it to our floor. When it opens, a rush of scents, both familiar and stomach turning, whooshes out, and a growl rumbles from my chest, sounding more like Hunter's dragon than my phoenix. My bond mate, Liam, is in there, but he has company. Gianna is wrapped around him like a sloth, her legs gripping his waist while her arms circle his neck as she grinds on him, their mouths kissing with desperate need. I want to burn all the hair off this bitch's head. She knows exactly which buttons to push when it comes to Liam. I've been watching his bear become more and more unruly as it pines for a mate, which means Liam is susceptible to the pretty words of a conniving manipulative fox.

Neither of them notice me, and I clear my throat as I step into the elevator. Liam looks up as he pulls his mouth away from the dark-haired cunt. His eyes are glazed, and her lipstick is spread across his mouth.

She smirks at me as she drops to her feet, smoothing her skirt down and straightening her top. "Hi, Gem," she flutters her eyelashes at me and steps closer to run a finger down my chest in what I think is meant to be a flirty gesture, but it just seems contrived. That, combined with her scent which smells like wet newspaper to me, makes me step back, and I almost miss her eyes flash with frustration.

"Liam, what are you doing?" I ask him, ignoring the fox and narrowing my eyes on my bond mate. His eyes clear as he takes in my pissed off scent, and he adjusts the front of his pants as I huff in annoyance. Before he can answer, I turn my attention back to the wily female.

"You've been banned from the building and the

neutral zone. If you are caught in here, Liam will be in trouble," I warn both of them, and she shrugs, not giving one fucking damn.

"Nobody will know if you don't say anything. We're going straight to your apartment," she snarls, and I chuckle darkly.

"I'm pretty sure Prince Gryffin will have something to say. His dad was the one who fired you and had you blacklisted after all." She pales slightly, but my words finally get Liam's attention.

"Gryff's in there?" he asks, looking down the hallway in the direction of our apartment.

"For now," I mutter, and he tugs Gianna back into the elevator. The doors close, and it starts to move downward. She screeches and crosses her arms, glaring at him.

"What the fuck are you doing, Liam?"

"You can't be here, Gianna," he tells her. Her lip sticks out, and she begins to pout, but I can still see the anger in her eyes. I'm certain she's trying to get him to bite her in the hope that once one of us is mated to her, the rest of us will give her mate bites too. I'd rather cut off my dick than stick it in that piranha.

The doors open on the bottom floor, and he takes her by the arm and walks her to the building entrance, practically shoving her out the door. The glass doors close behind her, and as he returns to my side, I watch with amusement as she loses her shit. She screeches again and stomps her foot in anger before screaming something and flipping him off then storming away.

I whistle as he gets to me, and I shake my head. "Dude, what the fuck?"

He shakes his head, not looking at me as we start walking toward the mission rooms. "Fuck, I don't know what happened. She approached me in the locker room, and I was telling her I didn't want to see her again, and then the next minute, we're dry humping in the elevator and my teeth were aching to bite her. Thank fuck you came along when you did, because your scent was what brought me back to reality."

I frown. "That sounds like magic at work. Do you think she's wearing a spelled charm or something?"

He runs a hand through his white hair before rubbing his jaw, looking lost. "Fucking sure felt like it."

"You need to avoid her. If you see her, go in the opposite direction," I suggest, and he nods, quickly agreeing, but grabs my arm.

"Don't leave me alone. I'm worried if she corners me again, I won't have the strength to fight her off."

"Sneaky fox bitch," I mutter. "Don't worry, we're going to be assigned to the palace for the next few weeks once the new royal presents themselves, and she definitely won't be getting in there."

His sigh of relief is heavy, and I almost turn

around and chase after her to make good on my burning her hair off her head idea. Instead, I slap my bond mate on the shoulder. "Come on, I was just heading to the gym to work off some aggression. Why don't you join me?"

He falls into step with me. "What has your panties in a twist?" he asks. I can feel his gaze on the side of my face, but I don't look at him.

"I just came from the apartment where Gryffin is preparing to leave again," I mutter, my annoyance leaking into my tone.

"Ah, Gem, I'm sorry." He claps a hand on my shoulder and gives it a squeeze. My other bond mates aren't stupid, they know how I feel about the tiger. I try my best not to let it affect how we work, and I've been mostly successful until now, but Gryffin's obsession is affecting us. I'm certain it's part of the reason we haven't been gifted a mate yet. We've been a group for ten years now, which is the longest a bond group has gone without finding their mate. I feel like we are being punished, but for the life of me, I can't figure out why. Something has to give, or the five of us are going to splinter irrevocably.

The two of us are silent as we walk toward the incident room, but a sudden shout has us exchanging a glance and picking up the pace.

The incident room is wide open, and I find Hunter and Brodie with General Bryson. Hunter is arguing with his father.

"We don't have time to chase around after some

human. We are still trying to locate the other missing children and deal with the uptick in feral occurrences. Assign a different team the task of babysitting." Hunter's nostrils smoke, and his eyes shimmer with his dragon's annoyance.

Brodie is leaning against a wall with his arms crossed, watching the two with amusement. Liam and I join him.

"Hunter didn't take the news well, I see," I comment quietly.

Brodie scoffs. "What makes you think that?"

"Hunter, enough. It's a direct order from your king, and you will obey it. I have three other teams working on the missing shifter children."

"What about the missing humans?" Brodie asks, and I turn my attention to the wolf.

"What humans?" I inquire. This is new information for me, and from the look on Liam's face, him too.

Bryson leans against the table and hangs his head, and I can see the weight he carries from being in charge. I'm glad that's not me. He sighs heavily then visibly gets his shit together, throwing his shoulders back and straightening.

"In the last two months, humans have been going missing on a semi regular basis after visiting the neutral zone. We were originally unaware because the missing people were being reported to the human authorities. They have recently read us in on the reports."

"Why did it take them so long to let us know if they went missing after visiting this zone?"

Hunter scoffs. "Petty jurisdiction crap."

My mind processes the information swiftly, and my shoulders slump as I put two and two together. "Fuck! Are we assuming the missing humans are the ferals?"

Brodie hip bumps me before pushing off the wall and taking a seat at the table Hunter and Bryson have between them.

"Yup," he says dejectedly.

"But how? And why so many? Most shifters know it's their life and the human's if they get caught changing humans without permission. Who would damn someone to that existence?"

Bryson's jaw clenches, and I brace myself for what is about to come out of his mouth. "We think that maybe whoever took the missing kids is using them to bite the humans."

Shock hits me like a two by four to the face, and I see Liam flinch. Brodie's and Hunter's shoulders sag, so I know this is not the first time they are hearing this, but as the information computes in my mind, it all makes sense.

"Of course. Scared children would lash out and bite if cornered, even though they are taught not to, and without an alpha command, they are stuck in animal form, unable to change back. But why?"

"Are they creating an army? That seems a little shortsighted when ferals are notoriously hard to contain. What could the benefit be? And who?" Liam asks Bryson who looks dejected.

"We don't know, and we have no leads. This couldn't come at a more inopportune time. The royals are distracted by the change of leadership. Hell, the new royal hasn't even been found yet, so I haven't wanted to add to their worries," Bryson admits, pulling out a chair and sitting down as well. He picks up a remote and turns on the screen on the wall. It's a map of Aramis showing all three zones. There are red dots all through the shifter zone, and I know they are the locations of the ferals we put down. There are also green and blue dots all over the map as well.

Hunter steps up and points to the green dots. "This shows the three children who are still missing and where they were taken from as well as Archie." He points to the green dot over the palace. "As you can see, they are all from a densely populated area, which makes it harder to figure out how they were snatched up."

"You would think there would be more witnesses," Liam comments, and Brodie shakes his head.

"They were all taken from a busy mall or just when school was let out. There were a lot of people around to add to the confusion."

"What are the blue dots?" I scan the map. There are a lot more blue dots than green.

"Those are all the missing humans," Bryson says, and I purse my lips.

"Holy crap, that's a lot of missing humans. Way more than the amount of ferals we have put down," I point out, feeling sick to my stomach.

"Yes, it is," Hunter rumbles his agreement, his dragon close to the surface.

"To answer your question, son, yes, I have teams tracking all the humans as well. They were all visiting the neutral zone when they disappeared." He presses a button, and more dots appear on the screen in clusters around the neutral zone. I lean forward to get a better look at what they are clustered around.

"These are all hotels or entertainment venues," Liam says, coming to the same conclusion I do.

"Yes, we think that someone is deliberately targeting them. I've scheduled extra round-the-clock patrols in these areas, pulling shifter only teams from the shifter forces. I'm hoping the extra presence will make it harder for anyone else to be snatched."

"What about restricting human visitors in the neutral zone until we can get to the bottom of this?" Brodie suggests, and Bryson rubs a hand across his forehead like he's trying to ease a headache before he nods.

"Yes, that is a last resort. The businesses would suffer, so we would like to avoid that if possible, but it may come down to that."

"That's not going to protect the humans who live in the neutral zone though," Hunter points out.

"No, but it would limit the casualty count." Bryson sighs and stands up. "But none of you need to worry about that. Keep fielding the royal tip line, and the minute the new royal appears, you stick to their ass like glue. Until they gain their magic, they are at risk. The last thing we need is for whoever is responsible for the ferals to get their hands on the new royal. It would be a disaster if they turned feral before they could gain their crown. It would throw the shifter kingdom into chaos."

Holy fuck. Bryson's words bring a rush of dread to my body. I had never even considered that may be the game plan. I can tell by the look on my bond mates' faces that they are thinking the same thing.

He doesn't wait for a response, leaving the silent room that's heavy with the new knowledge.

"Fuck, I don't know about you guys, but I need to eat." Brodie pushes his chair back and stands up, stretching.

"How can your stomach be hungry in light of all that?" Liam asks incredulously.

Brodie shrugs. "It isn't really, but seeing that pretty little human baker is just the thing I need to brighten this miserable day."

"Brodie," Hunter growls, and our wolf glares at him.

"Hey, don't even pretend you didn't go there yesterday to grab lunch."

Hunter grimaces, looking slightly chagrined. "The food is good, okay? And my dragon is a pushy fucker and insisted we eat there for some reason. Anyway, she isn't there. They said she was out on holiday for a couple of days."

A burst of laughter escapes my mouth before I can help it. He sounds so disappointed, it's comical. "And you happen to know that how?"

"The shifter girl who works there, Violet, goes to school with my brother and sister. I just happened to strike up a conversation with her, and she's a chatty little thing," he admits sheepishly, and I can't help laughing at his audacity. I never would have thought either of them would be interested in a human, but Brodie is right, she is a pretty little thing. She smelled good too, like cupcakes and frosting. My phoenix most definitely has a sweet tooth and would have happily rolled around in her scent.

"And you guys think I'm bad messing around with Gianna. Being interested in a human is ten times worse," Liam scolds them. Brodie just grins, but Hunter looks ashamed.

"Well, there's nothing that says I can't enjoy a view with my lunch. Come on, I'll buy you a hot chocolate. Yesterday, they had polar bear marshmallows," he cajoles Liam, whose eyes brighten at the idea of marshmallows in the form of his animal.

"Fine, but you're paying," he replies as the four of us leave the conference room and head for the doors.

"Hopefully we can finish our meal without

another ridiculous false lead on the new royal," Hunter grumbles. "We've already been out to two false alarms this morning."

"The sooner they find them, the better," I agree, knowing that Gryffin will have to return home to complete his father's orders. I hope that will be the last time he disappears on his wild goose chase.

SEVENTEEN

Colbie

I'd like to be able to admit that I took to surfing like a dolphin takes to water, but that would be a lie. It was freaking hard work, and the waves were a lot bigger up close than they appeared from the porch. Nox taught me to paddle, but after the twentieth time of being hammered by a wave and dragged around by the leash attached to my board, I gave up. I waded out of the water, my board under my arm.

"Where are you going?" Nox calls from beyond the breaking waves, sitting on his board like he was made for it.

"I think maybe I should wait until the waves are a little smaller," I tell him. "But don't let me stop you. I want to watch."

"Fine, but you almost had it on that last one," he lies, and I feel a rush of affection for him.

"Pretty lies," I tease him and continue my journey back to the beach. I run up and set my board on the rack on the porch then strip off my wet suit, wrapping one of the towels there around my waist. I grab another cup of coffee, keeping a close eye on the feral cat, but he barely cracks an eyelid from his perch on his ridiculous cat tree.

Carrying the mug, I grab Nox a towel and head back to the beach to enjoy the early morning sun and watch the poetry in motion that is Nox on a surfboard. I settle down and sip the coffee as his board slices through a barrel, showing only his silhouette wrapped in the wave's embrace. He's laughing with pure, unfiltered joy when he emerges from the other end, and my heart skips a beat. He pushes his hair back off his face before he dives from the board and into the water.

Fuck, I'm getting attached, and that's only going to lead to more heartbreak. How did this happen so quickly? I've only known him for a few days. Maybe it's because he feels like a kindred soul.

The sun rises in the sky, and the waves fill with more surfers who paddle around the point from the other cove. Soon, there is a congregation of wave worshipers floating just beyond where the waves crest, waiting for the perfect one to call to them. I can hear them talking amongst themselves, but I can't make out any words. I close my eyes, lie back, and let the sun beat down on my face, knowing this is going to be the last moment of pure peace that I'm going to get for a long time.

I must drift off a little, lulled into a false sense of comfort, because I don't know how much time has passed when a shadow casts across my face, and I crack my eyes open to find Nox standing over the top of me.

"Hey, pretty girl, you're going to get burnt if you aren't careful." He crouches down beside me as I sit up and blink a couple of times against the brightness of the day.

"Are you done?" I ask him as I watch a bead of water drip from a lock of his long hair, which looks darker when it's wet and has managed to work itself free from its confines.

"Yeah, come on, I'll make you some breakfast." He stands up and holds out a hand. I reach out to grab it, and he freezes, looking at the marks on my wrist which have somehow been exposed. The sleeves of my rash guard are pushed back, so it must have happened while I was napping.

My heart starts to race as his eyes narrow on the marks, which are somehow darker now, the gold almost shimmering in the sunlight.

"Colbie, what is that?" he asks, and I hear the suspicion in his voice. I hurriedly snatch my hand back and tug down the long sleeves to cover the marks, but it's too late, he saw them, and they have caught his complete focus.

I push up off the sand and brush it off me before tossing the spare towel at him. "Nothing," I tell him, not waiting for a response before I start walking back to the cabin.

I hear him following behind me and pray he lets it go, but when we mount the steps to the porch, he grabs my arm.

"Colbie?"

When I turn around to face him, his eyes blaze with both anger and more questions.

"That is not a normal tattoo, is it?" he asks, but he already knows the answer, so I don't bother replying. He ditches his surfboard haphazardly off to the side and reaches for both my arms, pushing up both sleeves. His fingers circle my wrists and the marks that sit there.

His gaze lifts to mine, and I see so many emotions swirling in his—hurt, anger, and confusion. "When did they appear on your arms?" he asks, and I shrug.

"Saturday night," I admit, and he drops my hands like he's been burnt.

"You're the new shifter queen," he whispers, sounding awed as well as slightly horrified. "That's what you were so upset about on Sunday."

Now that he's released me, I whirl and hurry into the house, straight to his bedroom. I tug off my borrowed swim gear and throw on my clothes from yesterday before quickly attaching the jeweled cuffs to my wrists again. I grab my phone off the bedside table. There are a couple of missed calls from my mom and a message asking where I am. I don't have the energy or emotional strength to deal with her right now. It's taking everything I have to keep my shit together at the moment. When I turn, I find Nox leaning against the door, watching me.

"Talk to me, Colbie," he begs.

"What do you want me to say, Nox?" I say flatly. "Do you want me to tell you that I am the very last person who wanted this? That the thought of it makes me feel sick to my stomach? That I am the worst person for the job? That I secretly want to run away and pretend it never happened? That I wish I could wear the cuffs for the rest of my life and pretend the marks aren't there or find someone to tattoo over them so I can forget about them?" I'm shouting at the end of my tirade, and tears spill down my cheeks.

He pushes off the doorframe and hurries toward me, gathering me into his arms and holding me tightly. I sink into his embrace as he murmurs words of reassurance, but they are empty promises. There is nothing I can do to stop this runaway train. I've spent enough time hiding. When I leave here today, I will return to the neutral zone, get my affairs in order, and then present myself to the shifters. There's no more avoiding it, the goddess made sure I knew that.

He leads me out into the living room and helps me onto the couch. Nox pulls a blanket over me and hurries around the kitchen, doing something. I watch, kind of in an emotional daze. He removed his wet suit and is only wearing a pair of boxer briefs, so all his golden skin is on display, but even that's not enough to get me out of the funk I'm sinking into.

When he returns, he has coffee as well as the plates of pie we didn't get to last night. He hands me one and puts my coffee on the table in front of the sofa before returning to grab his own. When he joins me on the couch, we are both silent as we eat our pie, but then he clears his throat.

"For what it's worth, I think you're going to be an amazing queen. I know we haven't known each other very long, but I can tell you're a good person with a kind heart, and I think that needs to be the core makeup of someone who is chosen to be ruler. I don't think you will let the power and status go to your head like some have in the past, and I'm sure the shifters will be proud to have you as their queen."

I scoff and continue to eat my apple pie. It's pretty good. "Easy for you to say. I'm sure you've never disappointed anyone in your life." I wave my empty spoon.

He frowns, pausing with his spoon halfway to his mouth. "Oh, I can assure you, I disappoint plenty—my parents, my friends, the people of my village, just to name a few."

We sink into silence, a pity party for two in the

making. "You know that any shifters you come across are going to know who you are, right? The magic in those marks will call to them, and it will get stronger the longer you leave it."

My mouth drops open, and I gape at him in shock. "How do you know that?"

"It's my business to know about magic. They may mistake it for magic in the cuffs, but eventually, they won't be able to ignore it."

I groan and slump down on the couch. "One of my employees is a shifter," I admit to him. "I was hoping for another day or two at least to get my grandparents situated and up to speed in my bakery before I had to present myself to the palace."

This gets his attention, and he whips around to face me. "You're going to do it?"

"Well, like you said, I don't have a lot of choices, and I may have gotten a visit from Aramis just before I ended up on your porch," I admit sheepishly, and it's his turn to gape at me with shock. I can't stop the little giggle that bubbles up out of my chest at his stunned expression.

"The goddess Aramis visited you? That's unheard of." He sounds awed.

"Yeah, I'm pretty sure she knew I was thinking of bailing and wanted to let me know there was no escaping this."

"That's slightly terrifying," he remarks before shoveling another bite of pie into his mouth.

"You have no Idea," I agree as I lean forward to

grab my coffee, washing down the last of my pie with it.

The silence is loaded, and I feel like squirming, but I hold my shit together. Suddenly, Nox jumps to his feet and starts pacing back and forth before stopping and looking down at me.

"Will you let me help you?" he asks, and I feel my eyebrows jump in surprise.

"What can you do?" I ask skeptically. "I can't hide out here forever, no matter how much I would like to."

He spins and hurries across the room and into his office, talking loudly. "You know how I do security and web design, but I also have an interest in everything supernatural? Well, sometimes on my research trips, I come across items of interest."

I frown, kind of lost with where he's going with this. "You've lost me," I call, but all of a sudden, he shouts, "Ha!"

When he returns, he's carrying a corded pendant much like the one he has around his neck —even the stones are the same gold and black— and he thrusts it toward me.

"I picked this up on a trip to the witch kingdom. This should hide the magic in those marks from any shifter you come in contact with at least for another couple of days, long enough for you to do what you need to do with your bakery."

I stare at him, feeling confused and hopeful all at the same time. I reach out and take the offered necklace. The weight of the pendant is surprising. I hold it up to the light, and the stones shimmer. I narrow my eyes, looking from it to the one around his neck. He sees my gaze and shrugs, unconcerned.

"I liked the stones. There's nothing magical about me whatsoever, but there was something that made me buy them." He looks out the window like he's lost in his thoughts for a moment before returning his attention to me. "Take it. I hope it gives you a small reprieve before your life dramatically changes."

I sigh and place it over my head, and my eyes widen with surprise as the marks shimmer and fade from view. "It works," I exclaim, and he nods, looking pleased.

"That's great."

We fall into another awkward silence, and I can't stand that our time together has ended like this. I go to apologize, but he interrupts me.

"Come back and visit if you can. I've really enjoyed our time together." He sounds as sad as I feel, like he's saying the words knowing the chances of it happening are slim. Shifters aren't allowed in the human zone without special permission. I'm sure as the queen of the shifters, I could probably get in, but I'm not sure a booty call is the right reason.

"Or we could meet in the neutral zone, at my café, for lunch maybe," I say hopefully.

"Sure, maybe. I'll text you," he replies, but I

know from the look in his eyes he's only giving me lip service. I don't think he's anti-supernatural, since he admits to having a fascination with magic and the like, but Nox is a self-confessed loner, and even the sparsely populated neutral zone probably has too many people in it.

I stand up, knowing that the longer we draw this out, the more painful it's going to be. "I need to get going. There is no point in putting off the inevitable anymore. The sooner I can get my grandparents settled in at the bakery, the quicker I can get this over with."

He chuckles darkly. "You sound like you're going to your death. I'm pretty sure it's not going to be that bad to be queen. Hey, you may even love it. What shifter form are you hoping to gain?"

I gape at him, unable to control my shock at his words. "Shifter form?" I say, and his eyes almost bug out of his head.

"Yeah, part of the magic gives you an animal. You will learn to shift. How else can you control shifters without having the same kind of power?"

I wobble slightly, and he puts a hand out to steady me. I shake my head. "I haven't even thought about it. Hell, I don't even know all the different kinds of shifters there are."

Once I'm steady, he lets go of my arm, moves over to his bookcase, and pulls out a large hard-cover book. "Here, take this. It's shifter 101."

I take the large book from him and open it, flipping through some pages. The information is everything one would need to know about shifters, even closely guarded information.

"How did you get this?" I ask, and he waves a hand.

"It's been in my family for years. Someone must have had shifter connections in the past."

I hug it to my chest. "Thank you. Hopefully I can get through it in the next few days or so, then I won't look like such an idiot when I present myself to the palace."

He reaches out and gives my hand a squeeze. "They would never think you are an idiot. Humans are deliberately kept in the dark, but I think you're going to do amazing things, Colbie. Have faith in yourself." He sighs and steps toward his room. "Just let me throw some clothes on, and I'll run you home, okay?"

He walks toward his room, and it's all I can do to bite my lip and hold in the sob that wants to escape. Tears well in my eyes, but I don't let them overflow. Crying about this isn't going to solve or change anything, but I've been so happy the last few days, and I will hold onto these memories tightly for the rest of my life.

EIGHTEEN

Colbie

We don't really talk on the drive back to my grandparents' place. There is nothing much left to say. When he pulls up in front of their cottage, I brush a kiss across his lips.

"Thanks for everything," I whisper before hopping out.

"Good luck, I'm sure you're going to be amazing," he tells me, and without a backward glance, he drives away. I stand there, watching, until his truck disappears from sight, and only my grampy's voice calling my name has me turning my attention back to the present.

"You okay?" he asks, opening the gate and letting me pass through.

"Not really." I don't bother lying to him because he's always been able to see through them anyway.

"Ah, kiddo. I'm sure everything will work out for the best. Now, if you want to pack up the rest of your things, Granny and I have already put ours in the car. We will drive to the edge of the neutral zone and leave it in the long-term parking, then catch the public transport the rest of the way."

"Sure. Give me ten minutes, and we should be good to go," I tell him as he presses a kiss to the top of my head.

It doesn't even take me that long to gather my things, and before I know it, we're on the road. I lean against the window in the back seat of my grampy's truck and watch the seaside village turn into suburbia before it becomes a city. The freeway takes us around the main central business district and back into suburbia again. There's a small gap where the houses end and the neutral zone begins. It's like the humans didn't want to be too close just in case.

Regular traffic isn't allowed in the neutral zone, so people park their cars in a parking lot and then switch to the public transportation or electric scooters to get around. We have too much luggage for electric scooters, so we all climb aboard the bus that winds its way through the neutral zone. It takes about twenty minutes for it to get to my apartment building, and then we all hop off. I wince when I see my mother in the front room of her studio. The minute she sees my grandparents, she's going to be all over me.

I can't quite stifle the groan that leaves my mouth quick enough, and Grampy hears it and chuckles, but Granny frowns when her gaze follows mine.

"Oh dear, your mother is going to be so dramatic about this," she says, sounding put out, knowing her daughter all too well.

"Quick, if we hurry, she might not even see us, and I can avoid her even longer. Maybe I won't even tell her. We often don't see each other for days. She knows I've been visiting you, so she will assume I'm busy catching up on everything at the bakery." I hurry through the doors and into the foyer, smashing the elevator button. My grandparents follow me, and Grampy is still chuckling.

"Colbie," Granny scolds, sounding disappointed. "She's your mother, and she loves you in her own way. She will be devastated if she hears about this from someone else."

I lean against the elevator wall as the doors shut and close my eyes. Ugh, I know she's right, but I also feel like it's as much about keeping up appearances as it is caring about me. "I'm worried she won't be able to keep the information to herself," I admit, opening my eyes again. Granny and Grampy look at me with sympathy.

"You aren't wrong," Grampy scoffs. "Malina would shout it from the rooftops. Imagine what it will do for her business and social standing to be the mother of the shifter queen."

I shudder and wince. "God, I hope she doesn't want to insert herself into the shifter world. I'm not sure how that would go over."

"Aren't humans banned from the shifter zone without permission?" Granny points out, and Grampy snorts.

"Malina will assume she has carte blanche permission just because her daughter is the queen."

I groan again as the doors open on my floor and we head toward my apartment. "I'll have to ask the former king how he dealt with it."

Although it's only been a couple of days, my apartment smells musty when I open the door. While Granny and Grampy store their things in the spare bedroom, I open up a couple of windows to let in some fresh air. It's late afternoon, and I'm guessing the others already closed the bakery by now, so there's no point in hurrying there. Instead, I put my things away and decide I need to do a load of laundry. I gather everything in a basket, including the book on shifters Nox gave me, and head into the living room where my grandparents have made themselves a pot of tea.

"I'm just going to do some laundry." I gesture to the basket in my hands. "And while I'm waiting, I'll invite Mom to dinner so I can tell her, but you both need to be here to run interference," I tell them, and they agree. Granny and Grampy are experts in managing their daughter, and both are strong willed enough to stand up to her ridiculous demands and behavior. For me, it's easier to give in than deal with the guilt trip she gives me when I don't agree with her or follow her instructions.

"You know, this shifter thing might not be bad. It will get you out from under your mother's control. You'll be able to find yourself without her interference," Grampy says, trying to be positive about the whole thing.

"She's not that bad," I argue halfheartedly, but to be honest, she really is. She's dictated to me all my life. She's not abusive or neglectful or anything, but she's not really good at allowing me to be me. She tried to mold me into what she wanted me to be—stylish, polished, popular, and career oriented—and I never quite lived up to her expectations. I always felt like I was letting her down.

"Yes, she is, so this could be good for both of you. She will finally realize that you're amazing just the way you are." Granny smiles brightly at me, and I feel so much love for them. They really are amazing, and I have no idea how my mother ended up the way she is, concerned with appearances and social standing. Neither of my grandparents are like that at all. I have a feeling it has something to do with my father, but no one really talks about him, so I have nothing to go on. It's like when he left, they agreed they would never mention him again.

I take my basket down to the basement where

our laundry room is and put on a load. I look between the book sitting in the bottom of the basket and the elevator and decide to text my mother an invitation to dinner instead of going up there. If I do and she isn't with a client, then she will only grill me about my stay with her parents.

Instead, I take a seat on one of the comfy chairs that are positioned for people who want to wait for their laundry and open up the shifter book.

I get so lost in all the information that I don't even notice when the washing machine finishes. It's not until my phone beeps with an incoming message that I look up and realize two hours have gone by, and I have to move the wet stuff to the dryer. I quickly do that before checking my messages. It's my mother demanding to know where I am since I invited her to dinner.

"Fuck!" I slam the book closed and tuck it under my arm before hurrying up to my apartment. When I get there, there's an awkward silence between my mother and her parents.

"Darling," she calls as I hurry inside. "Imagine my surprise when I come upstairs to have dinner with my daughter who has ignored me for days and find my parents waiting." She sounds annoyed, but then, she often does. I've learned to ignore it. I will never meet her high expectations no matter what I do. She's wearing a stylish pair of black tailored pants, a sleeveless, emerald green top, and heels. My mother does not know the meaning of casual.

"Hi, Mom." I lean down and give her a kiss on the cheek before placing the book out of her line of sight. I don't want her asking questions about it just yet. "Sorry, I was doing laundry and got caught up in a book."

She giggles delicately. "Always have your nose in a book, don't you? I would have thought you would have grown out of that by now. How are you going to find any real friends if your head is always in the clouds?"

"We ordered some takeaway, dear," Granny says from the kitchen where she's dishing some steaming hot dishes into some serving bowls. Heaven forbid we actually eat out of the takeaway containers. *"We're not savages, darling."* The memory of my mother's voice echoes in my mind.

"Thanks, Granny." I smile gratefully at her as I take a seat at the dinner table with the rest of them. It's set for the four of us, and I feel Grampy give my leg a squeeze under the table as I reach for the glass of wine that is sitting at my setting. I have a feeling this dinner with Mom will require liquid fortification.

Granny brings the food over, and we're silent as we help ourselves to the various options. My mom watches on with disdain as she sips her red wine. Takeaway is uncouth as far as she is concerned. You either need to cook an elaborate meal or take her to an exclusive restaurant to impress her. She probably won't even touch the food, but I'm starving.

I don't even get a chance to shovel any into my mouth before my mom starts in on me. "To what do we owe this surprise?" she asks passive aggressively. She waves a finger between her mom and dad, and I want to kick her under the table. Granny and Grampy have been nothing short of amazing to me. When she was too busy being a famous designer and it was inconvenient for her to have a child, they happily stepped up and took care of me.

I wrinkle my nose, annoyed that I'm not even going to be able to eat my food before I have to address the question, but before I can answer, Grampy jumps in.

"Do we need an excuse to visit our only daughter and favorite grandchild?" he asks, sounding deceptively casual.

I shovel in some of my rice and curry, enjoying the delicious flavors that tantalize my taste buds. I'm pretty sure Mom is trying to frown, but she uses so many anti-aging witch potions that her face doesn't move, though her mouth is slightly turned down, so that's a indication sign she's annoyed.

"Not at all. It's just that Colbie usually goes to your place, like she did earlier in the week."

I sigh and put my fork down, knowing I can't avoid this any longer. I only hope the damn woman will keep her mouth closed long enough for me to get my shit together. I need two more days, so instead, I distract her.

"How was the retirement party for the royals?" I ask, and her eyes light up with excitement.

"Oh, darling, I can't believe you didn't accept the invitation. Queen Mia said they sent you one. You missed out on one hell of a party." She continues to tell us all about the party, gushing about the various dignitaries and celebrities who were there, the outfits, and the food, then she shares random little pieces of gossip.

This gives the rest of us enough time to eat dinner, clean up, and make a pot of tea. She's on her third glass of wine by the time she finally winds down, and none of us have had to say a word except for an occasional murmur of acknowledgement.

"That sounds like a lovely party, dear." Granny pats Mom's shoulder as she takes a seat on one of the sofas in the living room, placing the tea tray on the coffee table and then proceeding to pour everyone a cup.

My mom made herself comfortable while the rest of us cleaned up dinner. She declines tea and sticks with wine, but I happily take a cup from my granny. Leaning back, I blow over the top so I don't burn my mouth before taking a sip.

"Sounds more like a pain in the ass," Grampy grumbles, and I hide my smile behind my cup. He would hate the idea of dressing up and making small talk. I only hope he will suffer through it for me, because I don't doubt there will be a party to celebrate the arrival of a new royal, and I will want both of them there.

"Anyway, how was your trip, darling? You're looking a little strained. You really could use a holiday somewhere nice and sunny by the beach and get yourself a tan." She eyes me critically, and I consider not telling her my news. I really am tired and don't have the energy to deal with her today. I'm sure she will find some way to make this about herself.

"I'm a little tired," I admit. "I just needed to get away for a few days and sort a few things out in my brain. That's actually what I need to talk to you about and why Granny and Grampy are both here."

"Oh, do tell?" She doesn't sound particularly interested. Her eyes get that glazed look, which tells me she's thinking about something else and only pretending to listen, so instead of telling her my news, I remove the necklace from my neck and show her instead.

The marks reappear as soon as the necklace is removed, and they are even darker now. There's no denying them anymore, but it seems to take her a few moments to respond, and when she does, she shrieks.

"You got tattoos? God, could you be any more cliché?" she snaps, and I just stare at her. "Tattoos are so tacky. How are you going to find yourself a classy, distinguished man if you have tattoos? And around your wrists like shackles! God, Colbie, I thought I taught you better."

"Enough, Malina," Grampy snaps, and my mom shuts up. Wow, I want that superpower. "Let the girl explain."

I take a deep breath. "Mom, these appeared on Saturday night," I say slowly, and she purses her lips as she thinks. "Magically appeared," I add.

I see the exact moment she comprehends, because she shakes her head like she can't wrap her brain around the information. "You're the next shifter queen?" She sounds perplexed.

"Looks like it," I mutter, and she rolls the information around in her brain before her eyes light up with maniacal glee and she leans forward, forgetting all about her wine.

"What the hell are you still doing here? Why haven't you presented yourself to the palace yet? God, you're already failing at this." She stands up and starts pacing. "You ungrateful little brat. You're going to make a bad impression. They are going to think you don't want to be their queen."

I flinch at the barbs, and Grampy growls, sounding almost like a shifter himself.

"Malina, that's enough. It's a huge adjustment, and Colbie will do it at her own pace."

"I don't want to," I admit, and my mom looks like her head will explode.

"Why the hell not? You'll be the most powerful person in the kingdom of Aramis." I can see the exact moment she starts to scheme. She pauses, and a small smile crosses her lips. "Of course, you will need an advisor. I should go pack up my things and get ready to move into the palace when you do."

"What about your business?" Granny points out diplomatically while I stare at my mother in horror. What the hell makes her think she is qualified to be an advisor to a shifter queen?

"Pfft. That's not as important as assuring Colbie doesn't embarrass me or herself when she doesn't dress right or say the right things to the right people."

My cheeks heat, and I feel a pang of hurt in my chest before it turns to anger. Before I can say anything, though, my granny does for me. "Malina, you're human, and Colbie will soon not be. You will not be allowed to be an advisor for the shifter queen. They don't even allow humans to reside in the shifter zone." Granny's tone is cool as she calmly shoots down my mother's crazy scheming, but it doesn't dampen my mother's enthusiasm. She spins and looks me up and down and grimaces. I'm wearing jeans and a T-shirt and have my sandals on my feet. My hair could probably use a brush, and I'm pretty sure there's a stain on my top from dropping some dinner on it.

"This will not do." She waves her hand up and down. "I will go look in your closet to see what you have that is suitable." She doesn't wait for a response and hurries toward my bedroom.

The three of us are quiet, and I feel tears well in my eyes.

"We shouldn't have told her," Grampy grumbles, and Granny reaches over and pats my leg.

"Ignore her. Soon you won't have to deal with her at all. If there was any reason for jumping at the chance for the queen job, that is it."

"I just hope she will keep her mouth shut for a few more days," I murmur as Mom bustles back into the room, her nose turned up.

"Ugh, you have nothing fit for a queen in there. I'll just have to make you something new. You've waited this long, so another twenty-four hours won't make any difference. I'll get started on it now."

She doesn't wait for a response and leaves my apartment, letting the door shut behind her with bang.

I slump on the sofa and groan. "I guess I have twenty-four hours to get my shit together."

CHAPTER
NINETEEN

Colbie

After the disaster that was dinner, I head down to grab my laundry and check my mailbox. The lights are on in my mother's studio, but I have no more energy or mental capacity to deal with her. I'm sure she will make me something classy to wear, but it won't be my style at all.

I call it a night and head to bed to read more of my shifter book. It's fascinating learning about the different kinds of shifters and the different developmental stages. Shifters with animals like wolves and tigers can shift when they are very young, and they usually have their first shift by one, but shifters with mythical creatures like dragons, phoenixes, and unicorns don't shift until they are in their late teens.

I mean, it makes sense, since nobody wants a fire-breathing infant.

Then there is the information about bond groups and mates. I squirmed a little when I read about the mating rituals, something about knots and spurs that some male shifters have on their cocks, and breeding cycles called heats. It is all very overwhelming, but I can't help but wonder if I will experience any of that. I'm not sure how I feel about it, but I can't deny that I'm curious.

I learn that shifters are very long-lived compared to humans, but I kind of already knew that part, and because of that, they are not as fertile as humans. Most shifters only have one or two children in their lifetimes. The exception for that is bond groups. Bond groups usually share a singular mate, and she can have a child with each of her partners.

It's very late once I finally put the book down and go to bed, and I groan at the thought of getting up in a few hours, but I can't avoid the bakery any longer. I also needed to cram as much information about shifters into my brain as I could, because tomorrow, after I finish up at the bakery, I'm going to present myself to the castle. I can't wait around for my mom to blab to anyone else, and I don't want her to control any of my decisions. She is already forcing my hand a day or two earlier than I wanted.

The following morning, all three of us trudge to

work. Unlike my perfectly sunny morning yesterday, the early hours are cold and overcast. It's really starting to cool down now, and it won't be long before the leaves change color and fall from the trees. All three of us are wrapped in coats with beanies on our heads.

"Damn neutral zone not letting us have our cars," Grampy grumbles on the walk, his breath foggy in the cold morning air.

"Pfft," Granny scoffs. "The drive wouldn't be long enough to heat the car up. Stop being a princess."

"There's always the public transport service. On the days when the weather is really bad, I call a taxi," I tell them. "They are free for neutral zone residents. I'll contact the night watch today and get you added to my curfew permit and then call the council and inform them you are living and working here for now. That will give you the status you need to use the free service." My to-do list today is rather large.

"That would be great. I'd rather not walk in torrential rain or snow if I have to be up this early in the morning." Grampy rubs his hands together as we get to the door of the bakery, and I let us in. I turn the ovens on to warm up as they hang up their coats, then we get down to business.

By the time Olivia and Justin arrive, I feel confident between the four of them and Violet that my bakery will be in safe hands.

Justin and Olivia have met my grandparents before, so I only have to introduce Violet when she arrives.

I have to figure out a way of telling the three of them that I won't be around for a while, if ever again. I'm pretty sure they can sense my inner turmoil, because just before we're going to flip the sign over to open, Justin puts his hands on his hips.

"Damn it, Colbie, what's wrong? You're wound tighter than a top." One of the things I appreciate about Justin is that he doesn't beat around the bush.

"Come back into the kitchen for a moment," I request as Violet lifts her hand away from the sign.

"But…" She looks at the locked door, and I wave a hand.

"A few minutes won't matter. Nobody is waiting yet anyway." The rain is falling steadily outside, keeping our early morning customers in bed or indoors.

"What's going on?" Olivia asks cautiously as I lean against the prep counter, and the three of them join us in the kitchen.

Again, I'm not sure how to tell them, so I lift the necklace over my head, and my marks appear. Violet gasps and staggers slightly to the side. Justin puts out his hand to steady her, and she stares at me with awe in her eyes.

"So you can feel them?" I murmur, and she drops to her knees and bows her head.

"My queen." Olivia and Justin gape at her

before turning to look at me, their eyes locked on the marks around my wrists.

"You're the next shifter queen," Justin murmurs as Olivia gasps.

"Oh my god!"

"Get up, Violet. You don't need to bow to me ever." She doesn't listen, so I reach out to her.

She takes my hand and rises, still not meeting my eyes. "Why haven't you presented yourself at the palace yet? Rumors are flying around the shifter zone. Some are saying that Aramis messed up. Others are saying that the human thinks they are too good to be queen. The shifters are getting restless," she warns.

"It's a lot, you know. I just needed to take a few days to get my head on straight. I didn't want this," I explain, and she finally lifts her head and meets my gaze.

"And that's what's going to make you great, but you can't delay any longer."

I slip the pendant back over my head and nod. "I know. I just needed to make sure you were all going to be okay here. I would like you to work with Granny and Grampy to get them up to speed on everything. They won't be able to stay forever, and I'm going to need the two of you to take over. If this isn't what you want, then I need to start interviewing for a baker," I explain to Olivia and Justin, who both visibly startle before they exchange a glance.

"I would be honored." Justin bows his head to me.

"So would I. Don't worry, Colbie, we will look after the bakery like it's our own," Olivia assures me, and I feel myself relax a little now that I know it will be in the hands of people I trust.

"Well, let's open up then." I clap my hands together, and Justin and Olivia jump into action and hurry to the front to open the bakery, but Violet just stands there and gapes at me.

"What's wrong?" I ask her, looking from her to my grandparents. Grampy shrugs, not knowing what to say, but Granny is watching Violet carefully.

"Why are you waiting?" Violet asks, no judgment in her tone, only curiosity.

"It's not like I asked to be queen," I reply defensively. "I don't have the first clue about what to do."

"None of the royals did when they started. It's why you have advisors and mates, to help you through all this." She crosses her arms and has a stubborn set to her jaw. "Time to grow a set, Colbie, our people are waiting for you."

I look at my grandparents, and Granny is doing her best to hide a smirk, but Grampy is outright chuckling.

"I like this girl. Maybe she can be your advisor instead of your mother."

Violet's eyes widen, and she shakes her head vehemently. "Oh no, I couldn't possibly do anything like that. I'm not one of the upper class, and that's whom Her Majesty will chose her advisors from."

"Stop right there." I hold up a hand. "I don't ever want to hear you put yourself down like that again, and none of that 'Your Majesty' crap. I'm Colbie to you. Please give me that little bit of normality. And Grampy is right. I need someone I can trust, and you are the only shifter I know apart from Brock and Niles next door. I know you're still in college, but I need you, at least to begin with."

"I've actually finished all my classes for the semester, which is why I was looking for a job. All my friends are still going, and I didn't want to be bored, but they only have a few more weeks left anyway."

"Good, then it's settled." I look around my precious bakery and feel a wave of sorrow. Nothing is ever going to be the same.

"Okay, so how are we going to do this? Do I just walk into the shifter zone and announce myself?" I lift my apron off, hang it on the hook, and look down at myself. I wore jeans today, and they are still clean since Granny and Grampy did most of the labor while I organized all the paperwork. My top is also clean, so I'm not going to bother returning home. If I do, my mother might waylay me and force me to wear something that isn't me.

She gasps and shakes her head. "Absolutely not. Humans are not allowed into the shifter zone without an official escort." She cocks her head to the side like she's listening to something, and her eyes light up.

"Well, how do I get an official escort?" I ask, and she doesn't answer, just spins around and heads into the shop.

"What the hell?" Grampy grumbles, but Granny comes over and puts her hands on my arms.

"We are so proud of you, Colbie, and you know where to find us when you need us." She pulls me into a hug, which Grampy quickly joins. He presses a kiss to my head.

"Give them hell, sweetheart, and don't you dare take any of their crap. We will run interference with your mother, but I'm not sure how long that will last."

Tears well in my eyes, but I swallow around the lump in my throat and nod just as the kitchen door swings open, and Violet returns with Hunter and Brodie in tow.

Brodie smirks at me and looks around the kitchen. "When Violet said we needed to see something, I was a little worried there was going to be another shifter cub back here." His smile is warm and inviting, and I instantly feel lighter.

Hunter nods. "Glad to see you're back," he murmurs, and my eyes widen in surprise. They noticed I was gone.

"These two have been in both mornings and

afternoons for coffee, hot chocolate, and lunch," Violet tells me.

"So what did you want to show us?" Brodie turns his attention to the shifter girl, and she nods at me.

"Show them," she demands, and I smile. The timid, shy shifter from before is gone, and I'm pleased.

Granny and Grampy nod their encouragement, so I lift the pendant and place it on the counter. I don't want to lose it, because I'll never know when I might want to sneak away and pretend to be human—that's if it will even work once I gain the shifter magic.

I see the moment the two males notice the marks. Both of them stare for a moment before dropping to their knees in unison and bowing their heads. "Your Majesty," they murmur together, and Violet snorts.

"Oh yeah, I can see that becoming annoying for sure." She hip bumps me, and I feel grateful that she is in my life.

"Get up please, I don't want you on your knees." *Unless it's for another reason.* I keep that last comment to myself. Both men rise with grace. "So, um, I guess I'm the next shifter queen, and Violet says I need an escort to the palace."

They stare at me with no short amount of awe, and I feel the urge to squirm under such close scrutiny.

"I can't believe you're the next shifter queen," Brodie murmurs, and I wince, not sure if he's disappointed or pleased, but his next words make me feel so much better. "But I'm very happy about it." His and Hunter's eyes both glow with their inner animals, and I shuffle my feet, feeling awkward.

Violet clears her throat. "Escort?"

"Yes, of course." Hunter is all business. Both of them are, in fact, and I mourn the loss of the casual, friendly way they were speaking to me. "I'll let my father know, and he can make arrangements." He pulls a phone out of the pocket of his uniform, and my heart starts to race with panic.

"No." I hold up a hand. "Please, is there any way we can do this discreetly? Can't the two of you just escort me?" I plead, looking between them, and Brodie's eyes soften, even if he keeps his expression professional. He and Hunter exchange a look, and Hunter huffs a puff of smoke out of his nostrils.

"We can do that. My dad is going to kick my ass, but I will deal with it."

"You boys look after my girl, okay? She's going to need people on her side. Can I trust you to do that?" Grampy is staring the two shifters down like he has his own inner beast, and both men give him their assurance.

"I promise, sir. Our team has been assigned to watch her until her coronation and she chooses her mates. We will keep her safe," Brodie sounds even more serious than when he found me with Archie.

"We will go out back. Put the pendant back on for now. That will keep you hidden until we can get where we need to go."

I give my grandparents hugs and kisses goodbye then follow the guys into the alley. Violet follows us, but she stays in the doorway of the bakery.

"Aren't you coming?" I ask her, and she bites her lip, looking from me to the two men.

"It sounds like the queen has chosen you. Neither of us are going to stop you," Hunter assures her, and she relaxes slightly.

"What about work?" She looks back, and I hear Grampy grumble, "Go, child. We might be older, but we can handle this."

Violet whips off her apron and returns to the kitchen to hang it up. I hear the rumble of my grandpa's voice as he says something to her, but I can't make out what the conversation is about. It doesn't take her long to return though.

"We need to get her to the edge of the neutral zone, then Hunter can shift and take us all directly to the palace," Brodie says as the three of them fan out around me—Hunter at my back, and the other two on either side of me.

"Shift?" I can't help the words from blasting out of my mouth, and Violet chuckles, making me feel very nervous indeed.

"Oh boy, Colbie, I hope you pulled up those big girl panties, because you're about to ride a dragon."

CHAPTER
TWENTY

Colbie

I don't think my brain actually processed what Violet said, because when we get to the border of the neutral and shifter zones, and I watch with undisguised awe as Hunter shifts. Standing before me is a twenty foot, dark purple dragon, and all I can do is reach out and run my hand over its shiny scales, but before I can touch it, Violet slaps my hand away.

"Ah, maybe don't touch the pretty fire-breathing shifter without permission," Violet stammers.

The dragon swings its head around and pins her with its green stare, blowing smoke out of its nose and huffing with annoyance. She holds up her hands and backs away.

"Then again, maybe he wants you to touch him. Who the hell am I to tell you what to do?" she mutters before grumbling under her breath, "Damn grumpy lizard. I'm only trying to teach the shifter ways. We don't want her going around stroking every shifter she comes in contact with, do we? That's like a man going around squeezing every woman's breast he sees. It's lucky he's wearing magickal clothes, otherwise he would have had to get naked in front of us all."

"Naked?" I ask, not hating the idea of seeing this man naked.

"Yeah, unless they are spelled, clothes get ruined when we shift, so most of the time, we get naked first. Don't worry, you'll get used to it," Violet assures me as I gape at her in horror.

Brodie chuckles, reaches up, and grabs my hand, placing it against Hunter's side and running it back and forth. His scales are surprisingly warm to the touch and kind of silky feeling. "Violet is right. You shouldn't go around touching every shifter you see, but Hunter really doesn't mind if you touch him. It's natural. You're going to be curious, and he especially likes it if you scratch between his eyebrow ridges."

I gasp in shock as Hunter's large head leans in and practically headbutts me, and Brodie points to a spot. I reach up and rub the area he pointed at, and a loud purring sound comes out of the dragon's mouth as he leans his heavy head against my stomach, his nostrils flaring in and out with large lungfuls of air.

"That's enough." Brodie pushes the dragon's head away, glaring at him. "Come on, up you go. I promise the big lug is actually a fairly smooth ride."

"That's what he said," Violet mutters behind us, and I can't help my snicker of laughter. I'm pretty sure I'm in a small amount of shock. Seeing the dragon just made this all very fucking real.

Brodie rolls his eyes but smirks at Violet's comment. "I like you." He points at her before cupping his hands and nodding at them. "Put your foot in here, and then use the spikes on his back to pull yourself. Settle into the spot between his head and his wings, then scoot along, and I'll climb up behind you. Violet, are you coming with us?"

She bites her lip and looks to me. "Is that okay? I don't want to offend him or anything, but I don't want to let Colbie go on her own. I can run if it's a problem, but I won't get there as quickly as you."

"Are we offending him by riding him?" I ask, stopping before climbing up the dragon like Brodie told me to. "I don't want one of the first things I do as queen to offend such a magnificent creature."

Brodie shakes his head. "No, it's an honor for Hunter to give you a lift. Trust me, he doesn't mind in the least." Brodie gives the dragon a sideways glance. "But mostly, shifters won't let anyone else but their bond group or mates ride them. He said he would make an exception for Violet and his queen."

Violet still looks unsure but agrees. Before long,

the three of us are mounted on Hunter's back, and my stomach is in my throat. I'm sandwiched between Brodie and Violet, with Brodie's strong, warm chest against my back. He leans in, and his breath brushes across my ear, causing goosebumps to erupt on my arms. "Here we go."

Hunter's large, iridescent purple wings stretch out wide, and I feel his whole body dip as he uses his powerful legs to leap into the air. The wings flap up and down to gain momentum. I can't stop the squeal of fright that leaves my mouth as we are jostled back and forth with the movement. If it wasn't for Brodie holding me tightly, I probably would have slipped off. His arms around my waist and his thick thighs against mine hold me securely, and I try to do the same thing for Violet, but she has a hold of two large spikes that sit behind his brow ridge and seems more than comfortable.

"Easy," Brodie murmurs, and one of his hands strokes my thigh. "I promise Hunter has never lost a rider. He's actually a smooth ride once we get airborne. It's just the takeoff and landing that's a little bumpy." My heart races as we lift above the forest and higher into the air. I shiver in the cold air and say a prayer of thanks that the rain has stopped for now, though it is still overcast. I look up and wince at the thought of flying through those clouds. Brodie must guess what I'm thinking.

"We're not dressed for cloud flight, so he'll stay below them. Hey, Hunter, the girls are cold," he calls out, and all of a sudden, the surface I'm sitting on starts to warm, radiating toasty heat beneath my thighs. "He can at least make the ride slightly more comfortable for us. After all, he's a living furnace."

Hunter starts to move faster, streamlining his body, and the wind whips past our ears, making communication a little tricky. Instead, I watch the world go by and have an internal panic attack about what's going to happen. The forest is large, and I gain a new appreciation for how far Archie ran on the day I found him. No wonder he was exhausted. We pass over a small village. In a large clearing in the forest, children run and laugh and wave at the dragon flying overhead, but finally, in the distance, I make out a large, white structure.

"That's the castle," Brodie says, leaning in close again so I can hear him. "It's on the outskirts of the largest shifter city and will be your new home."

We get closer, and Hunter finally starts a slow, circling descent into the courtyard of the huge structure. I can't even begin to guess how many rooms the place has. My anxiety revs higher the closer we get to the ground.

"Everything is about to change. My life is never going to be the same, is it?" I lean my head against Brodie's chest, forgetting where and who I am for a moment, just soaking in the comfort and strength he offers.

"Yes, it is, but I'm sure you will be nothing short of spectacular." His words make me warm inside, and I get the urge to turn around and kiss him, so I do, placing my lips on his cheek.

"Thank you," I murmur before facing forward again just as Hunter touches down gently.

Suddenly, we are surrounded by guards all carrying guns, but thankfully, none of them are pointing them at us. I feel a rush of panic, though, and grab Brodie's wrist.

"Please don't tell them who I am yet," I ask desperately, and I feel his whole body stiffen behind me, but he slides off the dragon and holds up his hand to help me down.

"Fine, but if I can give you some advice—shifters admire strength. Don't cower or hide from your destiny, Colbie." He helps me down before turning and holding up his hands to the guards in a nonthreatening way.

"At ease. These ladies are with me," Brodie calls out, and the guards melt back into their surroundings.

Violet jumps down, and in a flash, Hunter changes back. He doesn't say anything, just starts walking toward the palace, expecting us to follow. I look around. Hunter has landed in a paved courtyard to the side of the castle, and there doesn't seem to be much else here except for a building where I hear the whinny of horses. I'm assuming it's the stable.

"There is a central courtyard Hunter could have landed in too, but that would have attracted a lot more attention. It was better to come in this way," Brodie explains as we approach a portico that leads into the palace. Hunter opens the door and moves through, followed by Violet, but I freeze in place. Brodie steps up beside me and looks at me quizzically.

"What happens next?" I ask him, not looking away from the daunting entry. Brodie frowns and shrugs, running a nervous hand through his hair.

"Um, I'm not actually sure. I wasn't around during the last coronation."

I think about the book I read last night that is still on my bedside table. I'll have to ask my grandparents to pack some of my things, or maybe they will let me return to do it myself. I mean, I'm not a prisoner, right? The book said that the moment the newly chosen human crosses the threshold of the shifter palace, the magic that is their right will embrace them, and that the process will end when the queen is crowned. What the hell does that even mean? What freaking process?

I hear a commotion inside the palace and turn my attention back to what's happening. I see people waiting inside the room, quizzing Hunter and Violet. Brodie's hand on my arm brings my attention back to him.

"It's okay, Colbie, you just need to trust the goddess." His eyes are soft like he can hear my internal worries.

"Colbie?" A voice has me looking up. It's

Queen Mia, and her eyes are wide with surprise as they scan my body. "What are you doing here? Did your mother send you?" It's then that I remember I still have the pendant on, so I lift it over my head and tuck it into my pocket, leaving my marks on display.

She gasps and places her hand against her chest. "Oh, dear child." Her eyes fill with sympathy, and she takes a step forward and holds out her hand encouragingly. "Don't worry, the four of us will help you every step of the way, but you need to take that first step. It's the hardest, but we will catch you, I promise." Her voice is gentle and cajoling, like she's talking to a wild animal, and she's not wrong to assume that. A very big part of me wants to spin around, hurry into the forest, return to my life, and pretend none of this ever happened, but then I remember Aramis's warning. I can't change this, so instead, I straighten my shoulders, and I see Mia's eyes gleam with pride. I brace myself for whatever comes next and walk over the threshold of the palace and into my new life.

Brodie follows behind me, and I stop just inside a large foyer. Hunter is talking to a man whom I recognize as King Lucas, while Violet talks to the other two queens. I look around and feel my body sag when nothing happens. Obviously, I was worried over nothing.

I give Queen Mia a small, wobbly smile, which she doesn't return. Instead, she gestures to Brodie.

"Get ready," she tells him as my body starts to warm, and I look down to the source of the heat to find my body is glowing. I wave my arms like I'm trying to get the glow off me.

"What's happening?" I screech as my body seizes and white-hot pain explodes through my limbs. I can't control myself as I begin to convulse, and I drop, unable to support my body weight any longer. I'm vaguely conscious of being caught, but the pain is too much. I squeeze my eyes shut and open my mouth to scream, but nothing comes out. My vocal cords are seized as well, so I'm silent as waves of agony roll through my body in a never-ending tidal wave. It's too much, and I black out as my system overloads.

"Wow that seemed way worse than what I went through," a male voice mumbles. "I remember glowing and pain, but I never seized like that or blacked out."

"Where's the damn physician?" I hear Hunter growl. "What is taking him so damn long?"

"He was guest lecturing at the university today. We didn't think to keep him on hand until the new royal showed." I recognize that voice as Queen Evie. "Poor child. Let's bring her up to her room, and we can at least make her comfortable."

I hear a growl, and I realize I'm being held by someone when their grip on my body gets tighter.

"Okay, Brodie, you can carry her, but you need to listen to Evie." That's the final queen, Layla. "If we take her to her room, we can get her comfortable and ready for when the palace physician gets here to check her."

"Why is she still unconscious? What did the magic do to her?" Violet sounds distressed.

"We're not actually sure. My experience was very different. Can anyone feel her animal inside her?" Lucas asks, and I hear the worry in his tone.

"I can't sense anything, but her scent is stronger," Hunter replies, sounding agitated, and Brodie growls again as I feel him move.

No one talks, but I can tell we're moving. I try to open my eyes, but they refuse to cooperate. Same with the rest of my body. I try to figure out if I feel any different, but all I can feel are achy muscles and my throbbing head.

I hear everyone's footsteps as we move through the palace and whispered words, but I can't make out what they are saying. After what seems like a long walk, I hear a door open.

"Here, lay her down on the bed. I'll remove her shoes," Mia tells Brodie, who does as she asks, but he seems somewhat reluctant, like he doesn't want me to leave his arms. The bed is soft, and I moan as he places me down, but I still can't force my eyes to open or my mouth to make words. Brodie's hand is still in mine as I feel Mia gently remove the sneakers from my feet.

"Brodie, you need to let the girl go," King Lucas snaps, and I hear another rumbly growl, but his hand releases mine.

"We should let her rest until the physician gets here to check her over. I'm sure she's fine and just overloaded from that influx of power. It looked like a lot," Layla says sensibly.

"Is no one else worried about what that might mean? Why can't we feel an animal inside her? Did something go wrong? Did the magic reject her?" Evie's worried, and I can tell from the inhale of breath somewhere that at least one person hadn't considered it.

"Nonsense. It's never happened in the whole time the humans have been our rulers, and I doubt Aramis would ever allow it to occur. It's her magic and her chosen one. I'm sure her wishes will make themselves known in time." King Lucas sounds firm but frazzled, almost like he doesn't believe what he is saying.

"I would like permission to stay," I hear my friend say.

"Who are you, child?" Layla asks.

"Violet is here at Colbie's request," Hunter

rumbles, answering the queen before Violet can. "She works with her in her bakery."

"Good. That is good. I wish I had a friend with me when I went through this. All of mine were human. It's good that she has someone who will help her through this. Of course you may keep her company. Send for us if she wakes before the physician arrives," King Lucas says, approving her request.

I hear Violet clear her throat awkwardly.

"Speak up, child. We are not to be feared," Evie chides gently.

"Colbie's mother may be a problem." A rush of surprise overrides the lingering pain. How does she know that?

"Malina Karridge?" I can hear the surprise in Queen Layla's voice.

"Yes, she is a somewhat domineering woman, and she likes to make Colbie feel small, or that's what her grandpa told me just before we left. She will try to insert herself into a role as Colbie's advisor. Her grandparents warned us not to let her." Trust my grandpa to look out for me like that. He knows I have trouble saying no to her, so he made it so I didn't have to. Thank goodness for the old man.

"She's human, so she has no standing whatsoever. What she wants won't matter, only what Colbie wants. Now let's leave the poor girl in peace. Hunter and Brodie, please return to headquarters and advise Bryson that the royal has been found so he can call off the search and gather the rest of your team." King Lucas brushes away Violet's concern, but I have a feeling he's going to regret it. My mother does not like to be told no.

"Of course, sir," Hunter replies.

"Should we go to her place and pack a bag so she at least has some of her things? I'm pretty sure her grandparents would help us?" I feel a warm rush of affection for Brodie. I only hope that he doesn't run into my mother, though they both seem proficient enough to cope with her, and if not, they can dazzle her with their good looks. She's a sucker for a handsome man.

"Good thinking," Queen Layla replies. "The rest of us will wait for her to wake so we can talk about what happens next." I hear them all file out of my room, and the door closes behind them as a hand picks up one of mine.

"Come on, Colbie, we need you to wake up. Everyone is worried about you," Violet murmurs, but instead of obeying her plea, I sink deeper.

TWENTY-ONE

Brodie

I am still completely reeling as I come to terms with everything that just happened. I can't believe the little human, whom I admit to having a small crush on, is the next shifter queen. Is that the reason I'm attracted to her? Did my magic sense something in her that no one else, including herself, did?

Hunter and I hurry back through the palace, both of us lost in our thoughts. I feel a sense of wonder and excitement through our bond, but also a sense of disappointment.

"You know we won't be selected as her mates, right? Our bond prevents it. In fact, as soon as she walked through those doors and the magic hit her, marks should have started showing up on shifters all over the zone. It's only a matter of time before they begin to walk through the front door." He growls that last bit, and I know he's feeling exactly the same as me, because the whole time I was holding her, I was wishing she was mine, but I know she can't be, and the disappointment I feel is visceral. I want to snatch her up and run away with her and keep her all to myself.

"Fuck, I know," I snarl, unable to control my temper. I'm mad as hell that I'm going to have to watch Colbie while she is being courted by others. I've never resented being in a bond group before and actively looked forward to the day our mate was marked, but right now, I could burn it all to the ground. My wolf whimpers mournfully inside me and covers his eyes with his paws, sadness leaking from our soul.

"My dragon wants to set fire to any male who appears with bond marks. He's actively plotting their deaths and is sure he can get Gem's phoenix on board," Hunter admits ruefully, rubbing the spot on his chest where his animal resides. "How are we going to protect her with our animals doing crazy shit?"

We reach the courtyard we arrived in, and both of us sort of just stand there for a moment, lost in our thoughts.

"I don't know but we better get our shit together quickly, because I have a feeling this is not going to go as smoothly as we hoped." There are alarm bells inside my head at the fact that we couldn't feel an animal within the new queen. We should at least be able to sense it, but it's almost like she was wearing the pendant again. She feels completely human. Did something go wrong with the magic?

If she doesn't, there will be nothing to stop shifters from challenging her. There's a law that says she has to be strong enough not to cower even to the most alpha shifters. Part of the ceremony calls for any shifter who wishes to challenge to step forward. No one ever has because they can always feel how powerful the king or queen is, but Colbie doesn't feel like a shifter at all, and it won't take long for that to spread through the shifter population.

Hunter shifts, and we make our way back to the neutral zone and the night watch headquarters. He lands on the reinforced roof, and I climb down as he shifts back. Neither of us waste any time hurrying down to brief the commander on what happened.

Bryson is relieved that the new royal has appeared and commands our whole team to return to the palace. "Fuck, Gryff isn't here," I mutter to Hunter as we take our leave and head to our apartment to gather Liam and Gem.

"He's just going to have to catch up. I'm sure Dad will let him know where we are once he returns." I wince at the thought of being caught in the crossfire of Bryson's anger, but Gryff brought it on himself. He can lie in the bed he made.

We find Gem and Liam watching television in our apartment. "Where's the coffee? What took you so damn long?" Liam frowns at our empty hands. Heck, I'd completely forgotten that's what we were doing. We worked late last night and all needed the caffeine hit this morning, even though we weren't working again until this afternoon.

"The new shifter royal has made themselves known," I announce, and that has both of them sitting up straight, paying attention.

"Holy crap, when? Where?" Gem demands at the same time Liam asks, "Who?"

"You aren't going to believe this," I tell them as Hunter goes into his room and starts packing a bag. We'll be staying at the palace for the near future, so we're going to need to take some of our things there. "Remember the pretty little baker?"

"No…" Gem whispers, understanding what I mean straight away, but Liam just screws up his face in confusion.

"What about her? What does she have to do with the new royal?"

I roll my eyes at our bear bond mate. God, sometimes he's so dense. "Colbie is the next shifter queen. When we went in for coffee, Violet made her tell us. She needed an escort to the palace."

Liam's confusion disappears as his expression turns to a scowl. "You're kidding."

"Huh. Maybe that's why my phoenix was so

insistent we return to the bakery. He instinctively knew."

I wouldn't put it past him. Gem's phoenix has magic on levels we can't even begin to comprehend. It's like he's lived a thousand lives and just knows stuff.

"Fucking great, and now we have to make sure she doesn't get herself killed between now and being crowned. Has there ever been a more pathetic human who was chosen? Jesus, what was Aramis thinking?" Liam puts his head in his hands and props his elbows on his knees, shaking his head.

"Dude, what the fuck?" I smack his shoulder. "What is your fucking problem with her?"

He stands up and presses his chest against mine, getting in my face. "You know this changes nothing. You can't start anything with her, even if she's a shifter now. She's the queen and has chosen mates, and we are still waiting for ours. If I can't fuck around with Gianna, then you assholes have to keep your fucking paws off the queen, which means we'll protect her and nothing else."

"Whoa, no one said anything about fucking the queen." Gem places a hand on Liam's chest and gives him a push. Liam snarls and spins, heading to his room to pack his own bag.

"Fuck, what an asshole," I grumble.

"He isn't wrong," Gem murmurs quietly so Liam can't hear him. Nobody needs him gloating.

I sigh heavily and rub my chest. My wolf's

whining and pacing is becoming painful. "I know. It's going to be a fucking nightmare. Lucas told us we need to help her with her shift."

Gem's expression would be comical in its horror if it wasn't so tragic. "He wants us to teach her how to shift? What the fuck is he thinking?"

"He's not thinking. We'll either have to get her clothes that shift with her or hand the job off to someone else. I can't spend hours at a time getting naked with her without my cock reacting," I admit, and I can tell he feels the same way. She's gorgeous, and I can imagine what she looks like without any clothes on. Even now, my cock is stirring in my pants at the imaginary image.

Gem scrubs a hand over his face as Hunter returns. "I doubt any of us would be able to. Despite Liam's arguments, I could feel his attraction to the baker when we were there last week. None of us are immune to her."

"Let's not worry about it now. She was still unconscious when we left, and we still need to grab some of her things and then return to the palace. There will be time to worry about the rest once she wakes up." Hunter returns from his room with a duffle bag slung over his shoulder.

"She's unconscious? Why?" Gem asks, and Hunter and I exchange a glance.

"We don't know. They are waiting on the palace physician to look her over, but it might be better if you do. Your phoenix can do its healing thing," I tell Gem who quickly agrees.

"Yeah, of course. Hopefully we can help her. It might just be magic overload. That sometimes happens to mythical shifters when they first receive their animal. Maybe she has a mythical creature."

Neither Hunter nor I mention the fact that we can't feel an animal inside her at all, let alone a mythical one. Gem and I both head toward our own bedrooms and pack our bags.

"What about Gryff?" I call out, wondering if one of us should pack a bag for him.

"Fuck him," Gem replies. "He can pack up his own shit. We aren't his errand boys who are at his beck and call."

"But you wish you were," Liam retorts, stirring the pot, and I hear a muffled, "Ow!" Hunter probably smacked him on the back of the head. I close my eyes and inhale deeply. This is going to be a fucking disaster. Our once harmonious bond group is a fucking mess. How are we supposed to keep ourselves together as a unit on top of protecting the queen and helping with her training, all while I have to ignore my raging attraction to her? The next couple of weeks are going to suck.

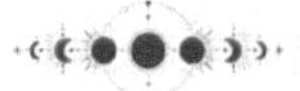

We stop in at the bakery to ask Colbie's grandparents about grabbing her stuff. We don't share with them that Colbie is unconscious and unresponsive, since there's no need to worry them just yet.

Jenny, Colbie's grandmother, accompanies us back to her apartment. As we enter through the foyer, an older woman who looks very much like Colbie, but with harsher eyes, intercepts us.

"Who is this, Mother? Where is Colbie?" she demands, putting her hands on her hips and blocking the way to the elevator.

I hear a muffled, "Goddess save us," from Jenny, but she smiles at the woman. "Malina, these men are here to collect a few of Colbie's things to take to her in the palace."

"Well, why isn't she here? She can collect her own damn things before she presents herself to the palace. I have her dress ready and waiting." She tries to peer around us like Colbie might appear from somewhere. "Is she waiting in the car? Go get her. Trust her to make this all about her. She has no thought toward me and everything I've done for her," she snaps, looking at Liam who crosses his arms and gives her his dead eyes.

"Ma'am, please move to the side and remember you are talking about our queen. Have some respect," he says, and I can feel through our bond that he's barely keeping a lid on his temper. Despite his misgivings toward Colbie, he respects her position as queen and won't have anyone else speaking negatively about her. In his current mood, though, it wouldn't take much to push him over the edge, and arresting the queen's mom probably isn't going to do him or her any favors. I step up and grip his shoulder, giving him a squeeze.

"Why don't you run back to the palace and get rid of some of that pent-up energy?" I word it like a suggestion, but he knows it isn't. He tears his dead gaze away from Colbie's mom, growls aggressively at me, then spins and leaves. I can practically feel him telling me to go fuck myself through our bond. I want to snigger with amusement, but that will only upset Colbie's mom more. I turn my attention back to her and find she is berating poor Jenny.

"I can't believe you let her go without me. You've always been too soft on her. I spent all night slaving over a suitable outfit, and now all that hard work is ruined."

To Jenny's credit, she keeps her temper in check and pushes past her daughter, pressing the button to call the elevator.

"Malina, what's done is done. Colbie needed to do it at her own pace, and it has nothing to do with you. Go back to your studio and work on your designs. I'm sure Colbie will invite you to her coronation, so until then, keep yourself busy."

A small screech leaves Colbie's mom's mouth. The three of us are smart enough to know not to engage. We skirt around her and step into the elevator.

"I will not wait. My daughter needs me. You will take me with you when you return to the palace. Colbie needs a familiar face she can trust and take advice from." Malina locks eyes with the three of us, but both Gem and I take a step back, leaving Hunter front and center as the focus of her ire.

"Pussies," he mutters to us, but his shoulders draw back, and his spine stiffens, a small amount of smoke drifting out of his nose. Malina's eye twitches slightly at the sight of it, and she takes a minute step backward, but we can smell her fear, and I see a flat smile stretch across Hunter's lips.

"Don't you know you should never run from a predator?" he says, but his words just seem to fuel her anger.

"I'm not afraid of you. I want to see my daughter." The doors to the elevator start to close, and I let out a small sigh of relief, ready to be done with this infuriating woman. I see why Joseph warned everyone about her now.

She puts a foot out to catch the doors, and they reopen. She crosses her arms and taps her foot, waiting for a response.

"I'm sorry, ma'am, but humans are not permitted to enter the shifter zone without written permission from one of the royals. As that position is currently in transition, all requests are being denied until after the coronation. Jenny is right, I'm sure Her Majesty will send you an invite, until then, you can contact her via phone, since she is still permitted to have that." Hunter doesn't wait for her to argue, using his own foot to nudge hers out of the way, and the doors close. We hear another screech of annoyance, but thankfully, the door blocks most of that out.

The ride up is silent, but in the mirrored walls, I see Jenny wipe at her eyes. She meets my gaze in the mirror. "I'm so sorry. Malina never used to be so self-involved. She used to be sweet and loving just like Colbie, but when she met Colbie's father, all of that changed. She became selfish, both of them caring more about material possessions and success than the more important things in life like love and family. Then Colbie was born, and for a while, I saw my daughter return to the person she used to be. She loved Colbie with all her heart, but then her husband left her for another woman—a woman with more money and power—and it destroyed Malina. Colbie was a constant reminder that Malina was never good enough for the man who promised to love her above all else."

The doors open on Colbie's floor, and we step out. "Shifters and the other supernatural races are lucky in that regard. Your mates are perfect for you. You never have to wonder what might have been or what you did wrong."

She pulls a keycard out and swipes it over the

sensor, and we step into the apartment. The space is filled with Colbie's intoxicating scent, and my mouth waters. Gem grabs the doorframe to steady himself, and more smoke leaks out of Hunter's nostrils as we all try to contain our reaction to it.

"No, Jenny, even the goddess gets it wrong sometimes," Gem says seriously, and I feel his pang of need inside our bond. All three of us know it isn't going to change one damn thing.

TWENTY-TWO

Colbie

The sweet sound of a child singing is the first thing I register as I struggle to wake up. My body aches, and my limbs are so heavy I can barely lift them. I crack an eyelid open, and I wince at the throb my head gives as the light attacks my senses.

"Ugh," I groan and put a hand over my face to block out the offensive brightness as I struggle to sit up.

"Colbie, you're awake! I knew my singing would help." Is that Archie? Why is he sitting on the end of my bed?

A hand on my arm helps me, and I can smell violets—sweet, fresh, and delicate but strong, like I'm sitting in a field of them. "Here, let me help you. Archie, go dim the lights a little." I feel him jump to do as she asked.

Huh, Violet smells like her namesake. I've never noticed before. I feel her put a couple of pillows behind my body as I drag it up the bed. Huffing from exertion, I lean back against them and try to crack my eyes open again. This time, I have more success, and I feel a small body jump back onto my bed as Archie appears in my line of sight, grinning like a loon.

"Colbie, did you miss me like I missed you? I told my papa that you and I are going to get married, but we're going to have to wait until I'm a little older, okay? Papa says I need to finish high school first, but you can live here with me, and we can hang out and play video games. I bet because you're going to be my wife, Papa and Mama will even let me play Shifter Quest if you ask them to."

Violet giggles as I try to wrap my head around everything that just came out of Archie's mouth. Before I can even form a response, the door to my room flies open, and I flinch back in surprise. Standing there is a gorgeous blonde woman who's about my height and age, with beautiful, deep ocean blue eyes that look fairly freaking mad at the moment, but she's not glaring at me. Instead, her attention is on the boy on my bed. He shrinks in on himself and holds out his hand, grabbing mine and mumbling, "Uh-oh."

"Archer Lucas Frankland. What did I tell you

about leaving Colbie be?" She storms over to the bed and looks down at him.

His hand shakes in mine, but I see him steel his spine and look the woman directly in the eye. "But, Mama, you and Papa told me that when the people we love are sick, we need to do everything in our power to make them feel better, so I sang to Colbie just like you sing to me when I'm sick, and she woke up." He sounds proud, and I see his mother melt at the super sweet words. Gosh, this kid is adorable. Heck, maybe I should wait for him to leave high school. He's ten times more charming than any adult male I've ever dated.

She chuckles and ruffles his hair, all the tension draining out of her body. "I can see she is awake. That must have been some powerful singing. Good job."

"Colbie, this is Princess Gracelin," Violet murmurs from the side where she's been watching the action, struggling to contain her amusement.

My attention sharpens as she mentions the woman's name. I look closer, and I recognize the familiar features of my old childhood friend in this elegant woman's face.

Gracelin turns her attention to me, and she studies me with the same intense scrutiny. She gestures for Archie to move over and make space then takes a seat in the bed, grabbing my other hand that Archie isn't currently clinging to and giving it a squeeze. "Hello, Colbie. I don't know how to thank you for what you did for my son."

"I remember you," I murmur, and she nods.

"Yes, we were friends a long time ago," she confirms, and another flash of locked away memories flutters through my mind like an old movie reel —tea parties, hide-and-seek, snuggling on the couch watching movies and eating popcorn, playing board games and laughing and shouting over winning or losing, then the heartache and tears of realizing my friends were gone and never coming back. My mother told me I had to go to my grandparents if I was going to cry every time the queens came and didn't bring their children. She said I wasn't special enough to be their friends any longer. Fuck, that hurt. How could she have been such a bitch to me? I had obviously locked all of that away.

"And you went away without saying goodbye and didn't come back," I say flatly, and her eyes shine with unshed tears.

"Yes, we did. Our mothers thought it would be better for all of us to have a clean break. Your mother hadn't told you we were shifters, and ours were worried we would shift in front of you and scare you. Apparently, we were pretty cocky once we gained control of our shifts." She winces. "They were probably right, especially Gryffin. He shifted as often as he could and liked to scare the castle staff by jumping out at them. Gretchin wasn't much better. They turned it into a competition to see who could get the loudest shrieks. They were menaces." The affection in her tone tells me how much she loves her brother and sister.

The door bangs open, and another girl walks in. This one is tall and slender but looks strong. Her black hair is shaved close to her head, and her dark skin glimmers in the low light. She has the same deep, ocean blue eyes as Gracelin, but they are currently glaring at her. "Gracelin, are you telling tall tales? I'm almost certain you were the one who started that game and convinced Gryffin and me to play it."

"Gretchin, keep your voice down. Poor Colbie only just woke up. She doesn't need your harpy tones in her ears," Gracelin scolds her sister who walks closer to us, her attention turning to the boy on the bed.

"Weren't you told to stay away?" She lifts one elegant eyebrow before tickling Archie. He dissolves into giggles and throws his arms around her neck, hugging her tightly. She pretends to choke like she can't breathe and flops down on the bed too. It's getting awfully crowded on my bed. If Violet joined us, we would have the makings of a slumber party. We just need popcorn and movies.

Violet clears her throat, getting everyone's attention.

"Uh-oh, we're busted," Gretchin whispers to Archie, who giggles again. Gretchin turns her attention to me and smiles widely, and I have a vivid memory of her smiling at me just like that when we were kids, except back then, she had braces.

"Hey, Colbie, looks like we're going to get to hang out again." I blink a couple of times, and once again, Violet clears her throat.

"Is someone going to tell the king and queens that Colbie is awake? We were instructed to let them know as soon as she woke up."

Gracelin and Gretchin exchange a glance, and both shrug, neither of them volunteering for the job.

"Not it," they exclaim together, and my friend rolls her eyes in exasperation.

"What happened?" I ask Violet. "The last thing I remember is stepping over the threshold of the palace and then excruciating pain."

"That was the royal magic shifting to your body," Violet tells me.

"Is it supposed to be that painful? Nobody warned me I would black out." I'm pretty freaking annoyed that no one explained what would happen.

Gracelin purses her lips. "Apparently what happened to you was nothing like what Dad experienced when it was his turn."

"And what exactly is the shifter royal magic? Am I a shifter now? Does it mean I can do other things? I can't believe I never thought to ask these questions before I stepped into this place."

"Yes, you should now have the ability to shift into an animal," Gretchin tells me, but she frowns as she says this. "To be honest, though, I can't feel your animal at all." She looks to Gracelin and then Violet for their opinions, and both of them shake their heads. "We should all be able to sense your inner animal, even if we don't know what it is. Our dad was the most powerful shifter because of the magic, and you could feel him before he even walked into the room."

"You can't feel anything?" I ask, my heart rate speeding up with my panic. What if the magic didn't find me worthy?

All three of them shake their heads, and tears well in my eyes.

"No, don't cry, Colbie." Archie throws himself into my lap and wraps his little arms around my neck. His hug feels nice, so I hug him back as I wipe the stupid tears away.

"I don't even know why I'm crying. I didn't want this in the first place. Maybe there really was a mistake."

"Dad will be able to help, and I'm sure he will be able to coax your animal out. That's another part of the shifter magic—the ability to control all shifters' shifts, not to mention the ability to help a human who has been bitten by a shifter to complete their transition. Shifters who decide to marry humans will petition you for permission to change them. It's not permitted without permission because a human will go mad without royal magic to help them through their first change."

I try to take in everything Gretchin just explained, but I'm stuck on the first bit. "If I'm supposed to have all that magic now, then how is your dad going to help me?" I ask, and Gracelin smiles.

"Until you are crowned, you both share the magic. It gives Dad the ability to guide you through everything until your coronation."

"And that doesn't happen until you pick your mates," Violet adds, clapping her hands. "Have any presented themselves for selection yet?" she asks the two princesses, sounding excited. "I can't wait to see who is chosen."

Again, Gracelin and Gretchin exchange a glance, and my stomach rolls with worry. "Not yet." Gracelin forces a smile, and Violet's excitement drops.

"It's been hours since Colbie arrived. Why haven't any marked possible mates arrived at the castle?"

"Oh God, the magic really did go wrong, didn't it?" I groan, and Archie squirms in my lap, patting my cheeks.

"Don't worry, it's because they know you're going to marry me," he reassures me, and I smile weakly at him. Gosh, he's a sweet kid. I hope he stays this way.

"Like I said, let's wait until we see Dad to start

to worry. How about you get up, take a shower, and put on some fresh clothes? Then, we can go find everyone and get to the bottom of this. It's almost dinnertime, and we were hoping you would join us." Gracelin takes my hand and gives it a squeeze.

"Yeah, don't worry, Colbie, the three of us have your back." Gretchin waves to her sister and Violet. Violet's mouth rounds with a kind of awe that makes me want to smile.

"Me too? Are you sure? My family isn't from the palace's social circle," she asks, and Gretchin scoffs, "Thank fuck."

Gracelin screws up her nose. "We never liked any of those snooty bitches anyway. They are only friends with us in the hope that our brother and his bond might look their way. The sooner their mate gets marked, the sooner we'll find out who our real friends are. It will be nice having two friends who don't care who he is."

"It can't be that bad," I argue, remembering how nice both girls were when we were kids. Surely they can't have changed so significantly over the years. Hell, Archie's lovely, so surely that tells me what kind of person his mother is.

"You wait. They'll all be kissing your ass soon enough," Gracelin warns me.

"Or turning on you," Gretchin mutters, and my nausea turns to dread.

"I'm not good at games," I say, and Gretchin

hops off the bed and grabs Archie off my lap before pulling her sister up.

"Luckily we are. Shifters can be real assholes, always posturing and trying to prove who is the strongest, and it's no different here in the castle. We will teach you, but first, get cleaned up. The best way to start is to look fucking fabulous, and we can definitely help with that." Gretchin points at a closed door that I'm assuming is the bathroom, so I push the blankets off, and Violet jumps up to help me. She holds my arm, my body still a little shaky from all the magic, and escorts me to the shower.

"You supervise so she doesn't pass out in there, and the three of us will pick something for her to wear," Gracelin instructs Violet, who nods her agreement.

"Oh, I didn't bring anything with me," I tell her, and she waves me off.

"Don't you worry. Part of the magic fills your closet for you, and we sent someone to collect your things from your grandparents. We will have you looking like a queen in no time."

With no arguments left, I let the girls steamroll me. I must admit it is much more pleasant than letting my mother do the same thing. There is laughter and fun as I reconnect with my old friends and get to know Violet and my future husband— which is how Archie insists I refer to him—better.

TWENTY-THREE

Colbie

Violet ushers me into the bathroom and turns on the light. Unlike the bedroom, which I really didn't get a chance to gawk at, the bathroom is fully on display in the bright light.

"Wow," Violet mutters as the two of us gape at the opulence. The bathroom is made of pink veined marble tiles with gold accents. There's a large, sunken tub in the middle of the room big enough to swim in, as well as a huge shower area behind a glass wall with four separate showerheads. There's a separate toilet, fluffy towels hanging from the towel bars, and shelves filled with all manners of luxurious bath products.

"I'm afraid to touch anything," I tell her, and she giggles nervously.

"I don't blame you, but I have a feeling the other two won't wait, so I would hurry up if I were you. Do you want me to wait in case you're still unsteady?"

I shake my head and remove my top and unbutton my jeans. "No, I think I'm good," I tell her, but her attention is not on my face. It's farther down, and she's frowning.

"Didn't you take that off before you stepped into the palace?" She points at my neck, and when I look down, my eyebrows jump in surprise. The pendant Nox gave me to hide the marks is back around my neck.

"Yes, I shoved it in my pocket. I don't remember putting it back on."

"Then how is it around your neck again?" she asks, sounding mystified and a little excited.

"I have no idea."

"Do you think that's why we can't feel your animal? It hid the marks, so who's to say it isn't masking the fact that you're a shifter."

"I don't know, we can give it a try though." I lift my hand to remove it, but Violet stops me.

"How about you take a shower and get ready first in case it is masking your animal, and when you remove it, you pass out again? Feeling your animal for the first time, especially if it's a mythical creature, can be very draining. It's going to fight with you to shift."

I drop my hand. "That's probably a good idea. I

don't need to pass out half naked and have to have someone carry me back to my bed." I think about Brodie, who I'm almost certain caught me the first time. He was standing beside me when the magic hit me. I would be mortified if they had to come back again and I was half naked.

"Alright, I'll leave you to it. There's a robe over there to put on when you're finished." She points out a hook hanging on the wall near the vanity. A big fluffy white robe hangs from it with a pair of fuzzy slippers sitting below it. "Come out when you're done. I'll make sure the princesses don't go too crazy with the outfit."

They were both wearing dresses fit for royalty, and Archie was dressed in slacks and a nice shirt, so I guess the dress code here at the palace is way more formal than I'm used to.

Violet doesn't wait for a response and leaves me alone for the first time since I woke up. I heave out a huge breath. I'm glad she's here, but I'm also glad to be able to have a moment to lose my shit quietly without anyone to see.

I strip off all my clothes, leaving the pendant on, and climb under the spray of water, groaning with how good the hot water feels against my aching body. I let my head hang, and tears fall as everything that happened so far catches up with me. God, I hope Violet is right and the pendant is just blocking the power. I have no idea how it got back around my neck. I don't think any of the others put it there, so I'm assuming the magic itself did, but why? Is it to make me seem powerless so people underestimate me, or is it to protect me from the huge influx of power and the possible animal inside me?

I'm anxious to finish up and try to take it off. I'll be devastated if the magic has gone wrong and I'm a dud. Although I didn't choose this or want it, it will be even worse if I was found unworthy. I'll be mortified, and there is no way I could ever face my mom again. She would be so ashamed. If it turns out I don't have magic, I'll give up my life in the neutral zone and move to the human one. Maybe Nox and I could live happily there together.

As much as I want to stand here and drown out the world, I wash and get out, not willing to risk the two princesses barging in and bossing me around. I'm pretty sure neither of them knows the meaning of boundaries.

Drying off, I wrap the robe around my body, tie it off, and walk out to my fate. The three of them don't mess around, and soon, I'm polished and coiffed into perfection, with the help of two ladies' maids who dry and do my hair and makeup.

They are dismissed, and I stare at myself in the mirror, awed with the result. "Holy cow." I can't believe what I'm seeing. They put me in a gorgeous long dress that is as simple as it is beautiful. It's a stunning lavender color with black and silver accents embroidered on the bodice. It has a full skirt and long sleeves, with a scooped neckline showing off the pendant on my neck.

Violet has also been polished and scrubbed, Gretchin shoving her into the shower after me and finding her an appropriate outfit as the queen's chief advisor, which is just a fancy name for the queen's best friend and confidant, which suits her perfectly. Despite only knowing her for a week, I'm clinging to her familiarity like a barnacle on a ship. Her dress is not as full and has short sleeves with a scooped neckline, and it's a lovely emerald green, which looks great with her blonde hair.

"Violet said that pendant was masking your marks." Gracelin points at the cord around my neck. "And it might be the reason we can't feel your animal."

My eyes drift to the missing marks on my wrists. The pendant is still doing its job.

"Yeah, a friend gave it to me so I could have a couple of extra days to get my affairs in order," I admit, and Gretchin purses her lips.

"Why don't you take it off, and we'll see if it's the reason we can't feel your animal?" she suggests.

It's just the four of us now. Gracelin sent Archie off when he got bored and restless as we were doing my makeover. He made me promise to sit next to him at dinner, which is where we are headed next— a meal with the king and queens. I freaked out, but the princesses promised me it was just going to be family tonight so I wouldn't be overwhelmed.

Tomorrow night, it will be a more formal meal, which will include advisors and their families so I can meet them and decide if I want to retain the same council the king used or create my own. It will also include any mates who have appeared with marks from the goddess.

I grimace when I hear this, but I am resigned to my fate. Maybe I'll feel instant attraction to them like Gracelin told me her dad did with their moms.

I brace myself for devastation but lift the pendant over my head and pass it to Gretchin, who's waiting with her hand outstretched. She winces when the pendant hits her hand.

"Fuck, that is powerful. It instantly deadens my connection with my panther," she mutters. "It's awful." She tosses it on the vanity, but I'm too busy dealing with the influx of power inside my chest. It isn't excruciating like the first time, but it's heavy and intrusive and feels like it's clawing to get out of my body. I double over and grunt in pain, trying to breathe through the sensation. Eventually, it calms down, though its presence remains very much there.

When I get my breathing under control and open my eyes, which I slammed shut, I'm speechless to find all three girls on their knees in front of me with their heads bowed.

"What the hell?" I ask, and Gracelin raises her head and looks at me without meeting my eyes.

"Your power is unlike anything I've ever felt. It forced the three of us to our knees. It's a little easier now, but I think you're going to have to command us to rise," she tells me, sounding awed.

"Please get up," I beg and hold out a hand to help Violet rise.

"Fuck me, you pack a punch," Gretchin says, smoothing out her dress. "I can't wait to see what your animal is. I bet it's a beast."

"I don't know how to control it," I tell them, rubbing a spot on my chest.

"That will come easier. You will learn to contain it when you don't need it and let it out on command, but for now, I think wearing the pendant would be smart. Having the element of surprise is a good idea. If people don't know how powerful you are, they might underestimate you. We can see who really supports you and who has ambitions beyond their station," Gracelin suggests, and Gretchin nods enthusiastically, so I do as they ask, picking up the pendant and placing it over my head. The heavy weight of the power is smothered, but I can still feel a remnant of it pushing to break free.

All three women sigh with relief. "Oh, that helps. We can feel your animal, but the immense power has been dimmed," Violet tells me when I look at her for confirmation.

"This is exciting." Gretchin claps her hands, sounding gleeful. "Challenge day might actually be interesting."

"Challenge day?" I start to feel a rush of panic, and Violet takes pity on me.

"Although the queen is chosen by the goddess, she allows her people some autonomy. Challenge days let people challenge the chosen to fight for their position to prove they have what it takes to rule over shifters. We're a violent, aggressive bunch, and you need to be able to bring them to their knees on command, which you obviously have no problem doing." Gretchin waves at where they were all just kneeling. "But if nobody knows that, then challenge day could be fun. Normally no one bothers because they can feel how powerful the king or queen is. You are an anomaly, and I wonder if there is a reason for that."

"Right? I bet it's to weed out the loyal and not so loyal. Nobody who was loyal would dare dream of challenging the goddess's decision, but there are always a few who dare to think they know better," Gracelin muses.

"I don't know the first thing about fighting in human form, let alone as a shifter." I feel sick and put a hand over my chest where the power inside me throbs with aggression, like they need me to hand over the reins and they will take care of everything.

"Then it's lucky we have two weeks. The two of us and a team of experienced night watch shifters will get you up to speed." Gracelin tucks her arm into mine and leads me across the room. Gretchin hurries ahead and opens the door, while Violet trails behind. She chews on her lip with worry, but she stays quiet, happy to defer to the two experienced princesses.

"Don't worry, we have your back no matter what," Gretchin assures me as she leads us through the palace at a pace that doesn't allow me to look around all that much. "We will make sure you come out on top and take out all those who oppose you. It's going to be a blast."

Her idea of fun and mine vary greatly, but it feels good to have the three of them supporting me. I feel like maybe this isn't going to be as bad as I thought it would be.

Dinner isn't as small as I hoped. When we get to the dining room, I am announced.

"Ladies and gentlemen, Her Majesty, Queen Colbie Karridge, accompanied by Princesses Gracelin and Gretchin and Lady Violet," a man standing in the doorway of the dining room says loudly, causing everyone at the table to stand and watch as we enter the room.

The king and three queens are there, as well as Archie and a man who I assume is his father when Gracelin joins him and kisses him passionately. Also standing at the table are Brodie and Hunter, as well as the two other men I recognize from Night Watch One. There's also another large man who looks very much like Hunter with a petite woman by his side, and two young adults.

Violet stiffens next to me, and I can practically feel her distress. Before I can ask her what's wrong, Lucas hurries over and offers me his arm.

"Please allow me to escort you," he says kindly and walks me to the head of the table next to his seat, and he pulls out the chair. I sit, and he pushes it in before returning to his seat, which is next to mine. Violet and Gretchin both take seats next to one another farther down the table.

"Please let me formally introduce ourselves. I believe you know my wives, but I'm Lucas. It is very lovely to finally meet you, Colbie." The king inclines his head gracefully, and I feel like he means what he is saying.

The three queens also murmur their greetings. Layla, who is on my other side, grabs my hand and gives it a squeeze of encouragement.

"Oh, I can feel your animal now," Mia murmurs quietly, "but there's still something that's slightly different about it."

"None of that now. Let's enjoy dinner first, and we can talk about official stuff later. I'm sure Colbie is starving. She slept right through lunch." Evie frowns at her co-wife, who apologizes.

Lucas continues his introduction. "Sitting next to Gracelin is her mate, Adam." The big, brawny man gives me a wave. Next to him, Archie bounces up and down on his chair. "And I believe you've met our grandson, Archer, before."

I smile at my young friend who waves enthusiastically and then tugs on his dad's shirt. "Didn't I tell you how pretty she is, Papa? She and I are going to get married. She agreed to wait until I finish high school. Colbie, you promised to sit next to me." Unfortunately for him, Adam was taking a drink when Archie announced this, and he chokes on it in surprise.

"Archie, honey, Queen Colbie's mates are chosen for her by the goddess," Gracelin says gently, and he stops bouncing, crosses his arms, and pouts his bottom lip.

"But I love her," he argues plaintively.

"And I love you," I assure him, seeing he's close to tears. "You don't need to be my husband for me to love you," I tell him, and I can see him thinking.

"Fine, I will be your sidepiece."

The table explodes into laughter and surprise at his announcement. I'm slightly bemused at a child knowing that kind of term and using it correctly.

Mia frowns. "Where on earth did you hear that?" she questions her grandson who leans in conspiratorially.

"I heard Councilor Mason telling one of the maids that she was his sidepiece before they cuddled and kissed in the supply closet down the hall from Grandpa's office. I don't want to kiss Colbie, but cuddles are nice, and she said we could play Shifter Quest together."

I said nothing of the sort, but the mischievous little kiddo is resourceful.

The laughter cuts off, and there are looks of surprise all around the table and a number of rumbled growls, which sound slightly aggressive.

"Councilor Mason is a mated man," Lucas tells me quietly.

"Mated vows are sacred to shifters, so being in a relationship outside of them is taboo," Layla adds. "It's the ultimate insult. It's disgusting, and it marks a shifter as untrustworthy. I would suggest that Councilor Mason not make the cut for your new council."

I make a mental note. I hate cheaters anyway, but it sounds like it's worse as a shifter.

Lucas clears his throat, trying to ease the awkward atmosphere.

"I know you know Brodie and Hunter, but what about the other two rascals, Liam and Gem?" He points to both men who incline their heads. Gem gives me a wink, and I can see Liam is trying and failing to contain his scowl.

"We've met before," I tell the king who continues.

"Our son is a part of their team, but he couldn't be here for this dinner," he says through slightly clenched teeth, and I get the feeling he's not impressed. "The five of them will be your security until you are crowned. They will also help you with shifter 101. They are going to be your go-to for any questions you might have, and of course you can come to any of us as well." He gestures to himself and his wives. "I will be giving you lessons on the politics of ruling, and the girls will be teaching you all the etiquette. It's exhausting, and a lot of it is mind-numbingly boring, but it's all essential.

"Lastly, let me introduce General Bryson, his wife Sable, and his son and daughter, Talon and Ember. He is the night watch and shifter army general and one of your advisors if you choose to keep him. I can't give him a reference worthy enough to encompass how helpful he has been, and despite the fact that he's my best friend and confidant, he's also very good at his job. You can also go to him for advice."

"He is also Hunter's father," Layla murmurs quietly so I have that important information. "They are all dragons and extremely loyal and protective. They are a good family to have as your support system."

I give a small nod of acknowledgement for her recommendation before smiling at the family.

"It's lovely to meet you all, and I look forward to getting to know you over the coming weeks," I say, hoping I'm not portraying how nervous I am. The four of them give me polite but genuine welcomes, and the food starts to come out, servers placing plates in front of us and offering a range of drinks.

Nothing official is discussed over dinner, and instead, we enjoy the meal, the conversation light and flowing authentically. I thought I'd be uncomfortable around all these strangers, but I almost feel a kinship with them, like we've known each other for years instead of only just a few hours. There's laughter and teasing, and I don't think I've ever enjoyed a meal quite so much.

TWENTY-FOUR

Colbie

Once dessert is cleared away, Lucas turns the conversation back to me. "Colbie, I was wondering if you would like my help to learn to shift? I think it would be a good idea if we don't leave it too long before you shift for the first time. You might psych yourself out. If you're too much inside your head, it's more difficult," he suggests, and I agree.

"There's a special room inside the palace where we help shifters shift for the first time. It's magic proof to protect the rest of the castle in case a mythical's magic gets away from them, or they have trouble controlling their animal. Shall we all move there?" Layla stands up, and it seems to me she's inviting the whole group to observe, but I don't know how I feel about that.

I bite my lip with worry, scared to question her, but then I remember I'm queen. I don't need to be afraid of these people. "You want me to get naked in front of everyone?"

My question shocks Layla, but she quickly shakes her head. "Oh my goodness, no. I'm sorry you thought that. That dress is shift proof, which means you can shift in it without worrying about it being destroyed. It's a special fae magic that's applied to the fabric."

"Shifters aren't too worried about getting naked, but we are a little more reserved in the palace. A clothing optional policy is not something we encourage. You never know who might be wandering about. We regularly get visitors from other kingdoms and representatives from the human zone. We don't want to scare anyone off with naked bits flapping about," Gracelin's husband, Adam, explains with a wink, and I heave out a sigh of relief.

"Thank goodness."

There's an awkward silence, and I look around the table, trying to gauge what it's about.

Gretchin scoffs and throws up her hands. "What no one wants to tell you is after the challenge part of the coronation ceremony, you will have to shift to show the shifter population you can. You will have to strip down naked to do that so no one can accuse you of using fae magic or a witch charm to shift."

"Naked in front of everyone?" I ask, not sure I heard her right.

She nods and grins. "Yeah, but by then it won't even be an issue, you'll see."

I'm not sure she's right about that, but I'm not going to think about it for now.

Lucas offers me his arm again. "Come on. Aren't you dying to find out what you can shift into? I know I was." I take his arm and allow him to lead me through the palace.

"I think I'm going to need a tracker to help remember my way around," I murmur to him as I take in all the beautiful furniture and elaborate art on the walls, trying to make note of landmarks for reference, and he chuckles.

"I was the same way. We will do as much as we can to help you, I promise, before we take our leave and move to our new home. It's the least we can do. The old bag who was queen before me was a bitch who didn't want to give up her power. She was not helpful in the least. She ripped my animal out, which was excruciating, and then disappeared to her retirement home without a backward glance. I had to figure everything out on my own. Thankfully, I had the girls to help me."

"Do you mind if I ask you about them and your relationship?" I look behind us. The rest of the party is following farther back. I think they are giving us time to talk privately.

"Of course, ask me anything," he encourages me.

"How soon did they arrive after you were marked, and how long did you have to decide?" I ask, not sure if I really want the answer to these questions, but knowing I need them.

"Well, I didn't get the luxury of hiding my marks when they appeared." He doesn't sound mad, just wistful. "I was at a party in the human zone, watching the magic happen on a giant screen, and when they appeared, I was surrounded by humans and escorted to the border where a night watch team met me and brought me here." He gestures to his face. "There was no chance I was going to be able to hide them no matter what happened."

"And the people selected as your mates?" I ask.

"In my case, it was all women. I'm not sexually attracted to men, so the goddess didn't choose any for me, though that hasn't always been the case in the past. They started appearing within hours of my arrival at the castle. All of them were invited to stay so I could get to know them, but I didn't need to. I knew the moment I met my three that they were the ones for me. It really was effortless. I tried to give the others a chance, but I knew in my heart whom I was going to mate with."

"How many were there in total?" I ask.

"I think twelve women were marked, but as soon as I made up my mind, even before I told anyone, those marks disappeared, and they were asked to leave the palace. I'm sure you will have more to choose from since you will have six mates," he tells me, and I stop mid-step, and he jostles to stop next to me.

"I'm sorry, what did you say?" I ask him, and he winces.

"Has no one said anything about that? Damn. There are six consort crowns. The magic also dictates the amount of mates a king or queen has. Mostly it has been three, which they say reflects the amount the goddess has, but a couple of times in history, it's been two or four."

"How many had six?" I ask, and he grimaces.

"None."

I feel nauseous, and I put a hand against my stomach. "I couldn't even manage a relationship with one man, let alone six. I can't do this." My breathing starts to rush in and out of my lungs, and I feel a little lightheaded in my panic.

"Breathe, Colbie." A steady hand on my back helps me focus a little better, and the soothing, commanding tone helps get my breathing under control. "In and out slowly." I blink and focus on who's giving me instructions. Hunter's bright green eyes are glowing. I've noticed they only do that when a shifter's emotions are heightened. I get lost in them, letting them ground me and help reel in the panic.

Swaying a little, I fill my lungs before releasing them and realize my panic has settled and a wave of calm now rolls over me. There's a soothing, purring kind of sound coming from somewhere, and I look around for a cat, but then I step closer to Hunter and lean in, listening to his chest. "Are you purring?"

His cheeks turn a little pink, and he steps back, his nostrils flaring. "Yes, sorry. My dragon was trying to make you feel better," he admits, and out of the corner of my eye, I see his mother and the queens exchange a curious glance.

"It helped, thank you." I hook my arm through Lucas's again and drag him forward, away from the others, to continue the uncomfortable conversation.

"So how many men have appeared since I've been unconscious? Please tell me I have a decent selection to choose from?" I hiss, still feeling somewhat agitated, though Hunter helped immensely. As I walk away from him, the power in my chest seems to reach out for him, and a yearning sensation takes hold of me, but I ignore it. Surely someone would have mentioned if any of the men at dinner were marked. I certainly didn't see any glaringly obvious wrist shackles.

There's an awkward pause before Lucas sighs and sags slightly. "None."

The nausea and panic return. "What do you mean, none?"

"Now, don't panic. I'm sure they will start arriving tomorrow. I'm thinking maybe the magic going haywire interfered with the process."

We arrive at a large, reinforced door, and he puts his hand over a biometric scanner. "One of tomorrow's jobs is to key you in to all the security around the palace, as well as show you the vault, but for now, I'll open everything for you."

A light flashes, and a small beep rings out as the door unlatches, and we step into a huge, circular room with a large domed roof. It's empty except for a small seating area around one side. The rest of the guests file into the seating area to observe, while Lucas toes off his shoes and gestures for me to do the same.

"Most shoes don't have the same spells as the fabric," he warns. "It's easier if you kick them off so your animal doesn't get tangled up in them when you shift."

I do that and put them off to the side out of the way. Before Lucas can go any further, Gracelin approaches, holding out a black velvet bag. "It's time to remove the charm. Drop it in here, and I'll give it back when you are done," she tells me, and Lucas frowns with confusion.

"What does she mean?" His eyes drift to the pendant and cord around my neck, and his eyes widen with surprise.

"Oh, I hadn't realized you put it back on."

Gracelin nods. "Yes, I think it's part of the spell. It encourages you not to notice it. She was wearing it after the first influx of magic again, and nobody put it back on her. It's why none of you could feel an animal inside her."

"That is some very powerful magic. Where did you get it?" Lucas doesn't sound angry, just curious.

"From a friend in the human zone who has an interest in magic." I don't give him any details, and he doesn't push for them.

I remove the pendant and drop it in the bag. There's a chorus of grunts and shouts of surprise, and when I look up, everyone is once again on their knees with their heads bowed, including the king.

He gapes at me in shock. "I have never felt anything so powerful before in my life."

I coax my animal to ease up on the dominance, and I see exactly when it pulls back. Everyone is able to get to their feet again.

"I'm not sure if I'm going to be able to help you," Lucas admits as Bryson approaches us and Gracelin returns to the viewing area, the bag containing my pendant held away from her body.

Bryson eyes me with caution and curiosity, but it doesn't feel malicious. "Your Majesty, will you allow me to assist the king in coaxing your animal out? I believe it's going to take more than just him."

"Please call me Colbie, and of course, any help I can get is much appreciated."

Lucas shakes his head like he's trying to clear his mind. "I don't know if the two of us will be enough. Whatever she is, its dominance and power are off the charts. I've never felt anything like her before, and I think I've met all the different kinds of shifters over the years."

"What if all the boys help? Surely when faced with that much dominance, we should be able to force a shift."

Lucas nods, and Bryson gestures for the rest of the men to join us. "I'm sorry, Colbie, this is going to hurt, but hopefully with all of us, it should be quick. If I do it on my own, it's only going to draw the shift and pain out."

I nod my understanding as we all move to the center of the room. Bryson and Lucas take their spots, and Adam and the four night watch males fan out around me.

"Everyone, step back a few steps. Let's give the girl room," Mia calls out from her spot, and when I look at her, her eyes are narrowed in concentration, but Evie gives me a thumbs-up and a smile of encouragement.

"You've got this, cupcake," Gretchin shouts, and I raise my eyebrows.

"Cupcake?"

"Meh, you smell like them, so it seems fitting," she replies, and I chuckle nervously but take a small sniff of myself. I can't smell anything, but I appreciate her attempt to distract me.

"Okay, on three I need you to command her to shift, but unlike when you're commanding a regular shifter and you only use a little bit, you need to use as much dominance as you contain. We're actually lucky most of you are on the higher end of the dominance scale, and unlike when you stop once a shifter starts to change, you have to focus on her through the whole shift. The first time is the hardest. Alright, is everyone ready?" Lucas asks after issuing instructions.

He gets nods and murmurs of assent, and then he counts down. I can't stop myself from bracing for the pain again, but there's a throb of reassurance from inside my chest. When Lucas reaches one, there's a loud, echoing boom as the seven men command me to shift.

I was expecting resistance and pain, but what happens is nothing short of miraculous. My body seems to fold into itself, the sensations gentle, calming, and encouraging. I mostly lose track of what's happening, the feelings becoming disorienting, and when I blink my eyes open, my perspective of the world has changed. My view is multifaceted, like I'm seeing through multiple pairs of eyes from all sorts of angles, and it takes my mind a little time to sort it all out, but eventually, it all seems to filter in, and my brain processes everything differently. There's still a sense of myself, but there's an overriding sense of otherness as well—a more animalistic me. A myriad of scents assaults me, and I try to filter through them, but they are confusing, and it's tricky. A few of them make my mouth water, like I want to take a big bite out of whoever smells like that. I lick my lips and do a double take.

"Holy fuck." It's a whisper, but I have no problem hearing it. I swing around to look at the person. With that action, I finally comprehend I have more than one head. "She's a fucking hydra."

I look down and notice I have a huge, serpentine body as large as Hunter's dragon, but I'm skinnier and don't have wings. I'm more streamlined, like I'm designed for gliding or swimming, and I have six heads with long necks. I'm a gorgeous blue green color, which I bet camouflages beautifully in the water. I lift a clawed front leg and try to take a step forward, but I misjudge and stumble and go down hard, my body awkward and uncoordinated. I'm unable to slow or stop the descent.

"Shit, watch out!" The men scatter so they are not trampled or squashed by my massive form.

A mournful wail escapes my mouth as I squeeze my eyes shut in the hopes I can pretend I'm dead, feeling embarrassed beyond belief at how uncoordinated I am. Someone approaches me, and when I open my eyes, Brodie stands there with a look of awe on his face, his Caribbean blue eyes shining with his inner animal. He smells so good, like the woods on a hot summer day—pine and cedar, crisp and refreshing, with a hint of warmth like the sun shining through the trees. He strokes a hand over my head.

"It's okay, we will work on that. By the time we're done with you, everyone will fear the formidable and magical shifter queen," he reassures me.

TWENTY-FIVE

Hunter

I stare with no small amount of shock as Brodie strokes one of the heads of the downed hydra. Holy crap, a six-headed hydra. I don't think there has ever been a hydra shifter in the past. Dad and Lucas are huddled together, whispering aggressively, but the rest of us ignore it.

A sorrowful yowl that is complex in its musical depths comes from all six heads. You can almost hear the embarrassment from the poor creature.

It was nearly comical how uncoordinated she was, and I know exactly how that feels. My first step as a dragon sent me tumbling to the ground, shaking everything in the nearby area. Thankfully the magic in this room stops that from happening. I can't refrain from reaching out to one of the other heads, stroking it gently over its eyebrow ridges much like she had done to my dragon earlier. When I look up, both Liam and Gem are doing the same thing. It's like we are all drawn to her and can't resist trying to comfort her.

Fuck! I snatch my hand away, knowing getting too close to her is just going to lead to heartbreak. No one may have presented themselves with her marks yet, but it's only a matter of time. We need to present a united and neutral party, here to protect her but not influence any of her decisions. It will be hard enough for her to pick a mate with her human instincts still riding her hard. Her new shifter instincts should point her in the right direction though.

Stop stroking the new queen. Have some respect, I snap telepathically to my bond mates.

Liam is quick to listen, scowling at the hydra like she lured him in, but Brodie glares at me. Gem doesn't listen one little bit, but I see flames surrounding his hand, so I'm assuming he's healing her somehow, and I don't berate him.

"Has there ever been a hydra shifter before?" I ask as the queens and Mom approach us carefully. Colbie doesn't move. It's like she's exhausted. Her eyelids on all six heads barely flutter. I'm not sure why, but maybe Gem can get to the bottom of it.

"None recently," my mother answers. She is one of the shifter knowledge keepers and has a wealth of information about the past. "I can't think of any since the war, to be honest. They were one of the first shifters targeted by the humans. They took out a lot of the mythical families because they figured they were the most dangerous." She's staring at our new queen with awe on her face. My mother is basically shockproof, because raising three dragon children fortifies a person against most disasters, so to see her ruffled is slightly amusing.

"What are the hydra's powers?" Queen Layla asks my mother as Gem steps back, removing his hand from the hydra's head.

He is standing at the far one, so he makes his way back over to us. We've all gathered in a little group off to the side. I kind of feel bad talking about Colbie like she's not even here, but I don't think she even notices.

"Is she okay?" King Lucas asks before my mother can answer the queen.

"Colbie is fine. I get the feeling she's embarrassed, and she got a little battered and bruised when she fell. That's a lot of body weight, but she's also exhausted. Don't you remember how draining that first shift is? It's not fair to ask her to shift back just yet. Give her a moment to rest and recharge," he says, his attention on the hydra. He has a contemplative look on his face.

What is it? I ask him telepathically, but instead of answering, he just gives me a small shake of his head. Okay, he doesn't want to talk about it here.

"A hydra's powers are quite impressive. They are virtually unkillable in this form" —Mom waves a hand at Colbie— "which is why the humans targeted them in their two-legged form. To start with, her claws and blood are poisonous, and then there is the ability to breathe acid, which has no neutralizing agent. It can eat through any substance, including metal and armor. Then there's the regeneration, which makes them virtually immortal. On top of all that, there are her fangs. She can bite someone and transfer her venom, which will give them the ability to regenerate, even from death."

"Holy fuck." Dad looks at the new queen with respect.

"There is also one last ability that was a secret only shared amongst other hydras. I've searched everywhere to find what it is, but as far as I know, it died with the last one. It was never written down." Mom sounds frustrated. She always says that no mystery remains unsolved as long as you try hard enough to solve it.

"I think I might know what it is," Gem says, drawing his attention back to the group.

"Did you see something when you were healing her?" Mia pushes impatiently.

"Kind of. Didn't really see something, but I brushed across something inside her psyche—something I don't think she even realizes is there. It was a ball of magic that isn't like any other I've felt before."

The king huffs, and the queens wear expressions

of disappointment. "It's probably just the royal power your feeling," Layla reminds him gently, and he shakes his head vehemently.

"No, I don't think it is. Remember when Gryffin sliced Lucas open during that sparring match and I had to heal him? He has also been hit on the head and had a slight concussion," Gem reminds us. We were fighting as a bond group against Lucas and Dad. It was our assessment to join the night watch. "I felt Lucas's royal magic then, and this is not like that at all."

"Okay, so something new. What do you think it is? Was it similar to anyone else's magic you've felt before?" Mom sounds excited.

"Yes and no." Gem's eyes shift to look at me, Brodie, and Liam, and he frowns before returning his attention to our parents. "I think that maybe Colbie is a dual shifter. I think I can feel another creature inside her."

The gasps and exclamations of surprise echo through the room. "A dual shifter? That hasn't happened since before the war either." My mom rubs her hands together with glee. "This is wonderful."

One of the hydra's heads lifts, like she was listening the whole time. She uses her front legs, which are very much like my dragon's, to push herself upright, gathering her back ones underneath her and lifting her huge body so she towers above us. With her long, elegant necks, she is easily taller than my or my dad's dragons, but her body is more streamlined and not as large as ours.

One of the heads drops down and nudges Gem in the belly, and he stumbles backward and laughs. "She asks that we all move out of the way in case this goes wrong. She's going to try to shift again."

"How is she talking to you telepathically?" Liam scowls. "That only happens between bond mates."

"And us. Kings and queens can talk telepathically to all shifters," he reminds my grumpy bond mate, and that seems to settle him slightly, but he's still eyeing Colbie suspiciously. "Is she going to shift into something new?" Lucas asks as we all move backward again and stand behind the viewing area with my brother and sister, Violet, and the two princesses. Archie has been chatting excitedly this whole time, and the five of them have been distracting him so we could all talk.

"My future wife… sidepiece, is beautiful," he announces to no one in particular. He claps his hands and bounces up and down on his mother's lap. He's right. She is gorgeous. Her whole body isn't covered in scales like mine is, but they do cover her long necks, the sensitive areas behind each of her legs, and beneath her belly. The rest of her looks smooth and shiny, like an aquatic creature, and she glimmers under the lights.

One of her heads dips down, and she licks Archie's cheek. Gracelin pales with worry, but Archie squeals with delight and pushes her away.

"Eww, Colbie, sidepieces don't lick each other."

Brodies snorts and mutters, "Want to make a bet?" Liam slaps him upside the head.

"It's okay, Gracelin, they have to consciously spit their acid. Colbie won't hurt Archie," Mom assures the princess. Fuck, I would be worried about the same thing, but my mom's words seem to ease Gracelin's concern.

Magic seems to permeate the air as Colbie prepares to shift again. It should be instinctual after the first time, and it feels very much like what other shifters feel like before they shift, just way more powerful. My breath gets caught in my lungs, and everyone around me is also having trouble breathing.

She's using too much power! Liam shouts inside our minds. My body shakes as I try to hold off my own shift. Everyone around me trembles as their animals try to push forward. Poor Archie has no chance of resisting. His body reshapes, and a small orange and black tiger cub curls up on Gracelin's lap, whimpering.

Suddenly, the hydra form folds in on herself—there one moment and gone the next. Violet screams, and my brother wraps an arm around her, pulling her into his chest and shielding her eyes. Instead of blood and gore and bits of Colbie spread across the room when the magic clears, there's a large, jet-black wolf curled in on itself, watching us with lavender eyes.

"Holy shit, that looked nothing like our shifts," Brodie mutters and takes an unconscious step forward. I bet his wolf is riding him hard at the sight of another one, but does he want to assert his dominance or submit to her?

"She *is* a dual shifter," Mom says with reverence in her voice.

"Well, this is certainly going to make challenge day interesting," Mia says with a smirk of satisfaction.

Colbie isn't done. Her body shifts again, and this time when the magic clears, she throws around a magnificent mane while stomping a hoof, her large, gorgeous wings stretching out wide.

"A pegasus!" my sister shouts with excitement.

"Wow, not one, but two mythical animals and three different forms." I can't help but hear the worry in Layla's voice. "Poor girl, it's going to take some hard work to get a handle on all those shifts."

The magic activates again, and we all hold our breaths, waiting to see what will happen next. This time, her small, curvy body is lying in the middle of the floor. She appears to be unconscious, and Gem hurries toward her and scoops her up, releasing his healing magic.

"Just even more exhausted. I'm not surprised. I'll take her up to her room, but I recommend we up her intake of food over the next few weeks while she practices. She's going to need all the energy she can get," he says after assessing her body.

"And the sooner she bonds to her mates, the sooner she can take energy from them. Hopefully they start arriving tomorrow, and it's an easy pick like it was for us," Mia says to Lucas, who is watching the new queen with the same kind of worry he has for his own children.

Brodie scowls at her words, but we don't have any right to say anything, and thankfully, he keeps quiet.

"I think she should wear that pendant that suppresses her animals and stops her from shifting. Control is going to be hard to learn, and we don't need her shifting into her hydra inside the palace and bringing it down around our heads," Adam says as he watches his wife stroke a reassuring hand over their son's body.

"Yes, that's a great idea." Gracelin holds out the pouch the pendant is in, and Evie reaches in and pulls it out.

She wrinkles her nose. "Wow, that is powerful. It suppressed my animal by just holding it." She places it over Colbie's head then pulls her hair out, and the tension seems to drain out of the unconscious girl.

"Come on, let's let her rest again. Poor thing has been through so much." Gem follows the queens and my mother out of the test room, followed by our siblings and Violet, leaving my bond group, Dad, and Lucas behind.

"Whoa, so not what I thought was going to

happen," Lucas admits, nervously running his hand through his hair. "A hydra. Who would have thought?"

"At least no one is going to want to fuck with that," Dad points out.

"Damn, how is she going to find any mates who aren't absolutely terrified of her?" Liam smirks meanly. "Let alone six of them."

Brodie glares at him. "Shut the hell up, man. That isn't helpful."

"No, but he's not wrong," I agree reluctantly. "Male shifters are notoriously arrogant. It will be a blow to their ego that their mate is so much more powerful than them."

"Aramis wouldn't choose partners for her who would be resentful. Trust me, whoever she ends up mated to will be the perfect fit," Lucas argues, the voice of experience.

"I think Lucas is right. I can think of half a dozen very powerful shifters in my army who aren't in bond groups, and those are just the ones I know of. Remember, the call goes out across the shifter lands. You'll see, everything will work out like it's meant to." My dad is quick to agree with his friend. "Now, you guys should head off to bed. You have your work cut out for you to get her up to speed with all her abilities. Hunter, talk to your mother, she may be able to find some books with more in-depth information about hydra shifters, not to mention the pegasus abilities. You're going to need to know those too, so you can work with her on them."

I don't have the first clue about pegasus powers, so any help I can get will be appreciated. "Yeah, I'll do that first thing tomorrow morning," I tell him. With that, we all take our leave.

"Oh, and boys, find out where the hell my son is, and when you do, let him know I want to speak to him." Lucas's tone is deadly. The man is usually so easygoing, but I would not like to be in Gryffin's shoes right now.

"He's following up on an anonymous tip about the shifter kids that are still missing. He promised to be back tomorrow. I'll let him know you need to speak to him," Liam says, flat-out lying to the king, and Brodie and I gape at him. It's not like Liam to cover for one of us. He likes to stir shit up and is happy to watch the fallout.

"A tip?" Bryson scowls. "Why did I not know about this?"

"We think it's a wild goose chase, which is why he went on his own. The village he's going to sits at the base of the Aramis Rift. It's unlikely to be true because it's so inhospitable there, but we didn't want to ignore it just in case."

Well, he's not lying about that. The village he is going to is exactly where Liam said, but the reason is wrong. It softens Lucas's anger, though, so Gryff better kiss Liam's ass when he finally returns.

"He better be. We're having a formal dinner to

introduce Colbie to the rest of shifter society tomor-row. It will be broadcast to all of them. It will look like sour grapes if the son of the former king is not in attendance, so make sure he's there." He growls the last bit, his tiger pushing forward.

We assure him we will before the three of us take our leave.

"Fuck, he better be back," Liam growls as we head toward our suite, "or I'll kick his ass myself."

TWENTY-SIX

Gryffin

The door to our apartment swings open, and I enter feeling dejected and resigned. I promised Gem if I didn't have any success this time, I would give up. I was sure I would find something this time, but the village of Zalfari was weird. Most shifter cities and towns coexist peacefully. It doesn't matter what your animal is, you're judged on your individual strength, but in Zalfari, it seemed like what animal you are determines your social status. The head alpha was, ironically enough, a lion shifter name Leon. He was an aggressive asshole who made it clear he wasn't happy I was there, but I could tell he wasn't the most powerful shifter in the village, so how did he end up as the one in charge? He blocked me from questioning a lot of the residents, and I only got to speak to a few, all of which denied anyone with any bond marks that matched mine.

I wasted a whole day getting the runaround and eventually had to give up and return home. I wasn't sad to see the back of that town. It was on the edge of the Aramis Rift, the inhospitable mountain range casting shadows over the snow-covered village. It's the last inhabitable place before the mountain range and is made up of shifters who patrol the border and the tunnel through the mountains that leads to the vampire kingdom. Anyone who tries to get through the rift without using the tunnel never returns. Rumor has it the Aramis Rift is where feral shifters escape to if they want to avoid the death sentence that comes with being turned without help from a royal.

I toss my backpack down next to the couch and look around the obviously empty apartment. Where is everyone? It's supposed to be our night off, so at least some of my bond should be here. I walk into my bedroom and find a note on my bed.

Shifter royal has appeared. We have reported to the palace as requested.

It's Hunters writing. I drop the note, swearing as I hurry to grab my phone out of my bag. It's on silent, and I find half a dozen missed calls and messages from my parents and various members of my bond group. The last message I received is from my sister.

> Gretchin: Dude, you are in so much trouble. Dad is pissed! 💀 💀 💀

I groan and grab my backpack, shoving my phone back in, and hurry out of the apartment. Once I leave the night watch building, I shift, pick up my backpack in my mouth, and run through the neutral zone. It's late, but not late enough for curfew, so there are still a few people about who quickly get out of the way of the large, black and white tiger, so my journey to the shifter zone is quick.

Once I hit the forest, I pick up the pace, my paws easily eating up the distance as I weave my way toward the palace. The scents of the forest invade my nose as I breathe evenly, my tiger not getting tired despite the long distance it has already run today. I can feel small creatures around me, but I ignore the urge to investigate and focus on getting to the palace as swiftly as possible.

I cover the distance in half an hour and slow down and creep carefully into the grounds. I don't set off any alarms because my form is keyed to the magic protecting it, but I also don't want to run into any guards who might delay me further. I head toward the side entrance, but a sound in the stables has me slowing down, dropping my backpack, and creeping forward in a crouch.

I remember Archie was tempted out of the safety of the palace by the stable kittens, and I wonder if he hasn't learned his lesson after what happened the first time. I love my nephew, but he can be a handful. I don't bother shifting, instead moving quietly into the barn, my tiger stalking whoever is in here. If it's just one of the stable hands, I'll melt back into the darkness and continue my journey into the palace, but if it's someone who shouldn't be in here, then they are going to regret it.

I hear a whisper of a voice but can't make out if it's male or female. My whiskers twitch, and an intoxicating scent reaches my nose, making my mouth water. Holy crap, what is that? I want to bury my head in it and roll around until it covers my body. It smells like cupcakes and frosting.

I crawl a little farther, my tail twitching and my ears pricked for any hint of whoever it is. My claws almost ache with the need to grab hold and never let go. What the fuck is wrong with me? As I get closer, I reach out, trying to get a feel for the person who is tucked away in one of the empty stalls. They are definitely a shifter, but a low level one. Their power feels miniscule, and I can finally make out the voice of a woman. She's giggling and talking nonsense, and when I peer through a crack where the door of the stable hinges to the wall, I see her surrounded by kittens. Some are snuggled in, cuddling with her, and others are leaping and playing around her.

My gaze rises to her face, and I'm stunned by how gorgeous she is. Lush, plump lips perfect for nibbling are turned up in a beautiful, serene smile. I can't see the color of her eyes, but her long, dark lashes match the silky mane of jet black hair that flows around her shoulders as slick as a waterfall. She's sitting cross-legged, and her long dress hides her bottom half, but the top half molds to her perfect curves like a lover's hands. The scooped neckline gapes a little as she leans forward, and the tops of her round globes push forward, begging for me to run my tongue over them.

My tiger forces out a chuff, wiggles his ass, and crawls forward playfully, pushing past my control and taking the reins. I can't do anything to stop him, and her sharp intake of breath lets me know she's at least heard him.

"Archie, is that you? If your parents catch you out here, nothing is going to save you this time," she calls out in warning instead of panicking and retreating, which would have triggered my tiger's instinct to chase.

She knows my nephew? Maybe she is palace staff or even his nanny whom I have not met.

My tiger doesn't stop. Her eyes widen when she sees him tummy crawl into view, and her mouth rounds in a perfect O that I can't help but think would look good wrapped around my cock.

"Oh, definitely not Archie," she says cautiously and gathers the kittens closer like she's going to protect them. They have no sense of self-preservation, though, and start hissing and spitting in my direction, the fur on their tiny little backs sticking out at all angles, trying to make themselves look bigger.

My tiger rumbles at them, and it's all it takes for them to scurry away, finding hiding spots far away from us. The girl still doesn't move, and my tiger wiggles his butt and stalks even closer. The surprised look on her face turns to one of amusement, as if she thinks his actions are funny. He is pleased she is not scared of him. They both watch each other closely, and I note her eyes are a magnificent shade of lavender, much like the dress she's wearing. As he gets closer, her intoxicating scent makes us giddy. Could this beautiful woman be our mate? She certainly smells good enough to eat, but surely if she was, the guys would have let me know. I can't see our bond mark anywhere on her, but there isn't a lot of exposed skin.

We finally get close enough to lay our head in her lap, and that's exactly what my besotted tiger does. He sighs with relief and rolls onto his side, exposing his belly. Holy crap, he wants her to rub it like she was doing for one of the kittens.

She snorts, unable to control her laughter now.

"I know somewhere inside you is a human, and I can't help but wonder if I'm supposed to rub your tummy or not. That's kind of weird." Her fingers clench like she wants to but isn't sure if she should. He bats a huge paw in her direction, almost like he's begging, and I feel mortified. I'm never going to be able to look her in the eye once I shift back.

"I'm assuming your creature is fully in the driver's seat, otherwise this is definitely a little weird," she says, finally making the decision to give him what he wants. She leans forward and rubs his belly and coos to him.

"What a big, beautiful, majestic…" She pauses and lifts her eyes to look. "Boy," she finishes, and he stretches, giving her better access, enthralled by her attention. I look a little closer, seeing if I can recognize her. There is something familiar about her, but I can't quite put my finger on it. I'm sure I would remember running into such a stunning creature when I visited my family in the past.

Her fingers drag soothingly through our fur, and I feel our eyes drift closed. We're worn out from all the running we've done today, and a little nap in the lap of a beautiful woman who smells delicious is his idea of heaven.

She giggles, and I feel her settle back against the wall of the stall. "Okay, kitty, you can have a little nap, but then I need to return to the palace before anyone notices I'm gone."

She's silent, and I drift off to sleep. The next thing I know, I wake up alone in the stall, and the pretty girl is nowhere in sight. How the fuck did she get away without us noticing? I ask my cat, and he shrugs, showing her leaving quietly, not wanting to wake us. I didn't wake, but he noticed and allowed her the charade. When I berate him, he insists he has her scent now and can track her anywhere.

I decide maybe it's for the best, and he gives me back the reins. I move through the castle, the magic doors opening for me in animal form. My claws are noisy on the marble floors, and as I move toward my wing, I'm waylaid by one of my sisters.

"Finally made it, did you, idiot?" Gretchin is leaning against the doorway of her suite, which is on the same floor as ours. She has a mug of something in her hand, and when I sniff, I can tell it's hot chocolate. "Dad is pissed. The new royal appeared today, and you weren't here like he requested."

I don't shift back. I'm not in the mood to argue with my sister. Instead, I push past her, stalk into her room, and jump up onto her sofa in her lounge area. I roll around on it, leaving black and white fur all over the thing, scent marking it so her own cat will be pissed at the intrusion, before jumping back down and leaving again.

"Real fucking mature, asshole," she screeches and slams the door in my face, but I chuff with amusement. It saved me from a lecture. If only it would work with my own team. I continue down the hallway and brace myself for whatever their reaction is going to be.

I shift as I get to our suite and open the door. It's silent inside. It is late, but I hadn't expected all of them to be asleep. I sent them a message before I left that I was on my way. Not even Gem is waiting for me, which is very unlike him. He must be really mad at me. I consider waking him, but I'm not in the mood to be scolded, so instead, I make my way to my bed.

I think about showering, but there's a part of me that is pleased I smell like cupcakes and frosting, even after shifting back. I don't want to wash it all down the drain, so instead, I get to my room and strip before climbing into bed. Right then and there, I decide to give up my search for the sixth member of our team. The rest of them must be right. He doesn't exist or really doesn't want to be a part of our bond, so who am I to force him?

What if this means we never get a marked mate? Someone who bears the same mark as the rest of us, our perfect counterpart to spoil and cherish? Well, if that's the case, I'm sure we can find someone who will make us just as happy. The gorgeous girl from earlier comes to mind, and I have to resist the urge to stroke my hard cock to the memory of her hands running through our fur. Instead, I grit my teeth, roll over, and bring up thoughts of the asshole alpha from the village today.

That's enough to dampen my desire. Tomorrow, I'll make everything up to my bond group, starting with Gem.

I'm up early for breakfast the following morning, not bothering to shower. I find my bond mates already awake as well.

"Look what the cat dragged in," Liam drawls, leaning on the door of our suite. The four of them are already dressed, and I'm assuming they are heading to breakfast as well.

Brodie and Hunter mumble their hellos, but Gem flat-out ignores me, pushing Liam out of the way and opening the door to our suite.

"I'm going to check on the queen and escort her to breakfast. I'll see you all there," he says when Brodie asks where he's going. He leaves without a backward glance, and I flinch from the force of his anger.

"Dude, you have some serious ass kissing to do." Brodie claps me on the shoulder as we walk through the hallways of the palace. "You're lucky Liam covered for your ass yesterday, so I think your family will be okay, but Gem is butthurt. I hope you'll honor your promise to him."

"You covered for me?" I look at my bond mate in surprise, and he shrugs.

"You're an idiot, but you're our idiot."

A smirk crosses my lips, but before I can reply to him, Hunter crowds me, his nostrils flaring, and he scowls. "Where have you been? Why do you smell like that?"

I'm wearing the same night watch uniform I had on yesterday. It smells just like cupcakes and frosting from when my tiger rubbed all over the pretty girl from yesterday. My smirk grows.

"Last night when I got back, I heard someone in the stables, so I decided to check it out. My tiger got loved on by a pretty palace maid who was cuddling with the kittens out there. She smelled fucking delicious. I'm hoping maybe I can find her and convince her to come play with me maybe tonight after dinner. I'll ask Gem if he wants to join us." I feel giddy with my decision. It feels right, and I can't wait to share the maid with the phoenix. If we just so happened to touch one another, it would be even better.

The three of them stare at me, speechless. Liam and Hunter growl aggressively, but Brodie bursts into laughter, slapping them both on the shoulders. "Easy, guys. I think that's a wonderful idea. I'm so glad you've decided to give up your relentless search for our sixth, but I think you're going to have to rethink that 'maid.'" He says "maid" in a kind of sarcastic tone, and Hunter and Liam snicker like schoolboys. What the fuck is their problem? We start walking again, and I look carefully at every staff member we pass. All dip into curtsies or bow as I pass.

"I'm just not sure where to find her, but how hard could it be? How many staff members does the palace have?"

"Over a hundred," Hunter states dryly.

"Oh, I'm sure you won't have any trouble finding her. She may even just drop into your lap," Brodie says cheerfully.

Breakfast is a casual affair. A buffet is placed on the side of the room, and we all help ourselves before taking a seat at the table. Liam and Brodie head directly to the food, but Hunter stops to say hello to his mother, and I do the same.

"Ah, Gryffin, there you are. We missed you last night," my mother scolds me as I place a kiss on Evie's and Mia's cheeks before doing the same to her.

"Sorry, but it couldn't be helped. I'm here now." I look around the room, but I don't see anyone unfamiliar.

"Uncle Gwiff!" Archie calls and waves at me. "You're here! I want to introduce you to my side-piece," he shouts, and the table chuckles. Adam chokes on his juice he had unfortunately taken a sip of.

"Archie, you can't keep calling her that," he scolds his son who ignores him. I ruffle his hair, and

I'm about to ask him what he's talking about when Dad and Bryson enter the room. Bryson joins Liam, Hunter, and Brodie at the buffet, but my father beelines it toward me.

"Good, you're back." He hugs me quickly. "We need to start work with the new queen immediately. Your mothers and I will instruct her this morning, but your bond group will take over this afternoon and work on self-defense, shifting, and gaining control of her magic. It is a priority. Leave the missing shifters to the rest of the watch for now."

He gives my mothers absent kisses before moving to the buffet without waiting for a response from me, but I guess there's nothing left for me to say.

"Did any mates show up this morning?" Gretchin asks as I give both her and Gracelin kisses on their cheeks before heading to grab some food.

There is an awkward silence that has me looking around to see what's going on. My three mothers have frowns, and Mia shakes her head. "No, not yet."

"Maybe the magic did go wrong," Evie says quietly, and I frown.

"What are you all talking about?" I ask, but before I can get a straight answer, the steward makes an announcement.

"Queen Colbie Karridge, Lady Violet, and Prince Jeremy Saunders."

I smirk with amusement. The guys all got prince

titles when they bonded with me, but they hate the pomp and ceremony.

My smirk soon drops, though, as the doors open, and Gem enters. On his arm is the gorgeous creature from last night. Holy shit, is she the new queen? Something inside me shrivels with misery. I'm never going to have a chance.

Colbie

The dining room is bright and cheerful this morning, and the smell of breakfast makes my stomach groan loudly. I put a hand over it and feel my cheeks warm with embarrassment when Gem chuckles next to me.

"You must be starving. You used a lot of energy shifting last night," he says kindly, and I try to ignore everyone's attention on me.

"I really am. I feel like I could eat a horse," I tell him then wince with guilt. I'm not sure I should use the phrase now that I can shift into one.

"I'll fix you a plate," Violet offers, brushing past me and heading toward the breakfast buffet. I watch her to make sure she's okay. She was nervous this morning about how she's going to fit in, but I don't think she has anything to worry about. Talon and Ember, Hunter's siblings, both greet her warmly, as do the two princesses. Brodie gives her an empty plate when she approaches the buffet, and I let out a sigh of relief. I think she's going to be fine.

"Ah, Colbie, there you are," Lucas says as we approach the table, my hand still tucked into Gem's arm. He knocked on our door this morning and asked if he could check me over. He explained that he is a phoenix shifter with the power of healing, and I couldn't really argue with that. His powers felt like the comfort of a warm fire when he ran his hands over my body. He was very professional about it, but I couldn't help wondering what his hands would feel like if he wasn't being so professional. "How did you sleep? I'm assuming Gem has checked you this morning?"

"Yes, I did, and she is a little low on energy, but nothing that a good meal won't fix," Gem answers.

He's right, I am exhausted, although my body seems to be in one piece with no aches or pains, just a mild headache, and I think that probably has to do with my lack of sleep. When I finally regained consciousness last night, I was in my bed, and Violet was asleep in a chair next to it. I didn't bother waking her. Instead, I ate the plate of fruit and crackers that were on my bedside table and tried to go back to sleep, but my mind wouldn't let me. I just kept replaying everything that happened a few hours before. The memories of shifting into a hydra, then a wolf and a pegasus played through my mind over and over, as did the jumbled sensations of unrestrained magic burning my nerve endings. The whole thing was really weird. Instead of different consciousness every time I shifted, it was like it was the same, but our form and abilities shifted, the inner thoughts remaining unchanged. I was so tired, though, it was like I was just along for the ride. I couldn't communicate or make heads or tails of anything.

Finally, I gave up on sleeping and went for a walk. Violet didn't even stir, and there wasn't any palace staff to be seen as I traipsed through the hallways, looking for a way out. I needed some fresh air. I was having trouble catching my breath with my anxiety. Once I found a door and stepped outside, the sight of the stables made me smile. I remembered Archie's excuse that he wanted to play with the stable kittens, so I went in that direction. Despite my violent interaction with Stormheart, Nox's rabid beast, I actually love cats, and it was exactly the distraction I needed at the time.

I was finally relaxing for the first time, my thoughts on nothing but the adorable bundles of fluff in front of us when I felt an intruder. The magic of my animal inside me perked their head up and started rolling around inside me in excitement. There was no fear or aggression, just pure joy as a fucking huge white tiger crawled its way into the stables. I couldn't believe my eyes, and if the kittens hadn't scattered, I would have thought I was asleep and dreaming.

His deep, ocean blue eyes connected with mine, and he chuffed as he crawled a little closer and laid his head in my lap. I didn't know what to do. Somewhere inside that huge creature was a human, but I think his animal was firmly in the driver's seat. What self-respecting man would act like that? Then it occurred to me that maybe he was one of my mates, but didn't want to scare me off, so he chose to show himself in his tiger form. With the way my own animal was reacting, it wouldn't have surprised me, so I just went with it, giving him a belly scratch and holding still when he decided to nap on me. My eyes closed as I listened to the sound of his heavy breathing, almost like a soft snore, and my mind finally felt empty. I'm not sure how long I dozed, but eventually, I had to get up. I shuffled my body, supporting the cat's head with my hands so I could move out from under it. It cracked its eyes open, yawned, and went back to sleep, so I left it there and hurried back to my room.

I stripped off my dress, which was covered in tiger fur, and threw it in the laundry before digging through the closet for a T-shirt to wear, then I climbed back into bed and fell asleep quickly after that.

"Colbie?" Lucas is looking at me with concern, and I realize I didn't answer him.

"Oh, sorry, yes, I'm okay. A little tired, but I'm really hungry."

"Well, we will make sure there are plenty of snacks for you this morning," Evie tells me as Brodie approaches, carrying a plate full of food.

"Here, I told Violet I would look after you," he says, smiling at me, but then he freezes, and he leans in a little like he's sniffing me. "Why do you smell like…"

Gem interrupts him. "Tiger. Apparently our little queen needed some fresh air and found herself in the stables last night." He already scolded me for wandering around without an escort. I argued that I wasn't a child who needed permission, and he said it was for my safety. I couldn't really protest after that. I mean, it's not like I could defend myself against a shifter if they wanted to attack, and I don't know if I can shift on command or even how to fight if I could. "A tiger approached her when she was cuddling with the kittens."

There are a couple of exclamations of surprise.

"Oh really?" Brodie turns his attention away from me and toward another man who is standing at the buffet with the others. I frown, watching Hunter lean in and smell the man. What is it with shifters and smelling people? "Did he shift and introduce himself?" I turn my attention back to the people around the table.

"No, he didn't, but I wasn't scared of him. He was adorable actually. He wanted belly rubs and then went to sleep with his head in my lap." As I tell them this, I remember something Violet said to me, and I gasp, clasping the pendant in my hands to steady myself.

"Oh my god. I just remembered Violet told me I shouldn't touch shifters like that. Fuck, I hope I didn't offend him. I was wondering if maybe he was one of my mates." I look hopefully at the queens. Surely it's not so bad that I acted familiarly with him if he is, but Mia winces.

"I'm sorry, Colbie. If he is, then he hasn't presented himself at the front," she says, but she looks guilty.

"Oh." I pick up my fork and stab it into a sausage before biting it in half. The men at the table wince, and Gracelin giggles, I should care, but my creature is starving, and being ladylike isn't cutting it at the moment. "Maybe the magic really did go wrong." I can't help but sound disappointed. I'm failing at this queen thing. I have three different animal forms inside me, but no mates. My mom was right, I am useless.

"I love having my tummy rubbed," Archie announces, oblivious of the weird tension at the table.

"Me too, buddy," Brodie mutters before returning to the buffet and having a quiet argument with the rest of his bond group, including the only man I haven't met yet. I'm assuming that's Gryffin, the king's son.

"Yes, well, eat up, Colbie, we have a lot to do. I am sure mates will present themselves soon enough. Maybe the goddess is waiting for you to get a handle on your shift first," Lucas suggests thoughtfully, his lips turning up in a smile. "Yes, I bet that's the reason why. She never gives you more than you can handle." He sounds pleased with his reasoning, and I grab hold of that tightly, because if I don't, it means accepting the fact that I really am a bit of a dud.

The conversation turns to tonight's dinner as the rest of the men join us at the table. Violet looks between the seat next to me and the one close to Talon and Ember, and I discreetly nod her in that direction. She smiles and gives me a nod back before joining them, and I'm distracted when I get an elbow in the side as Archie climbs into the seat beside me.

"Good morning, Colbie." He wraps his arms around my neck and gives me a sticky kiss. He smells like maple syrup, and I'm guessing he ate pancakes this morning.

"Morning, my little man," I reply, giving him a kiss on the cheek in return. He beams and settles next to me, chatting happily.

"Watching you shift yesterday was so cool," he says. "If I had six heads, I could eat everything I want and not get sick," he says, rubbing at his round little tummy, which is looking a lot better than when I originally saw him.

Violet told me that shifters, especially the young ones, use a lot of calories shifting, so it's important to eat a lot to fuel your magic and body.

"What animal has six heads?" an unfamiliar voice asks, taking a seat in the chair between Lucas and me.

I turn to see a pair of familiar ocean blue eyes staring quizzically at me. "Do I know you? I feel like I've met you before."

Liam mutters something, but an elbow from Brodie causes him to scoff and splutter. "Oh, Gryffin, you haven't met our new queen yet, have you?" Lucas says, and I can hear a slight hint of annoyance in his tone.

"Actually, Gryffin met Colbie many years ago." Gretchin snickers. "She had a superpower even back then. Her tears had the ability to have Gryffin at her beck and call."

His eyes widen, and the confusion in his eyes fades. "Cookie?" he asks, and I frown.

"What Gretchin forgot to tell you yesterday is that we used to call you cupcake back then, but Gryff called you cookie." Gracelin grins cheekily.

"Because of all the treats you used to bake us," he says, not taking his eyes off me.

"And because she smells like cupcakes," Gretchin adds.

"Yes, she does," Gryffin agrees slowly. "It's nice to see you again." His face lights up in a grin that has flashes of memories flying through my brain of him and me hiding from the girls and jumping out and scaring them, him allowing me to paint his nails when Mom wouldn't let me paint my own while his sisters were doing it, and us all playing dress up with him being a knight to my princess while the sisters were the evil witches. They really enjoyed playing the evil witches, but he protected me from all their schemes. I didn't know back then he was a prince.

I hadn't realized how much time the queens had spent at Mom's studio. She must have been dressing them exclusively for a while. I wonder what happened, or if they have been going all this time and I just didn't know. It's unlike my mom not to brag about that sort of thing though.

"Sir Gryffin." The name slips out before I can stop it, and the table dissolves into laughter.

"Uncle Gwiff, Colbie is my girlfriend, and I'm going to be her sidepiece because the goddess has given her mates already."

The rest of the table has already heard all of this, but Gryffin chokes on his sip of coffee at his nephew's announcement. "Sounds like solid goals. I fully support it," he tells Archie seriously, and his nephew beams at him. I feel my cheeks flush pink. Gryffin grew up well. He was a good-looking kid, but he's over-the-top handsome now, just like the rest of his group. His silvery, shoulder-length hair has a few artful streaks of black through it, and he has a striking jawline and chiseled cheekbones with full lips. There isn't an ugly one amongst his bond group. In fact, everyone assembled at the table is gorgeous.

"Are there any ugly shifters?" I blurt, feeling flustered. "The sheer attractiveness at this table is overwhelming. Please tell me I'm not going to be the only bland shifter out of the whole race?" I beg, and they all stare at me with surprise.

Gracelin is the first to recover. "Oh, believe me, we are just very lucky to have good genes. There are some very unattractive shifters in this kingdom."

"Both inside and out," Violet adds, and I see Sable give her hand a squeeze. I remember her telling me about having trouble with a girl at college.

"And in no way are you bland, Queen Colbie," Ember tells me earnestly, and I smile at the girl's lies.

"You're too kind, but I am aware of my short-comings. My mother has told me my whole life."

There's an awkward silence and a few angry scowls on my behalf.

Lucas clears his throat and fidgets, staring at my plate.

"Hurry up and get some more food in you, Colbie. Lucas is getting impatient." Layla nudges her husband, thankfully changing the subject and breaking the uncomfortable atmosphere.

"Mia told him he had to wait until you were finished eating and not rush you, but he is eager to get started this morning." Evie giggles, and Mia rolls her eyes.

"Way to go, Evelyn. Now you've made her self-conscious and are making her rush," Mia growls at her co-wife as I start to shovel more food in my mouth.

Conversation goes on around me, and the atmosphere is warm and inviting, just like being in the kitchen at my grandparents' place. I can't help but wish this is how this will always be, but I know it won't. Lucas and his wives and children will move out of the palace, and the rest are only temporary residents until I am crowned and mated. Bryson and Sable might stick around, but I will have to talk to them about their wants and needs. I'm not going to force him to stay in his job if he would like to retire and enjoy his life now that his friend is moving on.

I guess these are all decisions I need to make over the coming weeks. I get up and move over to the buffet to grab a cup of coffee. A server hurries over to assist me, and I wave them away with a smile. "The day I can't make myself my own cup of coffee is a sad day indeed," I tell them gently, and they return to their place against the wall.

When I return to the table, Gracelin and Gretchin are smirking at me, and I flip them off. They dissolve into giggles.

"Get used to it, Colbie. There are going to be times when you're going to have to allow them to serve you. It's all about keeping up appearances," Lucas instructs me firmly. "I know it's hard, and there is such a steep learning curve, but I have a feeling you're going to be an amazing queen. You just have to allow us to teach you."

The rest of breakfast passes by quickly. I can feel Lucas's impatience, so I stand up and put him out of his misery. "Okay, oh mighty king, teach me." I give him a sweeping bow, and he jumps to his feet and rubs his hands together.

"Let's go."

TWENTY-EIGHT

Colbie

I'm dead by lunchtime. Here lies Queen Colbie may she rest in peace, her brain fried with an overload of information.

I thought learning about shifter politics would be tedious and boring, but I've been completely captivated, absorbing everything the king, queens, and Sable have been teaching me, but it's definitely an intensive course. I don't even think we've touched the tip of the iceberg.

When Lucas sends me away to grab something to eat, I'm pretty sure I have a solid understanding of the people on the council and their various positions. They spent hours drilling me because I'm going to meet them all tonight, and not only them, but also other shifters who are gunning for their positions and hope to curry favor with me.

Mia said half the people there tonight will be sucking up to me, desperate to hold onto their positions, while the other half will be doing everything they can to usurp the current council members through sly comments, innuendos, and downright lies. Apparently tonight will be a cesspit of slander and malicious gossip, and I have to smile prettily through it all.

I groan loudly as Violet and I make our escape, heading toward the dining room where another buffet spread will have been prepared. "That was a lot," I grumble, and she tucks her arm into mine and gives it a squeeze.

"It sure was. I had no idea being in the upper class was like that. It must be so stressful to be constantly worried about your reputation. I'm kind of glad I've never had to worry about it."

The queens actually insisted that Violet had the same training as me to prepare her for all the crazy as well. I was so thankful to them for including her, mostly so I didn't feel so alone and out of my depths, but they were all so patient.

"I had no idea how many different kinds of shifters there were and that some of them had more magic than just shifting." Sable gave me a rundown, explaining the difference between regular and mythical shifters. They also pointed out which ones we need to be wary of tonight. A few of them like to push their dominance to try and get the upper hand. Without my pendant on, it wouldn't be an issue, but we're still trying to conceal how powerful I actually am. Without being able to control it yet, I'll have all the guests on their knees every time the wind blows in a different direction.

There's no one else in the dining room when we get there, and the two of us help ourselves to the food. I pile my plate high with potato and pasta salads and cold chicken pieces, before covering a bread roll with butter. I study the dessert options, but there is not enough room on my plate, so I decide to come back after I finish my first course.

We return to the table, grabbing seats next to one another. We're silent for a little while as we devour our food, but eventually, I catch up to my hunger and slow down.

"Thank fuck we don't have physical training this afternoon. I'm so tired, and if I have to smile and look pretty for hours tonight, I need a nap. Otherwise, I'm literally going to bite someone's face off," I joke, and Violet giggles.

"Are you worried about tonight?" she asks when she stops giggling at my dramatics.

"Not really. I give great customer service, and it can't be worse than dealing with irate coffee drinkers, but I'm worried that no mates have presented themselves," I admit. This is really bothering me. My mother's passive aggressive ways have really messed with my head, and I'm worried I'm not cut out for this and there are men out there with marks who hate the idea of being shackled to a short, curvy former human. I mean, it has to rub some of them the wrong way, right?

Her expression softens with sympathy, and I wince, but before she can respond, the door to the dining room opens, and one of the palace staff hurries into the room. He looks a little stressed, like he's not sure what to do about what brought him here.

"Your Majesty, forgive my intrusion, but you have some visitors. Shall I send them in?" He sounds as frazzled as he looks.

"Who is here?" Violet asks before I can respond.

"It's two male shifters and a human woman. She claims to be your mother."

No! Surely she wouldn't? How would she have gotten here? She would need permission. My stomach rolls with dread as all of these thoughts whirl in my brain, and my food threatens to make a reappearance. Violet grabs my hand and gives it a squeeze as the dining room doors open once more and my mother waltzes in, escorted by Niles and Brock. They appear beyond giddy to be here and look around the room with eager eyes. My mother has a haughty sneer on her face and stares down her nose at the food on my plate.

"Colbie, dear, you shouldn't make such a pig of yourself. Carbs are not going to do those hips any favors." She grimaces with disgust.

I wince and feel my cheeks heat with shame. It's

the same argument she gave me when I decided I wanted to be a baker. I almost gave it up, but Granny wouldn't let me. She and Mother had a huge blowout when Granny told her to shut up.

"Actually, shifters can eat all the carbs they want and not have to worry about weight. It helps fuel our animals, so when we rip people's heads off, we don't get tired," a menacing voice from a doorway that leads to the kitchen growls, and Niles and Brock squeak with alarm and clutch each other in panic.

My mother just glares at Liam as he strolls to the buffet and puts a piece of apple pie on a plate with a huge dollop of whipped cream before adding a couple of colorful donuts to it as well. He stalks toward us and places it in front of me, never once taking his eyes off my mother.

"Eat up, my queen. You will need your strength to deal with all the fawning idiots tonight." He doesn't look at me, just gives the plate a nudge. My mouth drops open in surprise. He's been nothing but indifferent toward me up until now. Violet fans her face like she's hot. I guess my mother is a lot.

"Humans are not being given permission to enter the shifter zone during the transition. How did you get here?" Liam demands, and a sly smile crosses my mother's lips as she reaches out and runs a finger over his broad chest, admiring him. He has a punk rock kind of look with his shock of white hair and the piercing in his eyebrow and lip. Liam is most definitely not the type my mother is usually attracted to, but she's going to work whatever angle she can to get her own way.

"You wouldn't deny the queen the support of her mother, would you?" she purrs and flutters her eyelashes, but he just removes her hand from his body.

"What help would you be? You know nothing about shifters. How did you get in here?" he barks.

She rolls her eyes and gestures to Brock and Niles. Brock stops clasping Niles's hand and gets his shit together, straightening the vest he's wearing.

"My father is on the council, and he gave permission." He adopts a self-important air, one I've never heard from him before, and I blink in surprise. I had no idea that Brock's father was on the council. He's never mentioned it before.

"And just who is your father?" a voice booms out, and when I look past my mother, Brock, and Niles, I find Lucas standing there with an expression of fury on his face. Standing behind him are the queens, their faces neutral. I've learned that's their public face, and I had better get good at my own.

"Vallen Tideman." Brock puffs up his chest to make himself seem bigger, but he looks like a real weeny against Liam and Lucas.

"Ah, yes. Tideman's son who was banished to the neutral zone for the sake of his reputation." Lucas's expression softens ever so slightly as Niles and Brock squirm on the spot. I am dying to know why, but I keep my mouth shut. There's time for gossip later.

"Layla, Mia, Evie, it's delightful to see you again," my mother calls, not able to stand the lack of attention on her anymore.

I watch as the three women internally speak to one another. It's the small, minute expressions on their faces that they taught me to look for. It means they are speaking through their mate bond. I guess they are trying to figure out how to play this. On one hand, I'm the new queen, and on the other hand, she's the woman who has been designing for them for years and also my mother. They could very easily destroy her career, but she would make me suffer.

Lucas doesn't give them a chance to respond. "No matter what my wives told you to call them in the neutral zone, you will address them formally here and give them the respect they deserve, and at least for a few more weeks, they are the queens." The look he gives my mother would probably shrivel any normal sane person, but it doesn't seem to affect her in the least. Narcissism at its finest.

I feel the pressure of his dominance in the air, and both Niles and Brock scurry to bow to their royals. My mom obviously can't feel it, but I see her calculating her response. In the end, she dips into a curtsy, the overly formal dress she is wearing making it possible.

"You will also give our new queen the same

respect. How dare you barge in without being invited?"

"She is my daughter, and I will do as I please," my mother snaps, losing control at being spoken to like that, and I see the moment she realizes she fucked up. She whirls around, looking at me with pleading eyes. "Honey, I only want to be here to support you," she cajoles, and I feel torn. Despite knowing she's only here for her own gain, she's my mother, but she also broke the rules, and I am now the shifter queen who has to see that they are enforced.

Before I can respond, the room suddenly fills with Watch Team One, Adam, and an unknown group of men who must be his team of shifters.

"Gryffin, Adam, can you and your teams please escort these three back to the border?" My mother turns to argue with Lucas, but he puts his hand up.

"Ms. Karridge, you may have received permission, but it was falsely given. I am still king, at least for a few more weeks, and my word is law. Be hopeful that your daughter will forgive you this trespass and still deign to see you once she is ready—ready being the operative word. As for you two, you should have known better. You know your father didn't have your best interest at heart. I will be placing a six month ban on both of you."

"But we live in this zone," Niles cries out. "Our home is here."

"You should have thought about that before

pulling a stunt like this. You will have to find a place to live in the neutral zone for the next six months, as you will not be welcome here." His attention switches to Brock. "Think very carefully about whether or not your father had your best interest at heart when he gave you permission, knowing banishment was a possibility for flaunting the restriction directive."

Brock's face clouds with anger, but he gives the king a nod, and both of them leave without a struggle, neither of them looking at me. Oh well, another semi friendship destroyed by my mother's manipulations. Should I even be surprised?

"But I need to discuss the queens' dresses with them." My mother scrambles for an excuse, and she looks pleadingly at the three queens who shift uncomfortably.

I stand up, smoothing my own dress down and picking up my plate of dessert. I don't want to make this harder than it is, so if I leave, whatever decision they choose is up to them. I don't want to influence them either way. "I will retire to my room for now. It's been a tiring morning, and I think I'll have a small nap before tonight's festivities. I'll see you all this evening. Goodbye, Mom. I will send you an invite to the coronation," I say mildly, and she grits out a smile, but I see the fury in her eyes. This didn't go how she wanted at all. Now she needs to work her ass off to salvage her reputation. I wish her luck.

Violet stands up and takes both of our first course plates and hands them to one of the servers, who is being very discrete by pretending not to pay attention. She helps herself to dessert, and then we leave the room.

The tension that I've been holding in my body releases the farther we get away from my mother. "Wow, I can't believe she convinced someone to bring her in. Those two are lucky they were only banned for six months. I wouldn't want to be in Councilman Tideman's shoes tonight."

"Make sure you point him out to me. I don't want someone like that on my council. What a shit stirrer."

Violet waves her free hand. "Oh, he'll claim it was a miscommunication or blame one of his lackies, and they will be out of job."

"Do you know what Lucas was alluding to when he spoke to Brock?" I ask her, and she winces.

"Actually, I do. It was quite a huge scandal. When Brock mated with a male, Councilman Tideman disowned him."

"Shifters are homophobic?" I'm kind of shocked to hear that. I would have thought with bond groups and sharing mates that possible same sex-couples would be common.

"No, not at all, but Councilman Tideman is." Gretchin steps out from behind a pillar I hadn't seen her leaning against and looks at my plate of dessert. "Bringing out the big guns?" she asks, and I grimace.

"My mother got into the castle," I say by way of explanation.

She nods and joins us for the walk to my room. "I heard. Anyway, Councilman Tideman had big plans for his three children. His oldest son will follow in his footsteps."

"If he keeps his seat, which is not looking good at this rate," I mutter, and Violet nods her agreement.

"And he was hoping his daughter would be marked as a mate for a powerful bond group. He's constantly throwing her at Gryffin and the guys. As for Brock, he was slated to join the army and move up the ranks and become a general—or that's what the councilor used to tell anyone who would listen. I was in training with Brock after we finished high school. His heart was never in it, and for a shifter, he has terrible coordination. Then he mated with Niles. They have true mate marks gifted from the goddess. Well, Tideman was livid. You could hear him screaming at Brock from the council's wing of the palace."

Yes, this is interesting news, as was learning that the council lives in the palace too. Can't say I was thrilled about that. Another point in the column of getting rid of them all and installing people I like.

"He kicked poor Brock and Niles to the curb and cut them off. Our moms helped them get back on their feet, find an apartment, and gave them a loan to start the business in the neutral zone."

"Ah, so that's why your dad and moms looked upset. They felt betrayed. They shouldn't be, my mom would have run circles around Brock and Niles by pandering to their egos, they would have been putty in her hands. She might have played the 'my poor daughter is traumatized' card and told them she could make everything better. They were conned."

"Doesn't matter, they broke the rules, even if they were set up." Gretchin stands firm, and I sigh.

"I guess I'm going to have to learn not to be so soft." I push open the door to my room and set my dessert down on the bedside table.

"Maybe, but don't lose your compassion. It shines so brightly in you, Colbie." Gretchin gives me a kiss on the cheek and waves at Violet. "I'll be back to supervise you getting ready for the ball," she says on her way out, but it sounds like a threat.

"You'll be here too, right?" I ask Violet as she takes her own leave. Her rooms are in this wing but down a different corridor. This whole section is for me and my supposed new mates, if any of them would deign to turn up.

"Of course. I don't trust her on her own. Gracelin and I will be back with a whole staff of cosmeticians and hairdressers. We will help you pick a dress when we return. For now, just relax, take a nap, and maybe enjoy a bubble bath. Whatever you need to do to make your animal calm and relaxed, because tonight is going to be trying, and we don't need you shifting and killing anyone just yet."

She chuckles and pulls the door closed behind her. I think she's joking, but I'm not entirely sure. God, I hope alcohol is provided tonight. I can always drink myself calm. Comatose is probably not a good look for a queen though, so maybe only one or two.

TWENTY-NINE

Colbie

I take Violet's advice and try to take a nap, and I actually succeed. My brain is exhausted, and I manage to shut it off for a couple of hours. When I get up, I enjoy a soak in my huge bathtub, releasing a little more of the tension in my muscles. The girls arrive, and I am plucked, curled, tweezed, and powder to perfection. The dress they select is a scarlet red satin with a full skirt and layered under-skirts, a fitted, sleeveless bodice that had a high neckline, and a row of black buttons up the front of the bodice to break up the red fabric. It's certainly a statement dress, and I do feel like a queen in it.

The debate about what to do with my hair rages around me, but eventually, everyone agrees with a messy updo, and Gracelin procures a small ruby and black diamond tiara.

"Gosh, I'm glad kneading bread keeps my arms toned," I mutter as I turn around and look at myself in the mirror for the first time. The girls worked miracles, and I don't look like myself at all. In the mirror opposite me is a gorgeous, curvy goddess. The dress accentuates my perky breasts, and the pair of spanks I have underneath makes my waist look slimmer and my tummy flatter. The skirt hides my hips and thighs perfectly, and the heels they forced me into give me a height that pulls off the whole look.

"Pfft, you're gorgeous. I'm jealous of your curves," Gretchin says, plucking at the teal blue mermaid dress she has on that looks stunning against her dark complexion. "This would look so much better with some junk in my trunk, but I can't get any weight to stick. It's the dreaded shifter metabolism at play."

"And the fact that you're in the military and always working out probably doesn't help either," Gracelin teases as she puts the finishing touches on Violet—another small tiara that she told Violet only had semi-precious stones in it when she freaked out and refused to wear it.

"Will that happen to me? Will I lose some of my weight? That would be awesome. I've always hated my thighs and ass."

"Who knows? It's different for humans who are changed. Some keep their original figures, and some don't, but with the energy you are using, I wouldn't put it out of the realm of possibility. Okay, done. Come on, we need to hurry up. We're already running late, and Dad will lose his shit soon. He's still pissed about your Mom from this afternoon. If there wasn't an amnesty on council positions during the transition, Councilman Tideman would have been out of a position after his stunt."

She hurries us out of the room and through our wing until we get to the public wing where the ballroom is located. "Right, you need to make an entrance, so wait here, and the three of us will go first, and then you will be announced and make your big entrance. You will be escorted down the stairs by your bodyguards, and Dad will meet you at the bottom of the stairs. He will then escort you to the head of the table. We will have a meal where you will be watched like you're a circus act, and then the tables will be cleared, and the mingling will occur. Moms and Dad will introduce you to our society's elite. There will be dancing and drinking, and you will feel like tearing your hair out by the end of the night," Gracelin tells me in a rush of words as she looks me over to make sure nothing has changed on our hurried walk from my room.

"We have a safe word. If you text any of us the word 'pineapple,' we will know you need to be rescued and swoop in to run interference," Gretchin tells me, producing my phone and handing it to me.

I gape at her. "But where do I put it?" I ask as

she tucks hers into the top of her strapless dress. I can't do that in this one.

"Pockets, my dear, pockets," she replies and gestures to the skirt. I feel around and am slightly giddy with glee when I notice that the dress indeed has pockets.

"This is awesome. I always tell Mom she should put them in her dresses. She told me I was stupid and we didn't need pockets when we had dates who have jacket pockets."

All three of them scowl at the mention of my mom, and I don't fault them for it.

"Okay, let's go. Good luck," Gracelin says, and Violet gives me a jaunty wave and allows the two princesses who have quickly worked their way into my heart to drag her along. I'm so pleased they've taken her under their wing as well. She's like the younger sister we all wanted.

"And remember to smile. You've got this." Gretchin winks as the doors open, and Violet slips through. I hear the herald announce her.

"Presenting Lady Violet Marsden, advisor to the queen."

There is an outbreak of whispers at this announcement, and I only hope that Hunter's brother and sister are somewhere close by to her at the dinner table. I did make that request, and hopefully being queen gets me a few perks.

"Presenting Princesses Gracelin and Gretchin,

secretary to the queen and bodyguard to the queen respectively."

When Bryson appointed Gretchin to be one of my bodyguards, I was stunned but pleased. I did double check if it was something she wanted and not being forced on her, and she assured me she'd ask for the position herself. I quickly agreed, happy that I have someone guarding my back I can trust. I was a little less sure about the secretary to the queen position for Gracelin. I felt like it was a downgrade, but it's what she was doing anyway. She lives for organization and did it on a small scale for a large shifter company prior to having Archie. She's been a stay-at-home mom since then, but she is ready to get back into the work-force. This way, she can bring Archie with her when he doesn't have school. It worked out perfectly for every-one, and she's dying to start bossing me around.

"Presenting Her Majesty, the new queen of the shifters, Colbie Karridge." That's my cue, and I step up just as the doors fling open.

The lights blind me slightly, but I resist the urge to shade them with my hand. Instead, I move forward so everyone can see me, pausing for effect on the staircase landing. The five rows of tables are full—one across the top for VIPs and then four perpendicular to it. Each table apart from the VIP table is able to sit upwards of seventy shifters. All of those eyes are on me. My stomach rolls with nerves, but an even stronger feeling of reassurance from my animal gives me the strength to keep going. I'm wearing my pendant, but it doesn't seem to dull my connection with my animal now, only dulling everyone else's sense of it.

I smile serenely as Watch Team One falls in around me, all resplendent in formal suits, and then as one, the six of us move down the stairs in sync, almost like it was rehearsed, but it wasn't. I haven't seen any of them since the drama at lunch. I'm dying to ask one of them how my mom behaved when they escorted her to the neutral zone, but it will have to wait.

I hear whispers, and with my new hearing, it's easy to make out what is being said.

"She doesn't feel very strong. What was the goddess thinking?"

"I heard that no mates have shown up at the palace, none at all."

"Gosh, I bet that skirt is hiding a giant ass."

A growl from my side has someone yelping in fright, but I don't dare turn my head to look. Despite some of the whispered words being my own fears, I know the truth—I am powerful, and when I can finally show them, they are going to wish they had kept their mouths shut.

I'm sure they know I can hear them, but they are trying to get me to react, so I tune them out and smile at Lucas as he holds out his hand. I place mine in his, and he bows over it before pressing a kiss on top. I dip in a curtsy, giving Lucas the kind of respect he deserves.

"Shall we?" he asks, holding his arm out, and the two of us move toward the table. Once we are seated, everyone else takes their seats.

Dinner is served, and thankfully, I have people surrounding me whom I know, so I'm not forced to suffer small talk with strangers during my meal. It would be a damn shame not to be able to focus on all the delicious food that is being presented to us.

I hear the occasional, muttered bitchy comment aimed at me though.

"Look at how much she eats. No wonder she needs such a big skirt."

I wonder if that's the same person who made the skirt comment before. Seems like they may be fixating on my ass.

I turn my head to look at where the comment came from. At one of the middle tables, there are two girls with delicate forms, almond-shaped eyes, and long, glossy dark hair staring at me with some serious hatred.

"Did you hear that, Prince Gryffin?" I ask the man who is sitting on the far side of Layla, who is directly next to me. I'm not sure how they worked out the seating arrangement, but I think Gryffin is strategically placed for my protection, while the rest of Watch Team One is seated next to him. Mia and Evelyn are on the other side of Lucas, followed by general Bryson and his family with Violet on the end. "Someone seems to have an obsession with my skirt. Do you think we can figure out who it is and give them the name of the designer?" I ask him, sounding unbothered, and he snickers while Layla hides her laugh by taking a sip of her wine.

"As you wish, my queen. I will listen carefully to the crowd to figure it out," he says just as loudly as I had. Dropping his voice, he mutters, "Naughty cookie, but well played."

"Indeed," Layla agrees. "That was masterfully handled."

No more whispers reach my ears, though I'm sure they haven't stopped completely, just not in hearing range of a tiger, which I'm assuming is fairly far.

Dinner is cleared away, and I have to mingle. It's excruciating, and I lose track of all the people I meet who kiss my ass. It's all fake and nauseating, and I'm reaching my limit when I am approached by a familiar face.

"Dad, will you allow me the pleasure of a dance with Colbie please? I'm sure she would like a break from all of this." He smiles charmingly, and his mothers twitter at him as his dad practically shoves me into his arms. My hand is hot in his as he leads me onto the floor. He spins me around before drawing me into his arms. Gryff wraps one arm around my waist and holds my hand up as he twirls me, waltzing in time to the orchestra. Dancing with him is like dancing on a cloud. He moves effortlessly and doesn't strike up a conversation, somehow sensing that I need a break to decompress.

I wonder what his animal is. I remember his mothers explaining how it works, and if I remember correctly, both of his parents are tigers, so that would make him a tiger… I freeze on the spot, and he frowns quizzically. "Are you okay?"

"What color is your tiger?" I ask him, unable to hide my suspicion, especially when I take into account the funny reactions when I told them all about my tiger cuddle experience at breakfast.

He winces and shrugs. "White," he admits, and I pull away from him.

"It was you last night, wasn't it?" I ask, feeling hurt, before spinning and moving away from him. I feel like a fool.

"Cookie, wait." He grabs my arm. "It was my tiger, I swear. He took over, and I was strictly in the passenger seat. He wanted a belly rub, and there was nothing I could do. I didn't know that you were the queen or that none of your mates had appeared. I wasn't trying to give you false hope. I swear," he pleads, but I shake off his hand and hurry away from him, pulling my phone out and typing "pineapple" to Gretchin. She won't let me down.

I'm done with all of this today. I'm sick of this bullshit. Why can't I do this queen thing on my own? The reminder that I can't take my full duties until my six mates appear is a kick in the teeth.

Gryffin's actions, while not malicious, were still hurtful, and the whispers around me all night have been speculating about the lack of possible mates, and if it's because I have no power. At one stage, I gripped the pendant around my neck so hard I thought it was going to shatter, but Lucas reminded me that without control, I could easily hurt or kill someone, so I dropped my hand. Gryffin's deceit was just the nail in the coffin.

I'm intercepted on my way off the dance floor, and I barely contain the growl that bubbles up out of my chest.

"Your Majesty, allow me to introduce myself since Lord Lucas hasn't deigned to do so." The man uses the title Lucas will hold once I am crowned. Technically, they should still be referring to him as King Lucas. I turn and find a handsome, gray-haired man beaming at me. He is accompanied by his wife and two children. I know exactly who this man is because I had Violet point him out earlier.

"No need, Councilor Tideman. Your reputation proceeds you," I say, pasting on a barely there smile.

He guffaws with laughter, and I take note that none of his family curtsies or bows to me as protocol dictates. "Wonderful, I look forward to getting to know you and helping you with your new position."

"Now then, no business talk at a party." Gretchin slides between us and herds me away.

Tideman protests, but she ignores him. "Sorry, Colbie is needed for a moment. No rest for the wicked." We lose them in the crowd, and I sigh with relief. I was not ready to deal with that, though I most certainly will.

"You done?" Gretchin mutters, and I sag.

"Absolutely," I tell her, and she discretely ushers us out a side door and takes a different route back to my room.

"We ran interference with Dad, so we are in the clear." Gracelin and Violet are waiting there when we arrive, and I heave out a sigh of relief at the bottles of champagne they each hold in their hands.

"Yes, yes, yes." I snatch one from Violet, and the four of us kick off our shoes and jump onto my bed, making ourselves comfortable. I don't even bother with a glass and just pop the top and guzzle it down. The bubbles tickle my nose, and it's a little tart for my sweet tooth, but if it does the trick of blurring my mind, then I am here for it.

"Ugh, I need to get out of this dress," Gretchin grumbles, climbing off the bed, and I wave at my wardrobe.

"Help yourself," I tell her, and it takes barely a second for all three of them to strip off their ball-gowns and replace them with some of the mountain of loungewear I have.

"That sucked," I say, flopping back on my bed, careful not to spill my champagne. "Did you hear them all talking about the mate thing?"

"Almost as much as I heard your lack of power mentioned," Violet grumbles and takes the bottle of champagne out of my hand. "Come on, get out of your dress. You will feel better."

"It wasn't all of them. Some of the people there tonight were lovely, but it's the assholes who are always the loudest," Gracelin says, and I see her sending a message on her phone. "Snacks are on their way." She jumps back on the bed with her own bottle of champagne in hand.

I put mine to the side and let Violet yank me up. I struggle with the little black buttons down the front, holding my dress together. "This was much easier at the beginning of the night," I mutter as the champagne takes effect.

"Here, let me." Violet pushes my hands out of the way and makes quick work of them. She shoves the dress off my shoulders, leaving me in only my bra. I shimmy out of the rest of the dress and toss it off to the side before spinning and going in search of my own loungewear.

"Colbie, what is that?" I hear Violet ask, and she grabs my shoulder, halting my movements.

"What? I can't see." I turn my head as she pokes at something in the middle of my spine.

"Have you always had this tattoo?" she asks, tracing something on my back.

"Tattoo? What tattoo?" I feel so confused. Gretchin and Gracelin approach me to see what Violet is talking about.

"Oh my god!" Gracelin squeals as Gretchin mutters, "Holy fuck."

"What?" I ask, getting annoyed. Violet takes my hand, drags me into the bathroom, and turns me around. My hair is up, so when I look backward into the mirror, I can see exactly what the hell she is talking about. It's a tattoo of a tree with a heart on the trunk and six branches curled up and outward.

My stomach is in my throat as I blink to make sure it's really there. I recognize it. I traced my finger over its exact replica not more than a few days ago. It's the same tattoo that was on Nox's chest.

"That's not just any tattoo. I think we just solved the reason why none of your mates have appeared yet." Gretchin crosses her arms and grins at me in the mirror.

"What do you mean?" I brace myself for whatever she has to say, because I am so fucking confused.

"That mark is the same mark shared by a bond group. You've been given a formed bond group as your mates instead of selecting them yourself. True mates!" Gracelin sounds dreamy.

Does that mean Nox is actually a shifter and was lying to me? I think about the pendant around my neck and the matching one he wore, and it all falls into place. Of course he fucking is. I can't believe he didn't tell me, especially after he knew my secret.

Violet obviously can't stand the wait, so she asks the question I'm too scared to. "Which bond group?"

Gretchin smirks and starts laughing. "Watch Team One. You are my brother's bond group's mate."

AFTERWORD

Phew, that was mean right? But don't worry I'm working on the second half and hopefully it will be coming your way in February. You can preorder it here, ignore the release date it's a placeholder.
Ardent Queen

I hope you enjoyed this new book. If you did it would be great if you could leave a review. .

If Unwilling Queen is your first Lexie Winston series you can find all of my other offerings by scanning the link below or searching for them on Amazon.

AFTERWORD

ACKNOWLEDGMENTS

It's always fun to start a new series and build a new world, and after being focused on the Galaxy Circus for such a long time this was a breath of fresh air. There's is so much potential with this world, but for now it will remain a duet until I have finished off a few of my other open ones. Who knows what will happen after that, the other Kingdoms will probably get their own stories.

To my cover designer Laura from Covers by Aura, thank you so much for your patience and dedication to my vision. You took my concept and knocked it out of the park.

Once again Jessica from Elemental Editing was my rock and made my words readable and pretty.

Thanks to Tegan and Amanda for beta reading and helping polish my work and catch any errors.

And lastly to you guys the readers. I love what I do, and probably would do it regardless if anyone read them or not, but you guys make it that much sweeter so thank you.

Until next time, happy reading

Lexie

www.ingramcontent.com/pod-product-compliance
Lightning Source LLC
Chambersburg PA
CBHW051311190726
48290CB00001B/106